HYDROGEN

BLACKWOOD ELEMENTS
BOOK 10

ELISE NOBLE

Published by Undercover Publishing Limited

Copyright © 2022 Elise Noble

v3

ISBN: 978-1-912888-57-3

Edited by Nikki Mentges, NAM Editorial

Cover design by Abigail Sins

www.undercover-publishing.com

www.elise-noble.com

Whoever said that diamonds are a girl's best friend clearly never had a dog.

1

LEAH

Just a small favour, my boss had said. It would do me good to get out of the office.

Well, she'd lied.

It might have looked sunny in Belvedere Park, where I was currently freezing my sweet patootie off on surveillance duty, but the bitter wind had left my toes shivering inside my high-heeled pumps and my fingers frozen to the book I wasn't reading. Since when had September been so cold?

This was why I'd become an executive assistant instead of applying to join the investigations team. Others preferred the challenge of working out in the field as a PI, the excitement, the glamour, but I loved my desk. I missed my desk. Twenty-three steps from the coffee machine, right next to a window where I could look at the great outdoors without having to wear a coat, and when I got bored with that view, I had all the hot guys in the office to ogle. Working for a security company did have its advantages. *Everyone* stayed in shape. What more could a girl want?

"Leah, any movement?" Dan asked in my ear.

"Nothing. And my ass has gone to sleep."

Usually, I got excused from surveillance work, but a perfect storm of big cases and a nasty stomach bug had sucked Blackwood Security's resources dry, and Dan was concerned that the suspected fraudster her team was watching might grow suspicious if he kept seeing the same faces. Hence the "favour." Everyone at Blackwood was expected to be flexible, and I *had* been trained in surveillance, so the request wasn't unreasonable, but that still didn't make it fun. A sigh escaped. *Suck it up, Leah.* I owed Dan, after all.

Because a week ago, I'd gone out clubbing, and at three o'clock in the morning, I realised I'd lost my purse as well as my dignity. When I'd staggered to Dan's apartment four blocks away, not only had she given me a bed for what was left of the night, but she'd also tracked my cell phone and retrieved my belongings from the thieving asshole who'd taken them.

This was her payback.

"Well, next time, don't puke in my living room," she told me over the radio.

"I'm never drinking again."

Most of the time, Daniela di Grassi was a good person to work for. I looked after her and another member of the Blackwood management team, Nick Goldman, organising their schedules and arranging their travel. Nick had gone to California for the week, but Dan was still in Richmond, tormenting me from her fancy leather office chair.

One more hour until I could go home, or possibly to the hospital if I succumbed to hypothermia first. In the meantime, I slipped my phone inside the biology textbook I'd borrowed from the prop room in Blackwood's basement and opened up DateMe.com, then began scrolling through the photos absent-mindedly in case anyone caught my eye. Such as that blond-haired guy in the shirt and tie.

I paused and opened up his profile, only to find he was six feet four. Well, six feet two—in my experience, men always exaggerated. But that was still a whole foot taller than me. No go. I'd have to spend my entire life in high heels and probably stand on a box too. My dream guy was more...compact, and ideally, he'd spend his days in a made-to-measure suit. Not that I didn't like muscles, of course, but I saw plenty of those every day at work, and there was something sexy about a man who hid everything with pinstripes. As long as I was the one who got to unbutton his shirt at the end of the day, of course.

Older was okay, but not too old. I'd tried one of those sugar-daddy sites last year, and been forced to weigh up the pros and cons of box seats at a Washington Nationals game versus being on the arm of a sixty-year-old. Well, he'd claimed to be sixty. He'd looked more like seventy. All those little sideways glances I'd received... Then my date's dentures had gotten stuck in a cheeseburger, and the decision was made: no more men over fifty.

I'd messaged one probable and two possibles by the time Dan said the magic words in my ear. Blackwood had supplied me with a tiny covert earpiece that was barely noticeable under my hair, so at least I wasn't totally alone in this urban hellscape.

"Changeover time. Tanner's on his way to the café opposite. Once he's in place, leave the park via the south exit."

"Thank goodness."

But why did Tanner get to sit in the café?

"And you're back in the park the day after tomorrow, so you might want to wear proper shoes."

"Yes, Mom."

I stretched out my icy limbs, and I'd just gotten stiffly to my feet when a blur of...of *something* hit me dead centre and knocked me on my ass. Something wet. Something hairy. Something smelly.

The dog slurped at my face as footsteps came running.

"Brian!" A guy grabbed the dog by the scruff of its neck

3

and hauled the thing off me. "I'm so sorry. He slipped his collar and jumped in the duck pond, and that green stuff got all over him, and..."

The stranger looked me up and down, his lips twisted in an odd mix of fascination and disgust. For a moment, I thought he was going to vomit, but then I realised he was trying not to laugh.

"It's not funny," I snapped. "I'm filthy."

Strands of slimy weed hung from my hair, my pants were covered in mud, and the beast had shaken water all over me. The stink of rotten eggs wafted past my nostrils. This was karma finally catching up, wasn't it? I'd made a small miscalculation while trying to find my friend Sloane a date, she'd ended up being stalked by a weirdo—okay, weirdos— and this was my reward.

Dog Guy studied me, assessing. What was I, a damn science project? His gaze paused on my chest, and I was almost ready to slap him when his eyes snapped back up to my face. Not to my eyes, though. He avoided looking straight at me.

"Uh, your shirt's gone...uh..."

I glanced down at myself. Mental note: Never wear a white top on surveillance. Ever.

"Ohmigosh! It's freaking see-through."

He started to peel off his T-shirt, and three ladies stopped to watch. *Way to go, Leah.* This was totally how to stay incognito on an undercover operation.

"Stop," I hissed. "Just stop."

Dog Guy dropped the hem and chewed the edge of his bottom lip. He did have rather nice lips, and it was a shame they were half-hidden by a scruffy beard. Somebody should teach him how to use a razor. And give him the number of a barber—his light brown hair was several months past needing a cut.

"My apartment's nearby. I can give you a new shirt, then call you a cab."

"I'm not sure—"

Dan's voice interrupted me. "Go with him, sweetie. Tanner sent me a photo, and you look like a swamp monster." Oh, great. That picture would be on the home page of the Blackwood intranet before I made it back to the office. "And the dog dude's cute in a messy sort of way." A pause, and she must have sensed my hesitation. "Don't worry, I put a tracker in your purse. If he turns out to be an axe murderer, just scream and I'll send someone."

Oh, that was comforting. But Dan was right. I didn't want to walk the twelve blocks home dripping slime onto the sidewalk, and no sane person would let me in their car looking or smelling like this. But my friend Johanna lived two blocks away, and I had a key to her apartment—she worked as a flight attendant, and I watered her plants sometimes when she was overseas. If I could make it to her place...

"I'm not cut out for this," I finished, then realised my words made little sense to Dog Guy.

"Okay." Dan finally relented. "Come back to the office."

Which was even farther away. And what if I ran into someone I knew? Like Johanna's sexy neighbour, the one I'd been flirting with for months? If he saw me channelling Solomon Grundy, I could kiss any chance of a date goodbye.

What should I do? Make a break for it, or borrow a shirt from the stranger?

2

LEAH

"I don't even know you," I told Dog Guy.

He held out a hand and then thought better of it. "Hay...uh...Haygood. Uh, Kevin Haygood."

"Fine, Kevin, I'll borrow a shirt. But you need to keep that monster on a leash."

I crossed my arms over my chest as Kevin led me across the park, but everyone still stared at me. I couldn't totally blame them—I would have stared at me too.

"I'm really sorry about Brian," Kevin said. "Normally, he gets out a lot more, but I've been working overtime this past month and he's been cooped up in the apartment all day."

"Maybe you should consider getting a dog walker?"

"I had a dog walker. She lasted three days, then texted me to say she was moving to South Carolina. Now I'm trying to walk Brian on my lunch breaks, and he's so happy to get out that he misbehaves."

What was Kevin's job? If I had to guess, I'd have said barista. Or waiter. Perhaps grad student on a break?

Kevin stopped on the sidewalk and stripped off his shirt despite my earlier protestations, then used it to wipe Brian's

6

feet. Okay, I had to admit his abs weren't bad. Could he be a gym instructor?

"Did he just strip?" Dan asked in my ear. "Take a good look, sweetie. Hey, you're going into Garner's building."

When Dan said Garner, she was referring to Terrence Garner, a thirty-seven-year-old computer repair guy who, as far as we could tell, didn't do much actual repairing. When Tanner had called to enquire about getting a hard drive replaced in his laptop, Garner claimed to be fully booked for the next month, but he didn't visit clients—didn't even own a car—and although he received the occasional package through the mail, we hadn't seen anyone dropping off a computer to be fixed.

And yet somehow, he managed to pay his rent.

Garner spent his days hanging out in his apartment in downtown Richmond and—possibly—the occasional evening conning elderly marks out of their life savings. The cops had identified eight victims of the fraudster Blackwood was hunting, all elderly, all living alone, three male, five female, and there were probably more. We'd nicknamed him "The Rat" because a favourite tactic was to gain entrance to their homes by claiming the landlord had sent him to check out a rodent infestation in the building. The first four thefts had happened last winter, and then the Rat had taken a few months off before returning to his cruel ways over the summer.

His last victim, a seventy-nine-year-old retiree named Molly Sanderson, had lost three thousand dollars in cash and several valuable necklaces. One in particular was an heirloom that had been in her family for generations. I'd seen pictures of it—emeralds and pearls set in a delicate web of gold. Molly had worn it on her wedding day, and her daughter wanted to follow the family tradition when she tied the knot herself next year. Her fiancé had hired Blackwood to get it back.

So far, we had few leads, but the owner of a local pawn

shop who Dan used as an informant from time to time told her that Garner had attempted to sell a necklace that matched the description of Molly's, and when the store owner asked for proof of ownership, Garner had gotten twitchy and left.

But if Garner *was* the Rat, he'd been careful apart from that one misstep. There was no sign of the jewellery in his apartment—we knew that because Dan had snuck in for a look around while Garner went to the grocery store—and nothing had surfaced on the black market. All we could do was watch him.

The initial plan had been for Blackwood to install bugs in his home, but firstly, Garner was a minimalist, a neat freak, and secondly, he appeared to have a cleaning fetish. Dan had gagged on the lemon scent that permeated his apartment, and every item he owned was lined up in a painful arrangement of right angles. There wasn't a speck of dust anywhere. Dan had vetoed the bugs in case he found them, and we'd tried to rent an apartment in the building instead, but they were all occupied. Hence my vigil in the park on an unseasonably chilly fall day.

I trailed Kevin into the building, which was nicer on the inside than it looked from the outside. Not fancy, but clean and welcoming. Three couches formed a U-shape around a low table, and a noticeboard was covered in flyers advertising yoga classes and items for sale and a local photography competition. Brian left damp footprints on the white tile all the way to the elevator, and Kevin frowned when he noticed them.

"Some of my neighbours aren't keen on dogs," he muttered.

Hardly surprising if they were all like Brian.

"Really? I can't imagine why."

The elevator rose upward, and when I glanced at the panel, I saw the third-floor button was lit. A knot of apprehension formed in my stomach. Garner lived in 303. And when Kevin stopped outside his door and fished around in his pocket for the keys, that knot tightened around my guts and left me nauseous. Because I knew what was about to happen.

"You live in 302?" I said, mainly for Dan's benefit.

Kevin glanced up at the silver numbers on the door while Dan squealed in my ear.

"Sure do," he said.

"Jackpot!" Dan would be dancing around her office now, probably with a hot guy and a glass of champagne. "Leah, find a way to spend time in that apartment. I don't care how you do it."

Oh, how did I know that was coming?

I mentally drafted my resignation letter as I followed Kevin into his man cave. The place was a nice size, but it looked even bigger without furniture. Had he just moved in? The only things in the living area were a dining table and a single chair, Brian's bed, and a whole collection of doggy toys.

"Kind of empty, huh?" he said. "We only moved in two weeks ago."

Yup, called it.

"You didn't consider picking a furnished place?"

"It's a corporate rental."

"Beggars can't be choosers?"

"Something like that. HR mentioned furniture, and I guess I should chase that up, but I spend most of my time at the office, and..." He suddenly brightened. "I have coffee. You want coffee?" Before I could answer, he gave his head a little shake. "What am I thinking? I'm sure you just want to clean up and get out of here."

I unclenched my jaw enough to speak. "Actually, coffee would be great."

"You're serious? I mean, sure. How do you take it?"

Cappuccino with a shot of caramel syrup, extra froth, and a generous helping of chocolate sprinkles. Did Kevin have milk? Did he even have a refrigerator?

"Uh, black is fine."

"I'll show you where the bathroom is and find you shampoo and a towel."

"I don't need a shower. I'll just wipe the worst off."

Kevin's grimace suggested that perhaps a washcloth wouldn't cut it. "What about the green stuff in your hair?"

I caught sight of myself in the mirror as he pushed open the bathroom door, and I nearly screamed. At this moment, I could land a part in a horror movie and skip right through make-up. And the slime wasn't the worst of it. Or even the colour—for the first time in my life, I'd gone brunette, and I hated it. But after my ex had called me an airhead blonde in our break-up fight, I didn't want to risk the same thing happening again.

"Is that a beetle in my hair?" Ohmigosh, it was. "Get it off!"

Kevin sprang forward, riffled through the duckweed for the offending creepy-crawly, and flicked it into the toilet. My freaking hero.

"Sorry. So sorry." He grabbed a towel from the rail and shoved it into my hands. "Use whatever shampoo you can find, and I'll leave you clean clothes right outside the door. Don't worry about the mess. I need to wash Brian afterward, so it'll only get worse."

"I think most of his dirt's on me."

Plus some slobber and a good amount of hair.

Kevin looked me up and down again, more slowly this time, which absolutely shouldn't have made my belly flutter the way it did because he was definitely not my type. In fact, I couldn't see how he was *anybody's* type.

"Yeah. Reckon it is."

I shoved the door shut, forcing him to take a couple of hasty steps backward, and sank down onto the edge of the bathtub. All I could hear was Dan laughing in my ear, and I had a strong urge to flush her along with the beetle.

"This isn't funny," I hissed.

"Sweetie, I've spent most of my day reviewing budgets and planning caseloads. This is the comic relief. Honestly, I snorted coffee over my screen when I saw the pictures."

"I quit."

"Resignation not accepted. Anyhow, this is a crazy stroke of luck. If you can gain access to the apartment, we can install wall microphones and listen to Garner."

"How exactly am I supposed to do that?" I asked, keeping my voice to a whisper. "I don't know the guy at all."

"He gave you the perfect opening—you can offer to walk the dog."

"What if he's an axe murderer?"

"Do you see any axes lying around the place? Chill, we'll do a background check."

"But I don't know the first thing about dogs either."

"I'll get Georgia to give you a crash course this evening. I will call her literally right this second."

"What if I told the guy I have a friend who actually is a dog walker?"

"Leah, Leah... The plan we already have is perfect. He likes you."

"He feels sorry for me."

"He offered you coffee, sweetie."

"Refer to my first answer."

Dan's voice softened slightly. "If you really don't want to, we can try to sell him on the idea of somebody else. But you'd be great at it."

"I have no idea what I'm doing."

"Which is *why* you'd be so great. You're completely

believable. Plus there's no guarantee he'd go for the alternate, and then we'd be stuck with the outdoor surveillance again."

I hated sitting in the park. I *really* hated sitting in the park. Whoever called it the great outdoors was lying. Probably some marketing executive who needed a slogan to sell tents or hiking shoes or bear spray or whatever.

Would hanging out in an empty apartment be that bad? It wasn't as if I'd need to speak to Kevin other than to agree on dates and times. He'd be at work. Plus if I did this for Dan and Kevin offered to pay me, I'd definitely be keeping the extra money. Call it the equivalent of hazardous-duty pay. Looking after Brian would certainly qualify me for the bonus.

Should I go with Dan's plan? I only had a few minutes to decide.

3

LEAH

Sometimes, I hated my boss. Fine, I'd offer to take care of Brian. And in between throwing tennis balls and feeding him doggy treats, I'd update my résumé and stick pins into a tiny voodoo doll with Dan's face on it.

Because I was never working surveillance again.

"Hey," I said.

Kevin turned from the kitchen window, and while his employer hadn't provided him with any furniture, I had to concede that they'd given him a nice view. If Terrence Garner lived next door, then crime really did pay. My kitchen window looked out onto a wall. Just a plain grey wall. Occasionally, a kid would come along and brighten it up with graffiti, but whoever was in charge of Richmond's community service program was too damn organised because the artwork always got scrubbed off a few days later. Sometimes a week. Never longer than two.

Maybe that sounded as if I were complaining, but I really wasn't. Dan might have driven me cray-cray, but Blackwood paid well, better than any other company I'd interviewed at, and I could have afforded an apartment like this if I hadn't had other priorities. Their names were Laken and Louis. My half-siblings. Our mom had opened the baby-name book at L and never bothered to turn the page, which was about as much effort as she'd put into every other area of our lives. Everything we'd achieved, we'd achieved in spite of her, not because of her. The strain on my finances had eased since my brother graduated, but Laken was still at Columbia, and although she had a partial scholarship, tuition was expensive.

So I'd learned to live with the wall.

"Hey," Kevin said.

"I don't suppose you have a blow-dryer?"

"Sorry. You look ni... Okay, I can't lie." His lips twitched at the corners. "You look as if you shrank in the wash."

Was it any surprise? Kevin had to be six feet tall, and my legs were probably the same size as his arms. The bottoms of the sweatpants he'd left out for me trailed along the floor, and the hoodie came to my knees. I looked like a hip-hop version of the Grim Reaper.

My eyes had narrowed all of their own accord, but I forced a smile and a hopefully sincere laugh.

"Right, I do. Thanks for the clothes, though."

"I'll get yours dry-cleaned."

"Honestly, it's fine."

Dan could pay for that. She owed me.

"Are you sure?"

"Totally. Do you have a bag I can put them in?"

"I'll find one. Uh, and here's your coffee. Want to sit down?"

He held out a mug, but before I could take it, Brian rushed in and shoved his nose into my crotch. Oh hell, oh hell, oh hell. *Deep breaths, Leah.* I knew nothing about dogs except for the fact that they scared me a bit. My little sister had been bitten by a terrier when we were kids, and I'd avoided them ever since. Meanwhile, Brian was snuffling away while Kevin tried to make up his mind whether to grab the damn dog or ignore his endeavours.

I stumbled backward, aiming for the chair, but I tripped over the pant legs and landed on the polished wooden floor instead. My cheeks burned as Kevin sat beside me, cross-legged, and held out the coffee.

"The floor? Uh, yes, good plan... I don't even know your name?"

"Leah."

"Nice name. It suits you."

What? I just stared at him.

"Anyhow, I was thinking it would've been awkward if we'd both tried to sit on the chair."

I kept staring, and he put his head in his hands. "I don't know what my problem is. Everything I say today comes out wrong."

Well, this wasn't awkward at all. I was stuck in a nightmare with Scooby-Doo and Shaggy, and according to my boss, I was staying there until we caught Garner. Small talk. I should try small talk.

"So, Kevin... What made you move to Richmond?"

"Nothing exciting. Just work."

"What do you do?"

"I'm... Did you want sugar in your coffee? I didn't put any sugar in."

"It's fine without."

"Do you want more milk? I bought a coffee machine, but I didn't get around to setting it up yet."

"Honestly, this is great." And I'd also asked for it black. "We were talking about your job?"

And I knew now that he wasn't a barista. This coffee was terrible. Really bad. As if he'd tipped half a canister of granules in and added the tiniest splash of milk. Not even cream.

"I'm an executive assistant."

"Really? Me—" Darn it, I couldn't tell the truth. "Me? I'm a student."

"Yes, I figured."

"You did?"

He gestured toward the textbook lying on the table. "I wiped the dirt off it. Reproduction in molluscs, huh?"

"What?" Horrified, I took my first proper look at the title. "Uh, yes? Gotta love molluscs."

Urgh. That was snails and stuff, right?

"Bet that's fascinating."

Was he kidding? He sounded serious, but who could possibly find molluscs interesting?

"I learn something new every day." How did the rest of the team survive? I couldn't even concoct the most basic cover story. "It wasn't quite what I imagined myself doing when I grew up, but life's full of curveballs, isn't it?"

"Indeed. And you were studying in the park this afternoon? Isn't it kind of cold for that?"

Thank you. At least someone understood.

"Yes, but it was better than studying at home. My roommate isn't the easiest person to live with."

"What's wrong with your roommate?"

What wasn't wrong with him? *Get a gay roommate,* Cosmo and Glamour said. *He'll help you out with colour coordination, accessorise the communal living areas, and vet potential boyfriends to make sure they're good enough for his new bestie.*

Well, I'd followed the advice, but Stefano didn't hold up his end of the bargain. He ate my food, sprayed cologne everywhere, left globs of hair product all over the bathroom, and last week, I'd come home to find him doing something unmentionable with a blond guy on *my* leather couch. At least he paid the rent on time, which was better than the girl before him, but he still drove me insane. I'd have liked nothing better than to kick him out and live alone, but I still had a year of Laken's tuition left to pay, so I was stuck living with a walrus in leather pants.

"Uh, he plays his music really loud."

"Can't you ask him to turn it down?"

"Uh, he has a hearing problem,"—I was such a bad liar —"so I'd feel bad about doing that."

I took a sip of coffee, and it scalded my mouth. Anything else want to go wrong today? Why, yes. Yes, it did. Brian tried to crawl into Kevin's lap, but Kevin pushed the mutt away, so Brian settled beside me instead, resting his chin on my thigh. Drool seeped into the sweatpants. I wanted to run screaming, but Dan's cunning plan meant I had to be nice to him.

"What about the library?" Kevin asked.

"The dust sets off my allergies."

"A coffee shop?"

"Student budget." Hey, I was getting good at this. "Brian's cute when he's not jumping on me. What breed is he?"

"Good question. I'm not totally sure. The veterinarian thought maybe he was a briard, but I'm leaning toward otterhound."

"He needs a haircut."

"Finding a new groomer is something else I haven't had time to do."

I took the elastic ponytail holder off my wrist and tied the hair on Brian's head into a little topknot.

"There, he can see again. Do you want me to ask around and see if anyone can recommend a groomer?"

"You'd do that?"

"I just offered, didn't I?" And I could already hear Dan yelling across the office for someone to call Georgia. "Hold on, I'll message a friend."

Brian was licking my hand when my phone vibrated two minutes later with the info. Georgia was the girlfriend of a sort-of colleague—Xavier was more of a freelancer who did work I wasn't allowed to speak of and definitely didn't want to think about—and she spent her spare time volunteering at Hope for Hounds. As it happened, the rescue centre had a grooming parlour on-site and they could fit Brian in for an appointment. All the profits from grooming and boarding were used to feed homeless dogs, so we'd be supporting the charity too.

"My friend knows a place with a slot the day after tomorrow at ten," I told Kevin. "I'll give you the address."

"Ten in the morning?"

"What are you, a vampire? Of course in the morning."

"I have to work."

Oh, perfect. He'd walked right into the trap I hadn't even realised I'd set.

"I don't mind taking him, if you want?"

"Why would you do that?"

Ah, crap. Kevin sounded a tiny bit suspicious. I took a deep breath and put on my best college-girl smile. I might have been twenty-eight, but I'd always looked younger, and I still got asked for ID every single time I went into a bar.

"Because I thought in return, I could borrow your dining table for a few hours to study in peace."

Kevin's turn to stare.

"Or not. It's just that you said Brian was on his own all day, and if you're busy working, he might like some company. And I swear if my roommate passes gas one more time, I'm gonna die from methane poisoning."

"How much would you charge?"

"Charge? Nothing. Nothing at all. I already—" Dammit, I almost said I already had a job. "I already love Brian and his soppy face."

Kevin glanced around his apartment, and I figured he was

working out the risks. There wasn't a lot to steal, but he still didn't know me from Adam.

"If it helps, I could get a reference from my summer job. I babysat for two different people. A twelve-year-old and a five-year-old."

That part was even true. I sometimes supervised Dan's son and his friends while she went out for dinner. He played pool better than I did, and he was teaching me to play the drums. Plus I'd looked after Tabitha Quinn on one occasion—the daughter of Blackwood's scariest employee—and what's more, I'd lived to tell the tale. Tabitha mostly spoke to me in Russian, and she was deadly accurate with her toy crossbow.

"Give him Ethan's details. Or Ana's," Dan said in my ear. Her boyfriend and Tabby's mom, respectively. If the reference thing didn't work out, Ana could always intimidate Kevin into letting me walk Brian.

"Okay. If you can provide a reference, then you've got the job. But I'm paying you. Otherwise, I'd feel as if I was taking advantage."

It would probably seem weird if a student turned down money, wouldn't it? "Minimum wage?"

"Deal."

4

LEAH

Day one of surveillance duty in Kevin's apartment, a Wednesday, otherwise known as a slightly more temperate version of hell.

After I left yesterday, I'd hopped into a cab and ridden back to Blackwood headquarters, where everyone had laughed at my outfit, and Marvin, who was basically a deputy assistant of gadgets, had given me a crash course in bug installation.

"It's quite straightforward. All you need to do is attach the microphone to the wall with these sticky pads. The batteries should last for three days at least, even transmitting at full power, and they're simple to change. We might need to refine the positioning a bit, but—"

"Wait, wait." I held up a hand. "Won't he see the microphone stuck on the wall?"

"Well, you'll need to hide it behind something, obviously."

"Then we have a problem. There's nothing to hide anything behind."

"What about a painting? Or a mirror?"

"There's literally nothing. The guy's just moved in. He has a dining table and a chair. Like, he doesn't even own a couch."

"Okay, then you're right. We *do* have a problem."

Although what was that old saying? That one man's trash was another man's treasure? If we couldn't plant the bugs, then there was no reason for me to spend time in Kevin's apartment. And if there was no reason to spend time in Kevin's apartment, then I could be excused from dog duty. My desk upstairs was calling. Georgia and Lara had organised a charity bake sale for tomorrow, and if I played my cards right, I could be first in line for pineapple upside-down cake.

"I can't put the bugs somewhere else?" I asked, just to check. Did I sound suitably disappointed? "Maybe I could stick one under the table?"

"We call them wall mics for a reason. And we've gotten lucky with the building's construction—the sensor will pick up vibrations through the brick."

"There's no other type of bug that would work?"

"A parabolic mic would be even harder to hide. The other option is to get into the target's apartment again and replace the regular wall sockets with transmitting devices, but those require installation and that isn't the work of five minutes."

Plus Garner had no routine and rarely seemed to go out for long. If he arrived home while a technician was dismantling his wiring, awkward wouldn't even begin to cover it. And we couldn't afford to get caught. Bugging people wasn't exactly legal, I knew that much, but I also knew that Dan sometimes bent the rules. If she picked up anything useful from the bugs, she'd focus in on Garner as a suspect and find a way of obtaining enough evidence for a conviction in a marginally more ethical manner. Her morals straddled the fat grey line between black and white. Once upon a time, that had made me a touch uncomfortable, but during my time at Blackwood, I'd seen the law fail too many people to get upset about it anymore. Dan got people the justice they deserved.

Most of the time.

So far, the Rat had proven to be elusive, but that was a problem for people with a higher pay grade than mine to solve.

"Gee, that's too bad. Welp, I'd better break the news to Dan."

I'd been working as Dan's assistant for just over three years now, and before that, I'd been a team secretary in the executive protection division, and before *that*, I'd staffed the front desk in Blackwood's downtown Richmond satellite office. Which was to say, I'd known Dan for a while. So it honestly shouldn't have surprised me when she saw the problem not as a disaster but as an opportunity.

"It means we'll get off to a slow start because you'll have to remove the bugs each time you leave, but we can keep the surveillance team in place for the rest of the time. And in a few days when you've gotten to know Kevin, you can take him a house-warming gift. A mirror or a painting, something like that. If we hide extra batteries inside the frame, you won't need to change them so often." Dan turned to Marvin. "We can do that, right?"

"Piece of cake."

"Perfect. And you realise the other neat thing about Kevin having no furniture?"

"No, and I'm not sure I want to."

"It means he doesn't have a girlfriend. If he did, he'd at least buy an extra dining chair and a couch. So you get a clear run at him without a jealous lover getting in the way."

"I don't want a 'clear run' at Kevin," I said through gritted teeth. "I just want to get this over with so I can go back to typing reports, arranging meetings, and booking travel. Oh, and spending time with a man who doesn't think sweats are an acceptable fashion choice."

"Did the hot guy ask you out for dinner yet? What was his name? Darren?"

"Darius. And no, but I'm working on it."

And it truly was work. Johanna lived in a fancy building with a gym, and Darius spent a lot of time on the treadmill. Exercise wasn't really my thing—I figured that if I hooked the right guy, I'd be able to afford lipo when I got older—but I'd been diligently borrowing Johanna's gym pass twice a week for the past month, and Darius knew my name now. I'd also spent too much money on sportswear, pulled a muscle in my leg, and put on a pound through rewarding myself with chocolate after every horrendous session.

"He'd be a fool to pass you up. Any other questions before you go?"

"Do you know anything about molluscs?"

Marvin gave me a "what the hell?" look. "Molluscs?"

"Unfortunately."

"Well, they're the second-largest phylum of invertebrates after arthropods—basically a muscular blob with a digestive system and a shell. Well, most of them have shells; some don't. Did you know there are around eighty-five thousand different species? The majority are marine, but some live in freshwater, and then there are the land-dwellers like snails and slugs. Fascinating little creatures."

"How do you know all that stuff?"

"Don't you watch the Discovery Channel?"

"Not if I can help it." But at least I knew who to ask for assistance if any mollusc-related questions came up.

"We'll only be an earpiece away if you need advice," Dan reminded me. "You've got this. Breathe."

How I wished I shared her confidence. "Breathe. Right."

"And try to find out where Kevin works so we can run a background check."

"Anything else?"

"Have fun, and don't blow your cover."

Have fun? Was she insane? Stupid question—I already knew the answer was "yes."

"I was worried you weren't going to show up."

"Sorry, I'm so sorry. My roommate wouldn't get out of the shower." In the end, I'd quit banging on the door and run the six blocks to Blackwood's downtown office, where there were changing rooms next to the weight room in the basement. "On days like this, I'd sell my soul for an en-suite."

"She likes to look her best, huh?"

"He, and I genuinely don't know what he does in there. I mean, he takes twice as long in the bathroom as I do, but he has half the amount of hair."

"Your roommate's a guy?"

"He seemed cool when I interviewed him, but it didn't work out quite as well as I hoped, and now..." I shrugged. What could I do?

"Beggars can't be choosers?"

I managed half a smile. "Something like that."

Kevin stepped back to let me into his apartment, and Brian bounded toward me the instant I stepped over the threshold, his fur beige rather than green today. Even though I braced for impact, he nearly knocked me on my ass.

"Brian!"

"Oh, it's fine." I waved a hand. A shaking hand. *Don't let him feel your fear.* "Dogs will be dogs."

"Maybe I should take him to training classes."

"Great idea," I said a little too quickly. "It'd be fun for him to learn tricks and stuff."

Two of the big bosses at Blackwood had dogs. Emmy and Black, husband and wife, each as tough as the other. They gave the words "till death do us part" a whole new meaning because I was pretty sure they killed people on the side. But only bad people.

Anyhow, Emmy's dog liked to stay at their estate, but Black often brought his mutt into the office. Barkley could shake hands, spin right or left, bark on command, roll over, back up, crawl along, and sniff out a morsel of cheese at fifty yards. Black pretended that having Barkley follow him everywhere was a chore, but he kept a box of treats in his desk drawer and there was a fancy doggy bed right next to his chair. The man did have a heart, despite what many claimed.

"Right now, I'd settle for Brian not eating my sneakers," Kevin said.

Thank the stars I'd worn old shoes today. He wouldn't eat them while they were on my feet, would he? I'd spoken with Georgia on the phone for half an hour last night, and she'd run me through the basics, but at no point had she mentioned footwear.

"I'll try to avoid him doing that."

"Let me show you where his things are. I've ordered a new harness to try to stop him from wriggling out of his collar, but the last time I did that, he chewed through the straps within ten minutes." Kevin led me through the apartment. "He likes his bed by the window, but he'll follow the sunbeams across the floor in the daytime. And his treats are in this jar. He'll beg for more, but go easy because he gets fat otherwise."

"How long have you had him?"

"Nearly two years. I wasn't intending to get a dog, but I found him half-dead on the street in Brooklyn one morning, so I took him to the veterinarian, and he had a broken leg and needed somewhere to recuperate, so..." Kevin spread his hands in an expansive shrug. "Here he is."

"That was really sweet. You're from New York? My sister lives in West Harlem at the moment."

"Spent half of my life there."

"You said work made you move to Richmond?"

"Temporarily. We're expanding one of our projects into

the development phase, so I'll be here for a few months at least. Uh, and by 'we,' I mean my boss and his colleagues."

Ah, he'd given me the perfect opening to knock an item off Dan's to-do list. Miracles did happen.

"Where do you work?"

For the first time since I'd met him, Kevin's smile turned into a frown. "Does that matter?"

Shit. "Not really. Just curious, I suppose. I have a couple of friends who work as executive assistants, and there's a world of difference between an EA at a food manufacturer and an EA at an investment bank. The food guys dish out free samples, but the bankers... Man, they're uptight." I froze. "You don't work for a banker, do you? I figured you were in advertising or maybe the entertainment industry."

"Why did you figure that?"

"Uh, the jeans? And the beard. And the fact that your hours are kinda flexible."

Although those criteria could have applied to Blackwood too. Dan and Nick didn't care what I wore to the office, or if I worked from home sometimes, or if I took an hour or two of personal time as long as I got the job done.

"Does everyone in advertising have a beard?"

"Only the douches." I clapped a hand over my mouth. "Once again, I'm so sorry. It's just that I spent six months dating a guy who directed infomercials, and I guess that's coloured my opinion on facial hair. And advertising." Dammit. "Tell me you don't work in advertising?"

"You don't think the world needs a solar-powered frying pan?"

Was he kidding? It sounded as if it should be a joke, but his delivery was dead serious.

"Uh, maybe?"

His face creased into an adorable smile. "Got you!"

Dammit, Leah, not adorable. More like adorkable.

"You don't work in advertising, do you?"

"No, technology. My boss is an engineer."

"Not at Allied Group?"

That was a big engineering firm, and they had an office over on Arboretum Parkway. How did I know that? Because I'd once had dinner with a guy from there who designed shampoo bottling machines, and although I loved hair products—don't get me wrong, anti-frizz serum was amazing—I didn't need to gain an in-depth understanding of the manufacturing process over three courses plus coffee. Right after that, I'd begun filtering engineers out of my online dating preferences. Life was too short.

"No, Hydrogen Labs." Kevin's smile slipped away, replaced by the faintest grimace. "Quite boring, but it pays the bills."

"Hydrogen Labs? I've never heard of it."

"They don't get involved with molluscs. But maybe I'll mention the solar frying pan idea in the next board meeting—I'm sure they could work with that."

If Kevin was going to board meetings, then he must be EA to one of the directors. The top EA. Nick was a director at Blackwood, but I didn't go to board meetings unless Sloane was on vacation or off sick.

"Campers all over the world would thank you. Well, not the world because I don't suppose there's much sun in some countries, but campers in Texas and California for sure."

"Amorphous solar cells work surprisingly well in low light."

"A-what?"

"Uh, never mind. We should talk about Brian, huh? You got glowing references, by the way, although the lady—Ana—she sounded a little scary."

"Her bark is worse than her bite."

Unless you got on the wrong side of her, in which case she turned rabid.

"Phew. Well, if I pay you for two hours a day, does that sound fair? And if you want to hang around for a while longer and study, then that's fine too."

"That's perfect."

"Call me if there are any problems?"

"Absolutely." I'd put Kevin on speed dial because with Brian's personality, I couldn't see how there *wouldn't* be problems. "What time do you think you'll be back? Just so I can make sure Brian's not on his own for too long at the end of the day," I added hastily in case Kevin thought I planned to throw a party while he was out. Because that would be so much worse than merely bugging his home to eavesdrop on his neighbour's conversations.

"If you're planning to spend some time studying, then I don't need to rush home. Maybe five thirty? Or six o'clock?" Hallelujah. "But if I get a chance, I'll drop by at lunchtime to check Brian's behaving."

Rats. I didn't need that, but at least Kevin had given me warning. And I could hardly bar him from his own apartment.

"I'm sure Brian and I will get along just fine. But thank you—that's thoughtful."

Kevin shot me a grin over his shoulder as he headed for the door. "Good luck."

I'd need it.

5

DOG GUY

"Kevin, I need to ask for a favour."

"Let me guess—you want me to walk Brian again."

"Actually, no."

"No?"

Kevin's surprise wasn't unexpected. Even though pet care wasn't in his job description, he'd always been willing to assist his boss in a pinch, and with Brian, those pinches had happened more often than they should. But today's favour was a more awkward request.

"I... Uh, I was hoping you could sanitise your social media accounts."

"Huh?"

"Basically, I need you to remove any pictures of yourself."

"I'm sorry?"

"Facebook, Twitter, Instagram, LinkedIn... Just take down the photos and untag yourself in any that others have posted."

Kevin deposited the tray he was carrying onto Hayden Lennox's desk, picked up his own coffee, and took a seat in one of the visitor chairs opposite, legs crossed at the ankles. Then he rolled his eyes.

"Go on, I bet this is gonna be good."

"So there was a small incident yesterday with Brian..."

"I *knew* he'd be involved somehow."

"He slipped his collar and jumped on another passer-by. She seemed okay afterward—I mean, she wasn't limping or anything—but I kind of panicked when she asked my name."

"And by panicked, you mean...?"

"I told her I was you."

"Oh boy."

"It just slipped out."

"I guess that's understandable after the lawsuit."

Yes, the lawsuit. Last summer, Brian had escaped in Central Park and knocked over a jogger. She'd brushed it off at first, said it was no problem, but she must have googled Hayden Lennox's name afterward because the next thing he knew, she was suing him for damaged clothing, a twisted ankle, and emotional distress. *Six figures'* worth of emotional distress. Plus she wanted Brian to be euthanised. Lennox's own lawyers had fought the case and won, but the whole episode had been stressful and he didn't need any more distractions right now, not when he had two ongoing projects, both at important stages. If the Richmond team managed to iron out the bugs in the new manufacturing process, they could make solar power far more affordable. When combined with Hydrogen Labs' existing battery tech— the tech that had made him a very rich man—the products could revolutionise energy generation the world over. Reduce the global carbon footprint, improve air quality... And then there was the passion project that took up his evenings. That one was far more experimental, but what was life without a few risks?

"I don't want any more legal trouble."

"But what does that have to do with my social media? The woman's probably forgotten all about Brian already."

"Not exactly. We were right outside my apartment building, so I let her borrow my bathroom to get cleaned up, and—long story short—I hired her as Brian's new dog walker."

"You did *what*?"

"I wasn't thinking straight, okay?"

"Thinking straight about what?" Haris Kohli, one of Lennox's two business partners, poked his head around the door. "Is there a problem with Project Helios?"

"Project Helios is running smoothly."

"Lennox accidentally hired some woman that Brian flattened to be his new dog walker, and now she thinks he's me."

"Why does she think that?"

"Because he told her his name was Kevin."

Haris's turn to roll his eyes. "Is she pretty? I bet she's pretty."

"She might be pretty," Lennox admitted. He'd become Lennox at college, ever since he lost the housing lottery and ended up with a roommate who was also named Hayden.

"Did you learn nothing from Liliana? Is your PhD in electrical engineering or self-sabotage?"

Harsh.

Harsh, but fair.

Liliana had moved out of his apartment in New York now, but she'd left a trail of destruction in her wake. Not just the physical mess—although Sol, Lennox's other business partner, had sent him photos and the place was a wreck—but the damage to his heart, too. Hell hath no fury like a supermodel scorned. She'd only been interested in the money, he should have realised that, but her betrayal still hurt.

Never again.

Brian might have been an asshole, but at least he was loyal.

"I didn't hire her for her looks; I hired her because she likes dogs, plus she doesn't mind hanging out at my place to study during the day because she and her roommate don't get along."

"So she's in your apartment right now?"

"Yeah."

"Your furniture-less apartment?"

"There's a table and a coffee machine." He'd spent yesterday evening setting the coffee machine up so it was ready for Leah in the morning. "That's all I needed when I was a student."

Buying furniture in Richmond hadn't seemed like a priority. Brian would only eat it, and it wasn't as if Lennox planned to live in the apartment for long. Once Project Helios was underway and his New York penthouse had been remodelled to remove every last trace of Liliana, he could go home. In the meantime, the borrowed apartment Sol had bought as a long-term investment was perfectly adequate.

"Between Brian and your taste in decor, I give her a week," Haris said.

"Maybe I'll get her a cushion."

Kevin snorted. "Don't forget his charming personality."

"She's there to walk Brian, that's all. I swear."

"If we're giving this arrangement a week, does that still mean I have to 'sanitise' my social media?" Kevin used little air quotes around the word "sanitise."

"If you wouldn't mind?"

Kevin had been with Lennox for five years now, since the days when Sol had to hustle for every dollar of investment money and Lennox and Haris slept in their shared office because they couldn't afford to rent an apartment as well as lab space. Kevin had walked in with his résumé one afternoon and offered to work a month for free because nobody else would give him a chance. Since the previous administrator had quit to work somewhere that was able to pay her more than minimum wage—things had been tight in those days—Lennox had given Kevin that chance, and he'd repaid the favour tenfold.

"There're probably twenty Kevin Haygoods in Virginia."

"I accidentally let slip where I worked too. Where you worked."

Kevin let out a long sigh. "Good thing you gave me that raise."

Make that elevenfold.

"I appreciate it."

"Do I need to scrub my Tinder profile as well?"

"You use Tinder?"

"You should try it."

"I'm never dating again."

"How about this?" Haris suggested. "If you scrub Tinder for a month, Lennox will pay your Saturday-night bar bills so you can meet a woman the traditional way."

"Hey—"

"Shake on the deal, Lennox."

Had Haris been taking lessons in negotiation from Sol? No, no, when Sol negotiated, he'd fuck you into a corner and make you believe you enjoyed it—his words, not Lennox's. There was nothing remotely pleasant about this discussion. Lennox felt like a jerk for even asking Kevin to erase his online life, but desperate men did desperate things.

"Fine, I'll pick up the tab. And, Kevin, could you please contact the IT department and have them remove my photo from the company website too?"

Haris was shaking his head before Lennox finished the sentence. "Whoa, whoa, whoa... You can't do that."

"It's only temporary."

"If my photo's there and Sol's photo is there, don't you think it'll look weird if yours is missing?"

Possibly, but Lennox wasn't about to take chances. "Fine. We'll get the IT department to replace my mugshot with a JPEG of a white box with a small blue square and a question mark in the middle. That way, users will think it's just a browser issue."

Kevin finished his coffee and put the mug back on the tray. "You've really thought this through, haven't you?"

"I'm an engineer. I have a doctorate in thinking things through."

Haris backed toward the door. "Yes, with your dick."

"That's a physical impossibility."

"Which is why you have a woman in your apartment who's under the impression that you're your assistant."

The truth stung like a ten-petawatt laser. Despite having an IQ of 179 and a bunch of letters after his name, Lennox still found himself in the first percentile when it came to social skills. He should have taken etiquette classes instead of that physics elective.

"It's strictly business."

Most of the time, the awkwardness didn't matter. He had his dream job, a small but perfectly adequate circle of friends, and a hand-picked team who understood him. He could spend the rest of his life tinkering in the lab and never again need to worry about making the rent. Or tiptoeing across the dating minefield.

"Yeah, right," Haris scoffed.

"It's true."

All Lennox needed was a reliable walker for Brian.

6

LEAH

"**K**evin's on his way up," Tanner said through my earpiece.

He was back on café duty again, but I wasn't feeling quite so bitter today seeing as I was inside as well. Good thing, because it was pouring rain. I'd been watching the weather forecast since I arrived at Belvedere Place, and if the tech gods had gotten it right, the black clouds should blow over by early afternoon.

Then I could walk Brian.

Yay.

I hurried over to the wall Kevin's apartment shared with Garner's, picked up the recording unit, and tucked it into my backpack. It really was a neat little widget. All I had to do was butt the microphone up to the wall, and it recorded the sounds from Garner's home and transmitted them back to Blackwood HQ. I could listen in via my earpiece too, and if I heard anything interesting, I'd alert Dan and Tanner.

So far, all Garner had done was binge-watch telenovelas. My Spanish was rusty, but as best I could work out, Julieta had been fired from her job as a hotel maid, arrived home to find her boyfriend in bed with her mother, and then realised she was pregnant. And that was all in a single day. Now I needed to find out what channel the show was on because it was far more exciting than the reports I was preparing. Being on surveillance duty didn't excuse me from my regular job, unfortunately, but Marvin had added a shortcut to my laptop. If I hit Ctrl+Q, PowerPoint disappeared and a half-written essay about cuttlefish popped up. Who knew that those were even molluscs?

Even if Tanner hadn't alerted me to Kevin's arrival, Brian would have. A full thirty seconds before Kevin's keys rattled, the mutt began sniffing around the door and whining. Did he have magic ears or an extraordinary nose? Or merely a spooky sixth sense?

"No, no, don't scratch the paint."

I grabbed his collar just as Kevin got the door open, and Brian must have had Shazam-like strength as well because he launched himself forward, taking me with him, and half a second later, my face hit the edge of the door with enough force to knock me on my ass.

Again.

You've got to be kidding. Someone up there was playing a cruel joke. If this was payback for the Sloane thing, then I'd apologised a million times for that. Plus she'd hooked up with a hot guy afterward, so it wasn't as if things hadn't worked out in the end.

"Shit!"

And ouch. Pain radiated out around my cheekbone, and for a moment, I saw two Kevins on their knees beside me. And three Brians, although that could just have been him leaping around in excitement.

Kevin hauled him away. "Go to your bed. *Bed!*"

"You okay?" Tanner asked in my ear at the exact same time as Kevin voiced the question in person.

No. No, I definitely wasn't okay. The whole left side of my face was throbbing, and if the tenderness was anything to go by, I might have fractured something. But I was *not* about to suffer the indignity of feeding the office gossip mill.

"I'm fine, I'm fine. Just a little spill," I added for Tanner's benefit.

"Sorry. Heck, I'm so sorry."

"Brian gets excited to see you, huh?"

"Always."

Kevin rose to his feet and offered me a hand, which felt kind of weird, but the chances of standing gracefully by myself while my head was spinning were slim. So I accepted, and ooh, lovely, he had sweaty palms.

"Thanks."

"Do you need ice? For your, uh...?" He circled a finger over his cheek as I sank onto the one and only chair.

"You have ice?"

I already knew he didn't have ice because when I'd looked for some earlier to go in my soda, the only thing in his freezer had been a package of petits pois and a pint of Ben & Jerry's. I knew which of the two I needed at that moment, and it wasn't the peas.

"Well, I don't have actual ice, but I might have frozen vegetables."

While I didn't love the idea of sitting with petit pois pressed against my face, I also wasn't a fan of swelling. And I had a gym date with Darius tomorrow night. Bruising, I could hide with make-up, but there only so much help contouring was able to give.

"Frozen vegetables would be great. Just *great*."

I couldn't afford to screw up my time with Darius. Finding a suitable suitor was so damn difficult these days. Of the three men I'd messaged on DateMe yesterday, the probable had replied with an invite to his apartment, and I just wasn't that sort of girl, one of the possibles had sent me a dick pic, and the other hadn't responded at all. Urgh.

"You sure you're okay?" Tanner asked. "Do you need to get out of there?"

"I'm staying," I whispered as Brian trotted off to the kitchen with Kevin. Five bucks said Tanner would tell Dan about the incident anyway. He sounded worried, which I guess was sweet, but at that moment, there was a lot to be said for indifference. "I think I'm okay."

"Did you say something?" Kevin called.

"Uh, just giving myself a pep talk."

"I have peas. A whole bag." When he reappeared, the bag was wrapped in a tea towel. Thankfully, it looked clean. "Do you want Advil too? There's some in the bathroom."

Why not? "I'd be grateful."

Kevin fetched painkillers and a glass of water, while Brian brought me a...carrot? He laid it carefully in my lap, then sat watching me, his tongue hanging out as he panted. Drool began soaking through my pants. I'd better get a damn raise after this.

"Here's your— Aw, he brought you a carrot."

"Yeah, I can see that."

"It means he likes you. Carrots are his favourite thing in the world."

Couldn't Kevin have adopted a dog that loved, say, red wine? Who wanted a carrot? But I put a hand over my heart and tried for sincerity.

"That's so cute." Wait. "Where did he even get the carrot?"

"Oh, he learned how to open the refrigerator."

"Wow."

"Yeah, I know, not very hygienic." Kevin held the peas to my cheek, his touch surprisingly gentle. "I had to get a new refrigerator with a different door, but Brian got sad, so now he has his own refrigerator for carrots."

"You have no furniture, but your dog has a refrigerator?"

A shrug. "Priorities."

Up close, I got a better look at Kevin. His eyes were a strange colour. Grey that faded to blue and then green at the edges of the irises. Good skin, and excellent bone structure, on the top half of his face at least. The beard needed help. A lot of help. Think hedge trimmer rather than barber. His teeth got a pass too. Genetics had been kind, but he'd ruined the benefits by doing up the top button on his polo shirt and teaming it with a pair of faded jeans. Was that the same shirt he'd been wearing yesterday? Not the one he'd used to dry Brian's feet, but the one he'd changed into? Was he enough of a geek to model his wardrobe on Steve Jobs and wear the same thing every day, or did he just not do laundry?

"I think I can hold the peas by myself."

"Uh, sure. Of course you can." Kevin rocked back on his heels and stood. "Do you need to go to the hospital?"

"It's only bruised."

"Right. So I thought I'd see how you were doing, but I guess the answer is 'not great.'"

"Brian was behaving pretty well until you got here. Really chilled out. Just lying down and scooching around the room after the sunbeam."

At the sound of his name, Brian pressed against my leg and laid his head on my knee. According to Georgia, that meant he wanted his head scratched. I gingerly patted him with my free hand, and he groaned with what I had to assume was pleasure seeing as he didn't move away.

"Oh?" Kevin sounded surprised. "Good. That's good. But in light of the, uh...face thing, I'll understand perfectly if you want to quit."

"Quit? What?" I couldn't quit. Nothing would make me

happier, but Dan would kill me. "Over a little accident? Nuh-uh. Us Missouri girls are tough—that's where I come from—and Brian hasn't had his walk yet today."

"His walk... Yes... Is cash okay? I figured it would be."

"Cash?"

"I said I'd pay you?"

"Of course—yes, cash is fine. Perfect."

"Do I need to order more coffee pods too?"

"I haven't been using the coffee machine. I—" *No, Leah, confessing your addiction to non-fat lattes with caramel drizzle isn't smart when you're pretending to be a student.* "I didn't know I was allowed."

"Please, make yourself at home." Kevin dropped a fifty-dollar bill onto the table as he glanced around the barren apartment. "Home-ish. Do you want a cushion?"

"You have a cushion?"

"No, but I could buy one."

This guy was an absolute dork. He made Marvin look stylish.

"How about I just bring a cushion from home?"

"That would be okay too."

"Great."

"So, uh, I guess I should get going. You're sure you don't need medical attention?"

"Really, I'm good with the peas."

"Text me if there are any problems?"

"I promise."

"Then, uh..." Kevin backed toward the door. "Bye."

"See ya."

When the door clicked behind him, I let out a groan louder than Brian's. How did people do this? Work undercover, I mean? Emmy and Dan fell effortlessly into the role, but for me, every interaction was a chore. And I was so scared of getting something wrong. Of screwing up more than I had already.

"Awk-ward," Tanner murmured in my ear.

Kevin's footsteps faded away. Tanner was right—this was awkward as hell, and I hated being stuck in the apartment on my own, but others at Blackwood did worse things for the job. I could cope. Emmy had gotten shot in the line of duty, for goodness' sake, and Dan had nearly been roasted alive.

All I had to do was walk a dog, and Kevin was harmless.

Or so I thought until the next morning.

7

LEAH

"Kevin's a *criminal*? Are you kidding me? I've been alone with him in his apartment."

I'd swung by the office on Thursday morning to drop off a birthday gift for Knox and made the mistake of looking at the results of Kevin's background check while I was there. And now he needed a new dog walker.

Dan, however, didn't seem to share my concerns.

"Chill, he stole a car. Who hasn't stolen a car?"

"Me! I haven't stolen a car." I jabbed a finger at her laptop screen. "And he assaulted a police officer. Don't tell me you've done that too."

"No, but I've been damn tempted on several occasions."

Emmy paused in the doorway. "I've assaulted a police officer."

Why didn't that surprise me? "Tell me he wasn't on duty at the time?"

"Oh, he was working, but he'd turned off his body cam and all the witnesses said it was an accident."

"What witnesses?"

Dan stuck her hand up. "And also Mack."

42

Again, I should have guessed. Mack was Blackwood's head IT geek as well as Dan and Emmy's partner in crime.

"What happened?" I asked, curiosity getting the better of me.

"The cop was a bad apple in the Miami PD. Let's just say there was a reason he'd turned off the camera, and it backfired on him. How did we get onto this topic, anyhow?"

"The guy whose apartment we're borrowing for the Garner stake-out has a record," Dan told her.

"A bad one?"

"Vehicular theft, the assault, and aiding escape. Seems as if it all stemmed from one incident. And the cops got their own back—check out the mugshot."

Did I have to? Dan was right about the retribution—the whole top half of Kevin's face was a tie-dye swirl of purples and reds, and his eyes were swollen shut. Plus the chin was a little weak—I saw now why he'd grown the beard.

Emmy stepped forward for a closer look. "Not even Mack could Photoshop that into something resembling human." Then she peered at me. "Nice black eye. I heard you got attacked by a dog?"

"A door, actually, but the dog was involved."

"Who knew surveillance could be so hazardous?"

"It's not funny."

"Absolutely not," she said, but her smirk didn't quite disappear.

"Good thing I'm going back to my desk today."

Dan's sly smile vanished entirely. "Your desk? No way. We need you in Haygood's apartment."

"Which part of 'criminal record' don't you understand?"

"He's been rehabilitated."

"How do you know that?"

"He has a dog. An apartment. A good job at Hydrogen Labs."

"Criminals can't own dogs? What about that Mafia guy with the Shih Tzu?"

"Well, I guess they can."

"And Garner—who you think is also a criminal—lives in the apartment next door."

Emmy gave a soft chuckle. "Leah does have a point, and didn't you say Garner gave off bad vibes?" Dan glared at her. "But we've still got to watch Haygood, obviously."

"And what even is Hydrogen Labs? Is it an actual lab? Or some marketing agency named by hipsters?"

"An actual lab."

"So Kevin could be cooking meth from nine to five."

"No, it's a legit company. They invented a more environmentally friendly battery and made millions."

"The name sounds familiar," Emmy said. "I'm pretty sure I've seen it in a prospectus somewhere. Hey, Black," she called to her husband in the office next door. "Do you recall any specifics about Hydrogen Labs? Did we invest in that?"

He ambled in, and I looked up at him. And I mean up. The guy stood six and a half feet tall, and speaking of criminal activity, it should be illegal to be that handsome, especially when a guy was a billionaire. And the sickening thing was, he and Emmy were perfect together. *Perfect.* I'd say a match made in heaven, but they both danced with the devil too often for that to be true.

"Not in Hydrogen Labs, but we invested in a new ethical hedge fund started by one of its founders. Sharp guy."

"An ethical hedge fund? Isn't that an oxymoron?"

"I guess that depends on your ethics. What do you want to know about Hydrogen Labs?"

"Are they likely to hire an asshole? Leah's camping out in an apartment belonging to one of their employees, and we just found out he's got a record."

"I'm not going back there," I said, but everyone ignored me.

"How long has he worked at Hydrogen Labs?"

Dan checked her screen. "Five years, according to LinkedIn."

"Sol King doesn't suffer fools gladly. He clawed his way up from the streets, the same way you and Emmy did."

"Sol King? Should I be familiar with that name?"

"Solomon King—their frontman. Also known as Midas. He does all the talking, and the geeks stay in the lab. Right now, the company's prosperous and it's growing, but it's still not that big in the grand scheme of things. Certainly small enough for Sol to know every employee personally. And if there was a problem with one of them, he's ruthless enough to kick them to the kerb without a second thought."

Dan gave me what I assumed was meant to be an encouraging smile. "So whatever issues Kevin had when he was a teenager, he's probably learned from his mistakes."

"Probably?"

"Has he worried you at any point over the past two days?"

I had to concede that he hadn't. In fact, he'd been sort of nice in a nerdy kind of way. "No, but I haven't had much contact with him."

"Tanner can stay nearby for now, and once things have settled, I can't see Kevin spending much time in his apartment. It's not as if he has a car. Getting home at lunchtime means either a cab ride or a bus ride."

"No car?"

"No licence. He lived in New York, remember? The subway's faster."

"He stole a car and he didn't even know how to drive?"

"Ah, young grasshopper, I drove for years before I got my licence," Emmy pointed out. "And depending on how you look at it, him having a record could be a good thing."

"How do you figure that?"

"He did stupid shit, but he wasn't smart enough to get away with it. Which means that fingers crossed and a following wind, he'll probably remain oblivious to the fact that y'all are using his apartment for an unauthorised surveillance op." She patted me on the shoulder. "Good luck."

"But I—"

Dan pulled her mouth down at the corners. "Are you heartless enough to make Brian miss his haircut? I checked out the photos—the poor mutt can hardly see. No wonder he keeps running into you."

"I—"

"I swear I wouldn't ask you to go back there if I thought there would be a problem. Emmy and I both got up to far worse than Kevin as teens, and we turned out okay."

"That's debatable."

"You're still worried?"

"A little. Surveillance duty isn't exactly in my wheelhouse."

Dan blew out a long breath. "I'll understand if you want to back out. No hard feelings, I promise. There're times when the Sanderson job feels like it's jinxed. But if you do this, I'll get Emmy to sign off on an extra week of vacation."

"Paid?"

"Of course."

Damn, that was actually a good offer. I could go visit Laken in New York or catch up with my brother, his wife, and my new niece. Or take a last-minute trip somewhere hot, maybe with Darius if I played my cards right. The Caribbean? I'd always wanted to go there. Plus there was a chance of finding Molly Sanderson's necklace, and she seemed like such a sweet old lady.

Did I truly believe Kevin was dangerous? Not really. I trusted Dan's judgment. Which was why I also believed her when she said the job was jinxed. With Brian in the mix, broken bones were a very real possibility.

"What about sick days? If I trip over Brian and break my neck, can I get extra sick days?"

"You're not going to break your neck."

"But if I do?"

"Then we'll sort out extra sick days. What time is Brian's barber appointment?"

"Nine a.m."

Which meant that if I was going to keep playing a part in this horror show, I needed to leave right now.

8

LEAH

At twelve thirty on Friday, Brian started whining, and I knew Kevin was nearby. The dog was a damn psychic. But why did Kevin keep coming home for lunch? Trust issues? This whole "act natural and he won't suspect a thing" charade was tougher than I ever thought it would be. Everything I said, everything I did, I second-guessed myself.

Still, I headed to the wall to remove the microphone before he arrived, and I couldn't say I was sorry for the break. Listening to Garner was more boring than binding reports. Apart from making one call to his brother-in-law—Garner's sister was sick but refused to go to the doctor, apparently—the man had done nothing but watch telenovelas all morning. Again. Seriously, how did he earn a living? Either he had money in the bank, or Dan was right and he was up to something shady.

"Kevin's on his way up," Tanner said in my ear. Today, he was in the park for a change, probably because the sun was shining.

"Thanks for the warning, but the dog got there first."

"Don't tell the boss or I'll be out of a job."

Brian and I were getting along better this morning. Probably something to do with him being nice and sleepy. First thing, I'd driven him to Hope for Hounds where Georgia's friend Pippa had trimmed off half of his hair, and when he could see again, we'd taken him out to an exercise paddock where he'd run around like a lunatic for the best part of an hour. He might have been smart in so many ways —I mean, how many dogs could open a refrigerator?—but he hadn't yet worked out that he couldn't catch birds. Or maybe he was just tenacious? Whatever, he was exhausted, which meant I got peace to work for the rest of the morning.

Until now.

Kevin knocked, then opened the door slowly, cautiously. "Is it safe?"

"You don't need to knock on your own door."

"I didn't want to surprise Brian again. Where is he?"

"In bed."

"In bed? Is he sick?"

"No, just tired."

Kevin crossed the living room in long strides. "Brian? Hey, buddy. Wow, look at you—you can see again."

Brian raised his head to give Kevin's hand a cursory lick, lumbered to his feet, turned around in his bed three times, then settled down to sleep once more.

"As I said...tired."

"He didn't escape again, did he? Go running across the city?"

"No, we borrowed a friend-of-a-friend's field."

"You're a miracle worker. I never thought I'd see the day he couldn't be bothered to get up for a meatball sub."

"You brought him a sub?"

"No, I brought subs for us." Kevin turned back to me. "I figured I owed you an apology for...you know." He motioned toward my face, then leaned forward to take a closer look. "The bruise isn't as bad as I thought it would be."

Because I'd used seventeen layers of concealer. "That's make-up for you."

"Oh. Yes, right. Anyhow..." Brian opened one eye as Kevin held out a paper carrier bag bearing the logo of the café opposite. "Peace offering?"

"Sure."

Even if Kevin *was* just checking up on me, it was sweet of him to buy me lunch. It meant I could tuck another ten bucks into "Leah's beach vacay fund," plus me and my black eye wouldn't have to venture out to the café. Tanner had probably eaten all the chocolate muffins by now, anyway. The guy was a gannet.

"I brought muffins too," Kevin said. "They'd run out of double chocolate"—see?—"so I had to get caramel swirl."

"Those are my second favourite."

"Sweet tooth, huh?"

"Yup."

"Might be hormonal."

"What? I am *not* hormonal."

Okay, maybe I was a little bit, but how did he know that from my choice of muffin?

Kevin took a hurried step back, both hands in the air. "I was talking about genetics. Your DNA. The liver produces a hormone that regulates sugar cravings, linked to gene FGF21, and people with a particular variant of that gene often have a sweet tooth and also less body fat. So perhaps that explains why you crave sugar? Not that I've been checking out your body fat or anything."

Tanner started laughing in my ear, and without thinking, I hissed, "It's not funny."

The half-smile slipped off Kevin's face. "No, no, you're right. It isn't funny, not in the slightest, and I'm sorry if I gave you that impression. Come to think of it, people with the FGF21 variant tend to be more apple-shaped, so maybe you don't have it after all?"

"Are you a biologist now?"

"What? Uh, no, of course not. *You're* the biologist. I just enjoy reading scientific journals in my spare time. Like...like a hobby." Kevin was halfway to the door now, and Tanner was still snorting in my ear. "I should get back to work now."

"What about your lunch?" I called after him, but it was a waste of breath. The door slammed, and I heard his footsteps running down the hallway outside.

"Shut up," I told Tanner. "Just shut up. It's *not* funny."

"Yeah, it is. But if it makes you feel any better, some chick gave me a really weird look."

"I hate you. I hate this job."

"Loosen up, babe. It's cute that Kevin likes you."

I froze. "What do you mean, he likes me? No, he doesn't. Not that way."

"When a guy trips over his own tongue the way he does, it means he likes you. We should start a pool. I'll call Luther, have him set it up."

"Don't you dare! Besides, nothing's going to happen. I have a gym date tonight."

"A gym date? What the hell is a gym date? Is that where you exercise horizont—"

"No, it is not." Tanner had a one-track mind. Okay, two-track if you counted food. And three if you counted guns. "It's where you meet a guy you like in the gym for cardio and conversation."

"Babe, with the amount of running you don't do, the two are mutually exclusive."

"Have I mentioned that I hate you?"

"Many times. What kind of tight-fisted asshole takes a girl to the gym? Was it your idea or his?"

Dammit, why had I told him about the gym?

"Okay, so Darius doesn't actually know it's a date. But he always uses the gym on a Friday evening—he says he likes to unwind from a week at work—so now I use the gym on Fridays too."

"Darius? His name is Darius?"

"What's wrong with being called Darius?"

"Does he get manicures?"

"Stop being so judgmental. And there's nothing wrong with a man getting a manicure. At least that way, he won't scratch you down...never mind."

"And Dan said this job would be boring," Tanner muttered. "Okay, translation: you're stalking a guy with short fingernails named Darius, and he's too busy with his clean and jerk to admire your power rack?"

"You're the one being a clean and jerk."

"Relax, it's a weightlifting term."

"I'm not enough of a Neanderthal to lift weights."

"You should try it sometime. Then he could admire your snatch."

Keep calm, Leah. How much of a ding would I take on my annual appraisal if I murdered a colleague?

"We do running and yoga, thank you very much. And some people prefer to take things slowly."

"Slow's overrated, babe. Go vinyasa his chaturanga. Say, do you have a spare sandwich up there?"

"Yes. And I'm feeding it to the dog."

I removed my earpiece, carefully turned it off, and went back to my laptop. This afternoon, I'd take my chances with Brian as my surveillance partner.

9

DOG GUY

"It's not funny."

"Oh, yes, it is. It *is*." Haris repositioned the laser a millimetre to the left and checked his calculations again. "All you had to do was make sure the girl wasn't incurring large medical bills, hand her the sandwich, and leave, but you told her she was shaped like an apple."

"Leah. Her name is Leah, and I told her she *wasn't* shaped like an apple." Lennox reached for a pair of goggles, just in case. "Can't you reheat your coffee in the microwave like a normal person?"

"This is faster."

"You spent an hour and a half setting up the apparatus."

"Yes, but...behold." Haris hit the power switch, and the coffee vanished in a hiss of steam. "*Arrey yaar*! That wasn't meant to happen. The liquid should have boiled instantaneously, not vaporised."

Lennox reached for the iPad and skimmed Haris's notes. "You forgot to factor in ambient temperature."

"I did?" Haris plucked the iPad out of Lennox's hands and

studied the screen. "I *did*. The lack of caffeine, it's affecting my brain. I'll remember to adjust when I heat up the ramen."

Ramen? Again? Haris had as much money as Lennox did, and yet he still ate noodles for lunch most days. Some old habits died hard.

"Or you could simply ask Kevin to buy you a sandwich. Call him. He went out to get food for me."

To replace the meatball marinara going cold on Lennox's dining table. Unless Leah had eaten it. Or—more likely—Brian. Why did Leah leave Lennox so tongue-tied? Yes, she was pretty, but hadn't he dated Liliana? For a year? She was a model, for Pete's sake, although admittedly, he'd spent the last three months of their relationship perfecting his avoidance tactics. "Pretty" shouldn't have been an issue.

But Leah... Leah was an enigma. A perfect stranger—emphasis on the "perfect"—who'd slotted into his life like the missing piece of a puzzle. Brian adored her. Lennox no longer spent every other minute wondering whether his dog had managed to chew his way out of the apartment, and he didn't have to rush through work to get home at the end of the day anymore, so why weren't his stress levels lower? The tension headache that had niggled in the background for months still wouldn't ease.

"What's that smell?"

Tally strode in, crinkling her dainty nose, and Haris shrank by an inch. Which shouldn't have been scientifically possible, but nevertheless it happened. The eyes didn't lie. Tally was pretty too, if one looked at things objectively, but Lennox's mouth didn't go dry when he spoke to *her*. They'd even tried dating back in their Columbia days, although after their one and only kiss, Tally had declared that the sparks weren't flying and they should therefore keep things platonic. Which had been a relief, if he was honest. Relationships were complicated.

"The smell is burned coffee," Lennox told her.

"How the hell did you burn the coffee? Doesn't your fancy machine have a setting to prevent that?"

"Haris did it. With a two-megawatt laser."

"With a...? For crying out loud. What's wrong with the machine? Is it broken? Can't you make a warranty claim instead of trying to burn down the building?

Somehow, her British accent managed to multiply her incredulity by a factor of three, and Haris shrank another inch. Dr. Tallulah Berkowitz had that effect on roughly fifty percent of the male population. Another forty-nine percent acted condescending toward her instead, as if brainpower were inversely proportional to breast size and possession of a vagina somehow negated her common sense. A characteristic both groups shared, however, was that they underestimated her. Tally was one of the smartest women Lennox had ever met. Possibly even *the* smartest. But he was part of that rare one percent who'd never found her intimidating, perhaps because they spoke the same language. She'd been a big reason for the move to Richmond. As his side project progressed, he'd needed the help of a biologist, and there was no greater expert on the mammalian olfactory system than Tally Berkowitz. Tally had agreed to serve as a visiting professor at the University of Richmond for a year while she helped her brother—who'd recently lost his wife—back onto his feet, and Lennox had lured her onto his team part-time with the promise of cutting-edge lab space and a generous research grant.

"Nothing." Haris slid off his stool. "Nothing is wrong with the machine. I'll get coffee. You want coffee?"

"White, no sugar. And don't forget to use a proper cup, not one of those flimsy paper things."

"Call Kevin," Lennox reminded him, but it was too late on all counts. Haris had skedaddled, and Kevin was back already, whistling his way through the door.

"One meatball marinara sub for you, and a tuna salad for the lady." He presented Tally's paper bag with a flourish and grinned. Somehow, he was also immune to her death stare, a fact Lennox knew had always puzzled her. "I got you a cookie too, Dr. T. Chocolate chip. Your hair looks lovely today—did you do something to it?"

"Other than tying it out of my face? No. And stop being obsequious."

"Ah, so coy. Len, do you want me to go get more of that good coffee for Leah? You must be running low."

"Who's Leah?" Tally wanted to know.

"Len's *dog walker*." Kevin added a wink, and Lennox had an urge to take the laser to his assistant's eyelid.

"His dog walker? Is that a euphemism I'm not familiar with? Something to do with dogging, perhaps?"

Thanks, Kevin. "No. No, to the power of infinity squared."

"You understand that infinity squared isn't actually possible?"

"Yes, of course I do, but I'm trying to make a point. I have a dog, and Leah walks him."

"I thought the dog walker moved to South Dakota?"

"It was South Carolina."

"Different person," Kevin added. "This one's practically living in Len's apartment, and she thinks he's me."

"I'm sorry, what? You'll have to back up. Start at the beginning."

When Tally fixed her gaze on him, Lennox understood he had no choice. She was like a dog with a bone. Or Brian with a carrot. So he told her the whole sorry tale, plotting Kevin's laser-induced demise as he spoke. Put into words, the story of Brian and Leah sounded even worse than the lived experience, and when he got to the part about regulatory hormones, Tally began shaking her head.

"And the Nobel Prize for idiocy goes to...Hayden Arthur Lennox. Congratulations on a well-deserved win."

"I didn't mean for any of this to happen."

"And yet it did. Look, if you like this girl, you've got to come clean about your identity."

"She's merely a paid employee."

"Which is why you took a cab halfway across the city to buy her a sandwich and a muffin for lunch today?"

"I just wanted to check she was okay."

"So you'd have done the same for the South Carolina girl?"

"Well, that would have depended on a number of variables, such as—"

"No. The answer is no."

Kevin gave Lennox a look that could have been amusement or pity. "Take Dr. T's advice, Len. You know she's never wrong."

"From a statistical point of view, the chances of her being right all the time are negligible."

"We're not talking statistics, we're talking the inner workings of the female mind."

Which was a mystery to Lennox, and one that he had to concede Tally was in a better position to solve, but math didn't lie either.

"What if I tell Leah and she just...walks out? Brian would never forgive me."

"Brian's a bloody dog." Tally rolled her emerald eyes behind wire-framed glasses. "He doesn't understand the concept of forgiveness. Kevin can exercise him."

"Hey, wait a minute..." Kevin said.

"Right now, it's early days, and the hole you're busy digging yourself into is almost as shallow as Liliana. Climb out while you can."

"But—"

"Len, shush. Assuming that you might one day want to copulate with this woman, whose name do you want her to cry out when she climaxes? Yours or the boy wonder's?"

Kevin winced. "Ouch."

A good point, well—if bluntly—made. Lennox's cheeks burned as he tried to push the image of a naked Leah out of his mind and come up with a good excuse to avoid a conversation he didn't want to have.

"If I got to know Leah, I might find she's not the right woman."

"True, but you set the bar so low with the duplicitous gold-digger that all this girl has to do is trip over it. Tell her the truth, Lennox. When you trot home at lunchtime tomorrow bearing chocolate eclairs, tell her the truth."

"You think I should take her chocolate eclairs?"

"For a genius, you can be incredibly dense sometimes. It doesn't matter whether you take eclairs or escargots or nothing at all. Just talk to her."

Just talk to her. Tally made it sound so easy.

The reality was anything but.

10

LEAH

There was the whine... Kevin was on his way again. How did Brian know? Could he hear him? Smell him? Or was it some weird doggy instinct?

"You're asleep on the job again," I told Tanner.

"Huh?"

"Kevin's gonna be here in three...two...one..."

"Shit," he muttered under his breath and through a mouthful of what I very much suspected was chocolate muffin. Outside, rain fell in a steady drizzle, so he was back in the café again. "That mutt's a freak."

Brian leapt around as I hobbled across the living room to retrieve the damned wall mic, my ankle throbbing with every agonising step. The doctor said the swelling should have gone down by now, but two and a half days on, it was still the size of a watermelon and the colour of an eggplant. Tanner had promised to help me walk Brian this afternoon, but in the meantime, I still had to make it to the other side of Kevin's apartment.

"Here." I tossed a carrot slice from the bowl I'd left on the dining table. "Go fetch."

Brian bounded after the treat, giving me a clear run to the surveillance equipment. Even so, I'd only just managed to stuff the unit into my purse and plaster a smile onto my face when Kevin opened the door.

"Hey, how are things—" His gaze dropped to my foot. Probably due to the hot-pink flip-flops I'd been forced to wear because none of my other shoes would do up. My toes were freezing. "Dammit. *Dammit.* What did he do this time?"

"He?"

"Brian. That looks like his handiwork?"

"Oh, no. No, it wasn't Brian. I, uh, I fell off the treadmill in the gym on Friday night."

Kevin blew out a long breath. "Thank goodness." Then his expression morphed into horror. "Uh, I mean thank goodness it wasn't Brian, not thank goodness you fell off the treadmill. There's definitely nothing good about that at all. Quite the opposite. Uh...uh..." He thrust a paper carrier bag toward me. "I brought you... Uh, here."

I recognised the logo of Claude's, Richmond's fanciest French restaurant, and my mouth watered automatically. Food to die for and prices that would give you a coronary. I'd only eaten there twice, both times when Nick took me out for lunch to thank me for going above and beyond the call of duty. And at the rate this job was going, Dan would owe me eight courses with wine.

"You shouldn't have." Two boxes nestled inside, and since Kevin was watching me expectantly, I figured I was meant to open them. Ooh, chocolate eclairs. I *loved* chocolate eclairs. And...snails? What the hell? "You *really* shouldn't have."

"Go on, what did he bring?" Tanner asked as I tried to school my expression into something other than disgust. But it didn't matter—Kevin was crouching at my feet, studying my purple ankle with morbid fascination.

"Snails?" I asked, more for Tanner's benefit than my own.

I quickly regretted it when the asshole started snort-laughing in my ear.

"You need to bake them for ten minutes. The chef wrote it down."

"Ten minutes. Got it."

"Did you have a doctor check your foot? My college roommate fell down the stairs once, and when his ankle swelled up like that, it turned out he'd fractured a metatarsal."

"The guy I was with drove me to the emergency room."

Kevin straightened. "The guy you were with? A boyfriend?"

"Not yet, but things sure are heading in the right direction."

I smiled despite the pain. How could I not? Talk about snatching victory from the jaws of defeat.

My tumble off the treadmill had been nothing short of spectacular. I'd been trying to skip to the next track on my playlist when I dropped my phone, and without thinking, I'd bent to pick it up. But hello? *Treadmill.* The phone hit the wall and I hit the deck, twisted my foot underneath me, and came to rest in a heap behind the machine. But of course, the humiliation hadn't ended there. I also had friction burns on both arms, one shoulder, and a boob. With Brian as my witness, I was never going to the gym again.

Darius had wanted to call an ambulance at first, but when I assured him that my injuries weren't that bad, honestly, he'd fetched his car and chauffeured me to the hospital. Ever been to the emergency room on a Friday night? It isn't fun, let me tell you. Wait times were four hours plus, and he offered to go and pick up Johanna so she could sit with me, but then I called Dan, and Dan called Emmy, and seeing as Emmy and Black had practically bought the paediatric wing, the boss doctor came to see me right away.

While Dr. Beech waited for the X-rays to come back,

Darius had helped me to fill in the forms—so many forms—and then we got talking. Really talking. In the gym, I'd been too busy panting to speak much, but in a quiet cubicle, Darius sat on the edge of the bed and asked me all about my job, my family, my hobbies. He did some kind of investment stuff that I didn't totally understand, but he enjoyed dining out—which was why he went to the gym so often, he said—plus he had season tickets for the Flying Squirrels. His pop had been a baseball player when he was younger, although he'd never quite made it to the major league.

And before Darius dropped me off at my apartment that evening, he'd asked me out to dinner.

"That's...that's great," Kevin said. "Congratulations."

"We have a date this evening." I was probably grinning like a loon by now. I just couldn't help it. "He's taking me to La Gallerie. Uh, that's a restaurant that's also an art gallery. You can buy the pictures on the walls if you like them. At least, you can if you have enough money, which I don't, but the desserts are to die for. Anyhow, did you have a good weekend?"

Bag in hand, I limped back to the dining table with Brian following. Did *he* like snails? I'd soon find out, but what about the shells? Would I need to scoop the slimy little suckers out? Because the thought of that was gross.

"My weekend? Uh, it was okay, I guess."

"You guess?"

Kevin took a seat on the floor, and Brian took a seat on Kevin. When Kevin scritched him behind the ears just right, the dog melted into a puddle of fur draped over Kevin's lap.

"I tried to buy furniture, but it didn't work out."

"I thought you said HR was gonna furnish the place?"

"They would if I asked, but I figured they probably had better things to do than buy a couch, and how hard could it be anyway?"

"Plus you'd probably end up with corporate beige. So what went wrong?"

"I found a store that sold couches. And I found a couch I liked. But they wouldn't let me buy that couch. Turns out if you want a couch, you have to order it three months in advance, and then they make it to order."

"And you don't want to spend another three months sitting on the floor?"

"No, and I might not even be here in three months."

"Which store did you go to?"

Blank look. "It was big."

"Kevin, do you need help with buying a couch?"

I don't know why I offered. Maybe because in that moment, he looked so adorably baffled that I felt sorry for him, and the words tumbled out of my mouth before I could stop them.

"You'd help me?"

If Tanner dared to snort again...

"I could go with you next weekend?"

"Sooner," Tanner said in my ear, his voice barely above a whisper and remarkably laughter-free. "See if he can go sooner. If he has furniture, we can hide the mic. Make sure he gets something to sit against that wall."

"Don't you have plans with your gym friend next weekend?" Kevin asked.

"Maybe?" Hopefully. "So why don't we go furniture shopping sooner? If we met during your lunch breaks, we could visit a store each day."

"We'd need to go to more than one store?"

"Don't you want more than a couch? How about a sideboard? A coffee table? Bookshelves? Some prints for the wall?"

"I could take tomorrow afternoon off, but will you be able to walk? That ankle looks nasty. Did you get it X-rayed?"

"Yes, but the doctor said it was only sprained."

"Do you have crutches?"

"Not really."

"Not really? I was expecting a binary answer."

"A what answer?"

"Binary. One of only two possibilities. Yes or no."

Right. "So they gave me a cane, but I feel dumb using it."

"Why?"

"Because I'm twenty-eight, not eighty-eight."

"You're twenty-eight with an ankle the size of Pluto," he said, then let out a groan. Blushed. Which was weirdly cute on a scruffy-in-a-hot-way grown man. "Sorry, I didn't mean to lecture. Want me to take Brian down to the park while I'm here?"

"I'll manage. That's my job, after all."

And I needed Kevin to leave so I could replace the damn wall mic.

"Don't worry, I'll still pay you for watching him. It's worth it just to know he's not gnawing on the baseboards."

Great. Another wasted hour, but I could hardly say no. And it *was* kind of Kevin to offer, gentlemanly, so I tried not to sound too peeved.

"Sure. I mean, thanks. And what about tomorrow?"

"I can walk him tomorrow too."

"No, I meant the furniture shopping?"

"Will you use the cane?"

Dammit, why did he have to be so concerned about my welfare? "Okay, okay, I will."

"Two o'clock?"

"Don't you need to check with your boss first?"

"I *am*... Uh, I am absolutely certain he won't have a problem with it. And I did work most of Sunday, so I'm due a break."

"You worked Sunday? Why didn't you call? I could've

come over to sit with Brian."

"Because it was a Sunday? And I was reliably informed by a colleague that most people don't like being disturbed on the weekends."

The more we heard from Garner, the faster this case would be solved, and the sooner I could go back to the office. And besides, I didn't have much of a social life. Evenings, I enjoyed going out when I could afford it, but not during the daytime. And anything was better than being stuck in my apartment with Stefano. He worked Monday through Friday, and on his days off, he liked to cook. Not cakes or cookies or anything nice, more meal prep for the following week, and he was on some weird diet that included a lot of fish. I'd banned him from ever microwaving it again, but my apartment still smelled funky for the first half of every week. And did I mention that he also imagined himself as a pop singer? What he lacked in talent, he made up for in volume.

"I wouldn't have minded. Brian's a cutie." I dropped my gaze to the furry bundle on Kevin's lap. Which end was his head? "Aren't you, boy?"

Brian lumbered to his feet and trotted over to me, then laid his head on my lap, which I had to admit was sweet. I fed him a carrot slice, and he looked up at me with those big brown eyes, begging for another. Okay, one more.

Kevin smiled, and my heart jumped. Was that a symptom of ankle pain? Must be.

"I'll take him for a walk," he said. "Do you need anything else while I'm here? Tylenol? Ice?"

"I'm good."

As Kevin walked out the door with Brian, Tanner chuckled in my ear.

"He likes you."

"He brought me freaking snails."

"Yeah, he *definitely* likes you."

11

DOG GUY

"Did you tell her?" Tally demanded, hands on hips. "Tell me you told her."

"I didn't tell her."

She smacked her own forehead. "Len, you had *one* job. Quarks alive, was it really that difficult?"

Kevin made chicken noises in the background, and Tally threw a pen at him, one of her favoured metal ballpoints. He ducked with practised ease despite the tray he was carrying. Normally, Lennox didn't condone violence, but just for once, he wished she'd hit her target.

"I was going to tell her, I swear, but it would have been a fruitless exercise. She has a date tonight."

"Not with you, I take it?"

"With some guy from her gym. He swooped in when she fell off the treadmill."

Tally winced. "Ouch."

"I know, it must've hurt like hell. Her ankle's purple and twice the size it should be."

"I was referring to you being friend-zoned, but I suppose

the sentiment works for an accidental edema as well. Although I still think you should have explained the situation."

"Why? What was the point?"

"You'll be here for, what, three months? A lot can change in that time. What if the chap from the gym turns out to be a pillock? Or a terrible bore? Does he lift weights? Did you know that side effects of taking anabolic steroids include shrinking testicles and a decreased sperm count? And if we're talking long-term, an increased risk of prostate cancer as well?"

"Knowing my luck, he's an endurance runner rather than a muscle-bound hulk."

"But how do you know? That's right, you don't." Tally tsk-tsk-tsked. "Always so negative, Len."

Kevin slid the tray onto the workbench and offloaded coffee. Cappuccino in a dainty floral cup for Tally, Americano in a "Trust Me, I'm an Engineer" mug for Lennox.

"I brought you cookies, Dr. T. Chocolate chip. And need I point out the obvious, Len? You also go to the gym."

"But not *her* gym."

Hydrogen Labs had its own facilities on both the New York and Richmond campuses, a necessity rather than a luxury since many of the staff worked unsociable hours. It was all too easy to get caught up in a project, and the next thing you knew, it was ten p.m. Of course, that had been in the pre-Brian days. Now if Lennox arrived home that late, Brian would have gnawed his way through the door and taken a stroll to the ASPCA.

Lennox liked to break for lunch early, go for a short run and lift weights for half an hour to ward off the mid-afternoon slump and improve his focus. Back in the company's early days, he'd used sugar as a crutch instead, which had left him soft around the middle and cranky by five o'clock. Sol had started him down the exercise route. The two of them used to pound the streets of New York, dodging tourists and breathing in traffic fumes.

Their paths had diverged now. After they completed their first big licencing deal, Sol had used his share of the spoils to invest in yet more companies, and now he was well on his way to owning the world. Lennox had stayed with his passion: creating. But despite the differences, they were still close. Sol and Haris were the two people Lennox trusted most in the world.

Some things changed, some things stayed the same.

"Then join *her* gym," Tally said, snapping Lennox out of his thoughts.

"I believe that's called stalking, and there are laws against it."

And besides, he didn't even know which gym she was a member of.

"Let's make a list." Kevin picked up a marker and headed for the nearest whiteboard. Then realised it was covered in Tally's scrawl and wheeled over a portable board instead. He'd learned the hard way not to touch her notes—when the ice cube she'd put in his Coke melted to reveal its Mentos core, the reaction had been quite something to behold. "Pros and cons. Number one, Leah's attractive. I checked out her Instagram."

Tally rolled her eyes. "You're so bloody juvenile. Start with 'Leah likes Brian.' She should get a medal for dog-sitting all day."

"Because you only lasted an hour?" Kevin reminded her.

"He ate my shoes *while I was wearing them*."

"That's a fair point. But as Len noted before, the fact that Leah's a paid-up member of Brian's fan club makes her too valuable to risk losing, so the two entries cancel out. And I have another con."

He printed *Distracting* in the right-hand column.

Had Leah been distracting? Possibly. Lennox had certainly given her more thought than was strictly necessary over the past week.

But Tally shook her head. "Following your hypothesis, that issue is cancelled out by the fact that Brian is no longer distracting."

"I don't mean right now. Think about it—Lennox has this way of picking needy women. Liliana used to call every freaking hour with demands, and that was before he tried to kick her to the kerb and the lawyers got involved."

"Liliana wasn't needy, she was entitled."

"Okay, what about the one who used to sit in the corner of the lab with a novel on the weekends because she hated to let him out of her sight? What was her name? Cara?"

"Carla. Creepy Carla." Tally shuddered. "Like one of those haunted paintings where the eyes follow you around the room."

Hearing his past mistakes dissected and itemised was more painful than Lennox cared to admit, and worse, he couldn't argue with the truth. The best he managed to come up with was, "A painting can't be haunted. Ghosts don't exist."

"Einstein proved that energy is constant and can't be created or destroyed, only transformed. So what happens to our souls after we die? There are things we can't explain."

"The energy goes into the environment when we decompose. There's no scientific evidence to support the existence of the supernatural."

"And yet you believe in dark matter."

Kevin collapsed dramatically over the workbench and covered his head with his arms. "Please, not the ghost discussion again. Don't you guys have a project to work on?"

"Yes, but first we're assisting Lennox with his love life."

"Sex life. Let's take things one step at a time."

"Lennox doesn't do well with meaningless hook-ups. He gets attached too quickly."

"You think? What if..."

Lennox backed quietly out of the lab. It seemed like the easiest option all around. He'd already made up his mind not to tell Leah his true identity—it was a complication he didn't need, not when Brian was happy and he was still recovering from the aftermath of Liliana. Ghosts didn't exist, but perhaps fate did? And at this point in his life, he wasn't destined to get involved with another woman, attractive or not. Tally and Kevin meant well, but they couldn't see the whole picture.

Didn't know how he felt.

No, he'd treat his time in Richmond as the escape he'd intended it to be. Take a few months to focus on the necessities—pushing forward Project Helios as well as keeping the bread-and-butter battery business running smoothly—plus devoting time to his passion project, the creation of a bioelectronic nose with the potential to revolutionise medical science. That had been Brian's fault as well—after the dog had managed to sniff out a single piece of kibble that had rolled under the couch and chew half of the seat away to reach it, Lennox had lain awake at night, wondering just how dogs' noses could be so sensitive. That had led him down the rabbit hole that was the canine olfactory system, and the engineer in him began wondering how to harness that power for the greater good. A functional artificial nose would change the world—it could sniff out cancer or diabetes as dogs could do, or detect explosive devices. Plus the technology might help patients suffering from anosmia. There were so many possibilities for Project Kibble.

Love? That would have to wait.

12

LEAH

When I was twenty and freshly broken up from the third idiot in a row that I'd dated—no, I didn't get a set of steak knives, although if I had, I'd probably be in jail right now—I'd opened a bottle of wine and written down the attributes my ideal man would have. I still had that list saved on my phone. I'd considered using it as my screen saver, but ultimately, I decided that I didn't need to die from embarrassment at such a young age.

Anyhow, that list had twelve items.

Enough money that he doesn't need to borrow mine.

Owns an apartment (preferably) or at least a car.

Excellent personal hygiene.

Stays in shape, but not like a bodybuilder.

Dresses well.

Not besties with his mom.

Wears shoes outdoors at all times (except on the beach).

Closes mouth when chewing.

Good taste in music.

Doesn't eat mayonnaise from the jar.

Not obsessed with women's beach volleyball.

Doesn't snore.

Yes, I realise that some of those were oddly specific, but they were born out of painful experience. And yes, perhaps a couple of the items were a little shallow too, but I was trying to choose a partner here. Possibly a husband someday. If I was going to spend the rest of my life with a guy, why settle for less than perfect?

But as I sat in La Gallerie with Darius, I realised I'd left one item off my list.

A spark.

I guess I'd always thought that if I met the right man, the spark would just kind of...be there, but I wasn't feeling it. Or did the spark come later? It was well known in the office that Emmy and Black, who were, let's face it, the best-suited couple *ever*, didn't do the whole romance thing for the first freaking decade of their marriage. Rumour said Emmy hadn't even liked him all that much to start off with.

And Darius was the perfect gentleman. He'd picked me up, opened the car door for me, offered his arm as we walked to the restaurant, and pulled out my chair. Complimented me on my outfit and studiously ignored the fact that I was wearing one flip-flop and one ballet pump. Helped me to translate the menu since he spoke French. Plus he was learning Mandarin because China was such a big player in global commerce these days, apparently.

He'd told me a bit about himself without coming across as self-centred, and he kept his attention on me, even when the woman at the next table got tipsy and asked her dining companion why he hadn't left his wife yet. Okay, yes, I'd been eavesdropping, but I bet you would have too. And that missing spark made it easy to get distracted.

"What do you think of the duck?"

The food wasn't the problem. "It's delicious."

Darius had recommended the almond-crusted duck

breasts, and they'd come with a chanterelle salad. Not what I'd usually have ordered—I stuck with the safe choices like duck à l'orange—but I was glad I'd stepped out of my comfort zone for once. He also got bonus points for not suggesting snails.

"I'm glad you think so." Darius's smile was warm. "This is my favourite dish on the menu."

"Not dessert?"

"I've never had much of a sweet tooth, but the crème brûlée is excellent. Can I tempt you with another glass of wine, or do you have to work early tomorrow?"

"Not super early." I held out my glass, and he topped it off. He'd selected the wine too, a crisp Chardonnay from the expensive part of the list. "Thank you."

"Tell me, how long have you worked at Blackwood? You said you were an executive assistant?"

Aw, he'd actually been listening during our conversation at the hospital last night. Which put him light years ahead of Simon, who, two months after we started dating, had introduced me to his sister as "some kind of secretary."

"That's right, assistant to a VP and one of the directors."

"Not Charles Black?"

"You know him?"

"Only by reputation. Seems as if he'd be a tough man to work for."

"I actually look after Nick Goldman, and also Dan di Grassi. But Black's okay. Not as scary as he appears."

"All hat and no cattle, huh?"

"Oh, he definitely has cattle."

Get on the wrong side of him, and he turned into a raging bull.

"Guess a man like that can afford to buy the whole damn ranch. Does he spend much time in Richmond? I heard he has fingers in a great many pies."

"I don't know anything about the other pies, but he sure seems dedicated to Blackwood."

"So he delegates the other projects?"

"Maybe, I guess, but I bet he still knows exactly what's going on. Black's basically a superhero without the fancy outfit."

"Just as well. Big guy, isn't he? I doubt they'd find a costume to fit."

The idea of a stony-faced Black trying to squeeze into a leotard three sizes too small made me giggle.

"No, I don't suppose they would. But enough about work. Tell me more about you—how do you like to spend your weekends?"

"I hesitate to call myself a party animal, but I do go to a lot of events. So often, fundraising shindigs are held on a Saturday night."

"You enjoy those?"

"Dinner, dancing, good company, raising money for great causes... What's not to like?"

I guess I'd always found them a tiny bit boring. Blackwood often took a table, and sometimes when enough of the management team didn't want to go, I managed to snag a spare ticket as part of Operation Perfect Man. Because that was where the rich, successful folks hung out, wasn't it? At fancy parties? I'd viewed those evenings as a necessary evil to be suffered in pursuit of my quest, but perhaps I'd gone in with the wrong attitude? How did the saying go? *Expect the worst, and you'll never be disappointed.*

"When you put it that way, fundraisers sound, well, fun."

"We could go to one together someday. I mean, if you're open to that. I don't want to act too forward."

"Oh, you're not being forward, not at all." And even if he was, I'd be a hypocrite if I called him out after my gym-stalking activities. "I'd love to go to a fundraiser with you."

Thanks to Bradley, Emmy's assistant, I even had a selection of dresses to wear. If you looked up the word "shopaholic" in the dictionary, he'd be right there, waving Emmy's credit card, and when he ran out of space in her closet, and Dan's, and Mack's, and Lara's, and Georgia's, and Tia's, and Sky's, and...you get the picture...he just started buying outfits for anyone else with a pulse.

Darius reached across the table and took my hand in his. His smile was warm and genuine, lit by flickering candlelight. "Then it's a date."

But there was still no spark. No zing of electricity. Not even a warm, fuzzy feeling. But it had to be worth persevering, didn't it? Dreams only came true when you put the work in; that's what Laken said. And she always put the work in.

Now it was my turn.

13

DOG GUY

"How was your date?"

Leah had offered to drive to the furniture store, but even though it was her left ankle that she'd injured, Lennox still didn't think it was a good idea for her to get behind the wheel. He'd been tempted to have Kevin—the real Kevin—arrange a town car, but that wouldn't have fit with his fake persona. So now they were in a cab. And Lennox was perhaps the tiniest bit grouchy because Leah was enamoured with a man who wasn't him. He held her cane while she lowered herself into the back seat, hoping the answer was, "Ugh, it was awful."

But he just wasn't that lucky.

"The date went well, I think."

"You think?"

"Darius was a gentleman. Kind, attentive..."

"But?"

"But what?"

Lennox climbed into the cab beside her and slammed the door a little too hard. "It sounded as if there was a 'but' coming."

Hopefully there was a "but" coming.

"But... I don't know... You're a man, so maybe you can help? It just felt as if there was something missing. A zing."

"A zing?"

"Like a spark. That rip-each-other's-clothes-off type of attraction. Darius was charming and sweet, but...no zing. Is that normal? I mean, you must have been on dates in the past, right?"

"Right."

"So if you meet somebody who's perfect on paper, does the whole heat-and-flames thing creep up on you gradually? Or is the relationship doomed from the start if it's missing?"

How was Lennox meant to know? He was zero for three when it came to relationships. He'd felt *something*, that was for sure, a bolt from above that shot straight to his dick, obliterating critical areas of his frontal lobe as it went. Lust wasn't the key to a lasting relationship—he'd learned that the hard way. What *was* the key? That was still a mystery. With Leah, he hadn't experienced the initial rush, although that could have been because he was busy apologising for Brian. But she'd grown on him. A smile from her was worth a dozen stripteases from a pouting Liliana.

"I don't think lust should be the principal consideration." Should he tell her how he felt? Yesterday, he'd settled on no, but if the date with Darius hadn't gone as well as she'd hoped, then maybe he stood a chance? "For things to last, a relationship needs to be built on friendship and shared interests."

"Shared interests?"

"Such as a love of dogs and an appreciation of science, for example."

"Darius likes good food, and so do I."

Okay, so she hadn't picked up on the hint. But seriously, food was all she had in common with her date? Who didn't enjoy a good meal? Well, Haris, who lived on ramen and Cheetos and neon-coloured soft drinks. But Lennox had long since come to the conclusion that Haris's taste buds were broken, so he didn't count.

"What about something slightly farther up Maslow's hierarchy?"

"Mas-what?"

"Food is a basic human need. Everybody likes to eat."

"Right."

No, wrong. Lennox had clearly said something *wrong* because now Leah's expression turned despondent, and in a panic, he rushed to fix the problem.

"But you met Darius in the gym, didn't you? Non-essential exercise is a shared interest."

Why did she look even more crestfallen? He should have studied for a doctorate in psychology instead of engineering because the female mind was still an enigma. But Leah liked to eat, and there was a taco truck up ahead on the corner... Haris had extolled the virtues of the churros on more than one occasion, so maybe a snack would help? Tally was always happier after dessert. And Liliana had never touched sugar, so perhaps that was why she'd been so gosh-darned miserable all the time?

"Did you have lunch?"

"Half a sandwich."

"What happened to the other half?"

"I blinked and Brian ate it."

For crying out loud. He nodded toward the food truck, noting the Health Permit sticker beside the menu. "In that case, I owe you half a sandwich. Want to substitute with a taco?"

"Really? I should let Brian steal my lunch every day."

For the first time in Lennox's life, he was glad his dog had the ethics of a seagull.

"Just let me know if he does, and I'll replace it."

In person, obviously. Having a bank of excuses to hang out with Leah sure would come in useful.

The taco truck had a trio of small metal tables set up next to it, and after they'd ordered, he settled Leah into a seat and then went back for the food. A homeless guy was sitting in a doorway not too far away, and when Lennox smiled, he tipped an imaginary hat.

"Is that guy a regular?" he asked the taco seller.

"*Sí, sí*, always he is here."

"Can you add a month of lunches to my bill?" Lennox was careful to keep his voice down. "Whatever he likes to eat."

"A whole month?"

"That's right."

The man beamed. "I give you the churros for free."

"That's much appreciated."

Lennox added a thirty percent tip to the total, grateful that Leah was busy with her phone. He'd never worked in the service industry, but he *had* spent years scraping by on research grants, and now that he had more money than he'd ever need, he liked to share. Small kindnesses meant a lot. In New York, he'd spent a year living in a one-bedroom apartment with Haris and Sol, and when they'd first moved into the building, one of their neighbours had kind of... adopted them. Mrs. Karowicz baked them a pie every week, and after they'd helped her to assemble a new, energy-efficient hydroponic system for growing her marijuana, they'd begun finding dishes on their doorstep every other day. Nobody made casseroles the way Mrs. Karowicz did, and sometimes, her offerings had been the only thing Lennox ate in a day. After the first big licencing deal, he'd gotten together with his two buddies, and they'd fixed up her place. And by "fixed up," he meant they'd bought the building and renovated the whole thing. Mrs. Karowicz lived in the penthouse now, and when

Lennox was in New York, he still found casseroles on his doorstep. Liliana had turned her nose up at them. In hindsight, that should have been a big red flag.

More fool him.

Leah unwrapped her food and took a deep inhale. "I didn't realise how hungry I was until I smelled that truck. Want a nacho?"

"I'll stick with my burrito. Do you like casseroles?"

"Casseroles? Huh? They sell casseroles too?"

Why had he asked her that? When it came to Leah, he had a bad habit of speaking before he'd thought things through.

"No, I meant in general."

"Oh. Uh, I guess? I used to make them on Sundays so I could reheat portions during the week, but now my roommate commandeers the kitchen on the weekends, and it's easiest to stay out of his way."

Asshole.

"Borrow my kitchen if you want."

She gave him a funny look. "Wouldn't that be weird?"

Probably.

"Does it matter? You're there in my apartment all day, and I don't spend much time cooking, so someone might as well use it."

"Well, okay then."

She focused on her food, and it might not have been gourmet chow, but it tasted pretty damned good. He'd have to thank Haris for the recommendation. The man could sniff out carbs at a hundred paces. Not quite as accurately as Lennox's prototype bioelectronic nose, but the addition of taste buds—albeit Haris's faulty ones—provided a degree of finesse that was difficult to replicate. Hmm. Could that be a project for the future?

"Ready to go?" he asked Leah when she'd finished eating.

"Almost. I just want to buy lunch for that guy over there

in the doorway." Rats. What were the chances of the taco seller not mentioning that Lennox had done precisely that? "Don't you think it's sad that he doesn't have a home?"

"Yes, very sad. Uh, why don't you wait in the car, and I'll buy him a taco? No point in you walking farther than you have to."

"Are you sure?"

"Absolutely."

Mental note: next time, just act like a regular person and buy one meal, then head back later for the other thirty. Still, it seemed luck was on Lennox's side today since he'd gotten away with his subterfuge. In the car, he found Leah discussing the list of stores she wanted to visit with the driver. Did they really have time for all that? Hopefully not, because then they'd have to spend another day together.

The first stop was a rug store.

"Do I need a rug?"

"No, you need four rugs. One for your living room and one each for the bedrooms, but we could just do the living room today. What's your budget?"

Unlimited.

"I can run to four rugs."

"Colour schemes?"

He shrugged helplessly.

"So let's go for a neutral couch plus armchairs and brighten the place up with the rugs and artwork."

"Artwork?"

"Your walls are bare."

"That's not okay?"

Leah just rolled her eyes. "Have you considered light fittings?"

"What do you think?" He rolled his eyes back, and she laughed as they drew up outside the first store. But when he opened her door, he realised there was a problem.

"Where's your cane?"

"Oh, shoot. I must have left it at the taco truck."

Something about the way she said it... "By accident or on purpose?"

"Uh..."

Devious, but he had to admire that. And two could play at that game.

"The cane is for your own good."

"People stare at me."

"You have two choices: either we go back for the cane, or you can use my arm instead. I'm not going to stand by and watch you injure yourself further."

"Can we go with option two?"

That suited Lennox just fine. "Sure we can."

And when she slipped her arm through his, warmth spread through him. Was this part of the *zing* she'd spoken about? Would the zing turn into a spark? And would that spark turn into flames? It wasn't a feeling he'd experienced before, and more than anything, he wanted to find out what came next.

But Leah was still getting a cane tomorrow. If hers had been stolen from beside the food truck, he'd make her a new one himself.

14

LEAH

Spending the afternoon with Kevin was a weird experience. I hadn't expected to enjoy it. But first, he'd taken me for lunch at Emmy's favourite taco truck—I knew it was her favourite because she snuck there every time she worked in the Richmond city office—and the food had been surprisingly good. And now he was acting as my crutch while we mooched around furniture stores. He had the manners of a Blackwood man, but without the whole "danger-danger-danger" persona.

We'd bought four rugs from the discount store, a second-hand dark-grey leather couch with two matching chairs that looked as if they'd never been sat on, and a sideboard whose price had been reduced by fifty percent due to having a scratch on one end. I'd picked out a chunky vase—in hammered metal rather than glass because *Brian*—along with some silk flowers, and those could sit next to the sideboard so nobody would even notice the damage.

Kevin didn't quibble about anything, and I wasn't quite sure what that meant. Did we have the same taste in decor? Or did he have no taste at all and just went along with my suggestions because it was easier? I honestly had no idea. He wore the same outfit every day like a uniform—jeans and a T-shirt—and he appeared to own precisely one pair of sneakers. But at least he hadn't shown up barefoot. And although he was a little unkempt, he did know how to use a shower. I wasn't embarrassed to be seen on his arm. And it seemed some girls went for the scruffy look because the cashier in the rug store had definitely been flirting with him, *right in freaking front of me*, although he'd acted utterly oblivious.

"What do you think of this?" I asked, spotting a gorgeous glass-and-steel coffee table lurking between a mustard-coloured couch and a set of dining chairs.

"If you like it, get it."

See?

"But I'm not sure it'll go with your dining table, because that's wood."

"So we can buy a new dining table? I'm not particularly attached to the one I have. The previous occupant left it behind, so I guess they weren't fond of it either."

"Or we could look for an oak coffee table?"

"But your foot hurts. Don't think I didn't notice you wincing just then."

"I'm okay." A small lie—my ankle hurt more than I wanted to let on. But we still had to buy artwork for the walls. "Why don't we get this coffee table for now? You could always sell it back to the store in a month or two if it doesn't work in your apartment."

"As long as Brian doesn't break it."

"I can see him knocking a vase over, but not a table."

"I love your optimism."

"So should we get it or not? It's forty-five bucks."

"Yes, we should get it. We can hunt for a new dining table

when your ankle's better, and in the meantime, you'll have somewhere to prop up your foot. What's next?"

"A picture for the wall."

"Is that really necessary today? You need to take the weight off that leg."

Absolutely it was necessary, and now I was kicking myself for not going to the art-slash-accessories store first.

"Just one more stop? Please?"

"One more, and then I'm taking you home."

Art on the Avenue was one of my favourite stores to browse. They stocked everything from quirky prints to original paintings by local artists, plus sculptures and handmade jewellery and pretty trinkets and even small pieces of upcycled furniture. Some items were obscenely expensive, while others were surprisingly affordable. Whenever I needed to buy a birthday gift or a Christmas present, Art on the Avenue was the first place I headed, but today, I could ignore most of the tchotchkes. I needed a painting on stretched canvas over a wooden frame, a frame with enough depth to conceal the surveillance equipment.

"What do you think of this one?" I asked Kevin, pointing toward a seascape.

"A boat?"

He sounded doubtful, and I couldn't blame him. The picture's only redeeming feature was the size of the frame. I needed something as chunky, but not as hideously ugly, to hide the microphone. Being honest, I was uncomfortable with bugging Kevin's home while he was there, but Nate had assured me that the wall mic he'd built was directional and also had filters to take out any remaining background noise, so we'd be able to hear what was going on in Garner's apartment but not in Kevin's.

We'd already learned one interesting little snippet thanks to my surveillance activities—until I'd overheard Garner's call to his brother-in-law, we hadn't realised he had a sister. Or rather, a half-sister—same mom, different dad—which was something he and I had in common. At first, I'd thought it was sweet that the two of them were close. Because if Garner had a caring streak, then maybe he wasn't our culprit? Dan had mentioned a second suspect—perhaps he was the guilty party?

But then it turned out that Garner's half-sister's husband wasn't such a nice guy. Mack's research revealed that Clarence McReady had ties to a white supremacist group in West Virginia, and he'd done jail time for threatening to shoot an off-duty cop. Did a disregard for the law run in the family?

I led Kevin deeper into the store and pretended to look at a whole bunch of perfectly lovely but unsuitable pictures. Then I saw it. Or rather, them. Two identical prints of downtown Richmond, a photograph taken from the flood wall on the south side of the James River, black and white apart from a rainbow splashed across the moody sky. Perfect in every way.

"This is it. This is the one."

"For the dining area?"

"Absolutely. The big wall next to the table." Then I looked at the price tag. Crap. "Ah, it's three hundred dollars."

I'd expected Kevin to balk, but he just shrugged, the same way he'd been doing all afternoon.

"You're right—it's a good picture. Great use of light." Kevin picked up one of the prints. "Are we done now?"

Phew. "Yup."

Or rather, not quite. When Kevin turned his head to check out a concrete-and-glass sculpture, I surreptitiously snapped a picture of the remaining print under the pretence of checking my emails and sent a message to Tanner.

Me: Need to buy THIS from Art on the Avenue and take it to Nate/Marvin. Can you do it? Please?

Otherwise I'd have to ask Dan, or Sloane, or come back later myself.

"Do you like this table?" Kevin asked.

Table? It was so much more than a table. The sculpture was stunning. A cutaway view of an underwater seascape, a concrete island topped with steel palm trees surrounded by a smooth expanse of turquoise glass. From a different angle, a small metal turtle swam past. How could anyone not love it?

"It's a real work of art." I flipped the tag over. "And also six thousand dollars."

Kevin chuckled. "Maybe we'll pass on that for today."

"Only today? When I'm fifty, if I'm lucky, I'll be able to afford the turtle."

Kevin merely smiled. "Sometimes, the unexpected happens."

Didn't I know it? I'd been pounced upon by a filthy dog, coerced into working surveillance when I really didn't want to, learned more about snails than I cared to know, ended up hanging out with a guy I'd normally have avoided, and then... started to like him? Go figure.

"Are you ready to leave?" I asked. "Or do you want to look around some more?"

"You should rest. We can always come back another day. Uh, I mean, if you want to. No pressure or anything."

"I think I'd enjoy that."

"Good. I mean, great. That's great. And I'd like to buy you dinner as a thank-you for helping with all of this stuff today."

My heart skipped. Kevin wanted to go on a date? That was...unexpected? And awkward. I mean, I was supposed to be undercover here, and the more time we spent together, the more likely he was to realise that I wasn't a student. And what was I meant to do about Darius? He was taking me to a fancy event this weekend, a fundraiser for a children's cancer charity. But dinner with Kevin... I didn't hate the idea. In fact, if the flood of warmth I felt was any indication, I actually kind of liked it.

Which was unsettling.

"I'm sure the last thing you feel like doing tonight is cooking," he continued. "So if you just let me know your favourite restaurant, I'll arrange for them to deliver whatever you want to eat."

Uh, what?

"You want to...buy me takeout."

"Yes, exactly. Arranging that is well within my capabilities. I *am* a personal assistant, after all."

"Okaaaaay."

Kevin's face fell. "What is it? Did I do something wrong?"

"No, no, nothing's wrong." I mean, he didn't need to buy me dinner at all. "I just thought... Never mind."

"Tell me."

"I just thought for a minute that you meant we'd have dinner together."

"Oh. Do you *want* to have dinner together?"

Now the ball was back in my court. But what if Kevin thought I was trying to two-time Darius?

"I always enjoy spending time with friends. And we're friends now, right?"

"Friends? Yes, absolutely. Uh, of course I'll take you out for dinner, but I need to walk Brian first. If I don't work off some of his energy, he'll get up to mischief while we're out."

"So why don't we order takeout and eat it together at your place? Brian's already been on his own all afternoon."

"You wouldn't mind that?"

"I'm good with it." Which was as much a shock to me as it was to Kevin. I'd always been a restaurant junkie, but I found that in this instance, the company was more important than the location. "Pizza and a movie?"

Kevin grinned like a big kid. "Sounds like a perfect evening to me. We can pick up your cane on the way."

My phone buzzed.

Tanner: Heading there now.

His message was a stark reminder that my time with Kevin was meant to be work, not pleasure. But hey, at least there would be pizza.

15

LEAH

Sheesh, this was boring.

A waiter topped off my wine—and boy, did I need it —as Darius hobnobbed with yet another captain of industry. Or something. For the most part, I'd lost track after he introduced me to the tenth associate vice president of whatever. Still, I smiled politely and nodded along with the conversation because wasn't this what I'd wanted? And when I felt Emmy's gaze land on me from across the room, I desperately tried to seem interested in the workings of the stock market. What was a price-to-earnings ratio, anyway?

The group sitting at the Blackwood table all looked as if they were having more fun than me. Right now, Emmy was probably bitching about her shoes, Mack would be working out which auction lots she wanted to bid on, and Dan had a glass of wine in each hand. Nick leaned in to listen to something Lara was saying, and Sky stopped a passing waiter to ask a question. Where was Asher tonight? At a race circuit? Now that he'd finished high school, he'd taken up sports car racing as a hobby, and it turned out he was pretty darn good at it. Rafael was sitting next to Sky, watching the room without being obvious about it.

"Leah, this is John Bonner. We worked on a joint deal with Dryden Pharmaceuticals last year."

I held out a hand. "Nice to meet you, John."

"Darius is a lucky man."

I said, "Uh, thanks," at the same time as Darius said, "There's no such thing as luck."

And then they carried on discussing mergers and acquisitions.

My part in the conversation was done.

Was this *really* what I wanted?

In truth, I wasn't sure anymore. On Thursday, Darius had taken me out for dinner again. Fancy restaurant, three courses and wine, and he'd been polite and attentive. He hadn't stared at the woman in the short skirt sitting at the next table. He'd tipped the server well. And at the end of the evening, he'd kissed me.

Still there was nothing.

No spark, no magic, no zing.

Was life an either/or situation? If you got the comfort and security, you lost the thrill? Not necessarily... Plenty of the Blackwood men treated their wives and girlfriends like queens, but their brand of excitement bordered on alarming. On occasion, their families could become targets too, and I had no desire to get kidnapped or shot at, thank you very much. I mean, Nick's former fiancée had *died*.

Should I give up on my dream?

I was so freaking confused, not only due to the Darius situation but because Kevin had tossed a wrench into the works on Tuesday. Why? Because on Tuesday, we'd shared a giant deep-pan pepperoni plus a pint of Ben & Jerry's and watched four episodes of a comedy series on Netflix. And then last night, we'd binged on Chinese and watched another four episodes. And it had been *fun*.

We'd sprawled out on his new couch, tossed crusts and pieces of egg roll to Brian, and laughed our damn heads off.

I'd never before considered dating a man like Kevin, but would it be a crazy idea? My goal in life had always been financial stability, but perhaps I'd lost my way over the years? I didn't need to marry a millionaire to be comfortable. I had a job, a *good* job with a 401(k) and great benefits. Sure, I'd have to budget carefully for the next several decades, but was that worse than feeling trapped in an unfulfilling relationship?

I had to conclude that the answer was no. At least Darius's preoccupation with everyone but me had allowed plenty of time for soul-searching. I'd let him down gently because he wasn't an awful guy, just not the right guy. And then I'd have to work out what the hell to do about Kevin. Because our whole friendship was based on lies, my lies, and he still thought I was a student. Maybe I could keep up the pretence until next June and then pretend I'd graduated? No, dammit, that wouldn't work. If we were still friends at that point, he'd expect to see a dissertation, a certificate, video of a graduation ceremony. What if I staged something? Dan certainly owed me a favour, and Bradley would probably help out.

Could I really keep lying for that long? I had my doubts. Kevin was definitely smarter than me.

And there was also the small matter of the bug hanging on his dining room wall. I'd have to keep that secret too, and the more time I spent with him, the more wrong that felt.

My only hope was that Garner would make a move soon. Late on Wednesday evening, the team in the surveillance room had overheard him talking about merchandise that would be available soon, and seeing as he still didn't appear to be working any type of legal job, we suspected the merchandise would have shady origins. But we didn't know exactly what the merchandise was or whether Garner was the shipper or the receiver. Was he an accomplice of the Rat rather than the Rat himself? We had no idea. But he *had* ventured out for a stroll yesterday, and his route had taken him through a neighbourhood with a large population of older residents. Had he been scouting for another victim? Or merely taking some much-needed exercise?

Darius was still talking, but guests were starting to mingle more, so I decided to meander over to Blackwood's table. Lara hated to dance, so she could probably use some company when the others hit the floor.

Would Darius even notice I was leaving? Surprisingly, he did.

"The ladies' room is out that door," he said, pointing to an exit in the far corner.

Seeing as Emmy and Black owned the hotel and I'd been there several times before, I already knew my way around, but I thanked him anyway, then headed across the room and slid into the seat Dan had vacated. She was always first on the dance floor.

Lara shuffled her chair closer to give me a hug. "How's your date going?"

"Not as well as I hoped," I admitted. "I love your dress. Bradley?"

"No, Izzy. She made my necklace too."

I bent forward to take a closer look at the intricate beadwork, royal-blue and hot-pink sparkles surrounding a mirrored cabochon. The blue matched Lara's dress perfectly.

"That must have taken her hours."

"She says she likes to keep busy. I guess that after..." Lara trailed off and stared over my shoulder, and I turned to find Darius standing there. *Now* I warranted attention? When I was mid-conversation with a friend?

"Aren't you going to introduce me?" he asked.

I swallowed a sigh. "Sure. This is Lara and Nick."

Darius offered a hand. "Nick Goldman, right?"

"Do we know each other?" Nick asked.

"Only by reputation. You're invested in Keltronica, as I recall? I saw your name on the list of shareholders."

"Right. Yeah, I'm Nick."

"You have a good eye for a deal." Darius leaned across the table, a hand held out to Black. "Darius Traver, Full Circle Capital. You must be Charles Black?"

"Just Black."

"Sure, sure. Can I say how terrific it is to finally meet some of Leah's friends? You're a hard man to get ahold of."

"There's a good reason for that."

Darius snickered, but he didn't realise Black wasn't joking. And wait... How did Darius know Black rarely took calls?

"Lucky we're both here tonight, then." Another laugh. Was Darius nervous? He sounded nervous, and he should have been. "Have I got a *great* opportunity to explore with you."

"What kind of opportunity?" Black kept his tone light, but if you knew him well enough, you'd recognise the danger signs. The barely contained annoyance. The calm before the storm.

"Right now, I'm representing a fantastic young company with a great business model. They provide shared, remote customer-care staff, and that industry is growing rapidly. Here..." He fished around in his inside jacket pocket. "I happen to have a prospectus."

Oh, sure, he just *happened* to have a freaking prospectus with him. I felt sick. And used. The clues had been there, I realised now—the way Darius had become so attentive as I filled in my employment details on all those forms in the hospital, his many, many questions about my job, the fact that he'd ignored me this evening until I came to talk to my friends.

He didn't give one single shit about me. All he cared about was Black's money. Maybe Nick's too, but mostly Black's.

Emmy rose, glass in hand. I longed to leave the table too, but I needed to stay and apologise for being an idiot. Plus I longed to kick Darius in the shin, but when I tried, my legs were too short.

Black smiled, but his eyes were cold, cold, cold. "I see you've been researching me."

"Always pays to do your homework."

"Well, in this instance, I'll give you a D-minus. If you'd taken more than a cursory glance beyond my net worth, you'd know my investments lean heavily toward real estate, the clean energy sector, and STEM companies. An outsourced call centre? What do you think, Nick?"

"Sounds like my idea of a nightmare."

"Agreed." Black rolled the prospectus up and held it out. "So take this, stick it where the sun don't shine, and walk the fuck away."

Darius actually had the gall to reach for my hand. What a jerk.

"Alone," Nick growled.

"Uh...uh..."

After a long pause, Darius turned on his heel, but Emmy was waiting, and with a perfect flick of her wrist, she tossed a glass of water over the front of his pants.

"Well, golly gee whiz. I'm *so* sorry."

I was totally straight, but I could have kissed her at that moment. With tongues.

"I love you," I mouthed, and she flashed me a grin as Darius fled the ballroom. *Thank goodness.* I'd have to avoid bumping into him when I visited Johanna, but at least I never needed to set foot in the gym again. My still-delicate ankle twinged in sympathy.

"Ouch," Sky said, holding out a glass of white. "Want some wine?"

"I *need* some wine. Guys, I'm so sorry about...all that. I didn't realise that he...that he..."

Emmy picked up an almost-full bottle. "Forget the glass; take this. And congratulations on completing a rite of passage."

"What rite of passage?"

"Everyone has to date an asshole at some point or another."

"Which asshole did you date?" Nick asked, and it was a fair question, seeing as he'd dated her in the past. So had Luke, for that matter—Mack's husband—and he was looking on expectantly too.

"Uh... So when I was fourteen, this prick asked me out for dinner, insisted we go Dutch, and then ate most of my chicken nuggets."

"Classy," Luke said.

"We weren't all born with a silver fucking spoon up our arse."

This time, Black's smile was genuine. "Mine was platinum. Come and dance, Diamond."

Emmy rolled her eyes. "And then there's this jackass."

But she took his hand and headed for the dance floor, leaving me with a headache, enough alcohol to do serious damage, and the weight of bad decisions sitting heavy on my shoulders.

Maybe life would be better if I swore off men for good?

16

DOG GUY

"I'll trade the sock for a carrot, how about that?"

Lennox faced off with Brian in the living room, one of them on each side of the coffee table. This morning, Lennox had made the mistake of hitting the snooze button, and when he finally rolled over, his head pounding, Brian had smacked him in the face with one half of his second-favourite pair of socks. Tartan cashmere socks that Tally had brought him from Scotland, and they were softer than clouds. Which Lennox knew was technically impossible since clouds were a colloidal mixture of water droplets and air, but they felt soft, and that was the important thing.

Brian spat out the sock and leapt over the table, scattering Lego bricks in his wake. The Lego had been another gift, this time from Kevin. Apparently, Lennox needed to "chill out" more.

"That'll teach me to use the laundry hamper," he muttered. "Where did I put the Tylenol?"

In hindsight, drinking so much Scotch had been a mistake, but how else was he meant to take his mind off Leah and her date? Usually, he could get lost in the workings of his bioelectronic nose prototype, but last night, he hadn't been able to focus on anything complex.

Did the evening go well?

Had she succumbed to Darius's charms?

Lennox fed Brian and forced down two slices of toast, then picked up the Lego. Instinct told him to go back to bed, but reason said he'd regret that later. And Brian needed a walk. Perhaps he could rent that field Leah took him to? Where did she say it was? He should have paid more attention to her words rather than constantly puzzling over his actions.

In the end, he sent a message. If she didn't reply for hours, at least he'd have gotten his answer as to how the date went.

But his phone chirped almost immediately with a contact card for Hope for Hounds.

Leah: Ask for Pippa or Georgia and tell them you know me—hopefully they'll be able to squeeze in a run in the freedom field for Brian. Do you need a ride there?

He stared at the phone. A ride? What did that mean? Leah hadn't stayed at Darius's place? She preferred to take things slowly? Perhaps she was a proponent of the "treat 'em mean, keep 'em keen" theory? Or...had that mysterious "zing" not materialised?

Kevin: You're not busy today?

Again, the response was instant.

Leah: What time do you want me to pick you up?

Guess that was a "no," then.

"I can't believe I was so stupid! Do I have 'mug' written across my forehead?"

"There's no writing on your forehead whatsoever. Unless you used some kind of invisible... Uh, no. The answer's no."

"He used me, and he embarrassed me, and he...he...he had a freaking brochure, and he tried to pretend that was just a coincidence? Did he think I was a complete idiot?"

Objectively speaking, the answer had probably been "yes," seeing as the man had indeed brought the brochure to dinner and tried to present it to a friend of one of Leah's friends. But Lennox figured it wouldn't be a smart idea to point that out to her. Likewise, he hadn't mentioned her lack of a cane, despite the fact she was limping. No, he'd simply offered her his arm when they arrived at the freedom field, and now she was hobbling around, complaining about men in general and Darius in particular while Brian ran laps.

"*He* was the idiot," Lennox tried. There, that sounded like something Tally would say.

Leah leaned into him. "Aw, you're sweet. And you know what? I'm gonna totally rethink my dating criteria. No more men with money." Well, that was awkward. "And if a man lies to me again, I'm gonna deep-fry his balls and serve them up to wild coyotes."

Fuck.

Should Lennox come clean? He was rather fond of certain parts of his anatomy. On the other hand, there were ninety-five million reasons to keep his mouth shut about his true identity, so why rock the boat? He still had Brian to think of.

Brian, who right now was heading in their direction at Mach one, ears flapping. A squirrel darted past along the treeline and Brian jinked left, putting himself on a collision course with...shit. Lennox made a grab for Leah's waist, but Brian clipped her already-injured leg, and her squeak of pain made Lennox wince in sympathy.

"Brian!" The squirrel was long gone, and the dog was unrepentant. "Bad dog! Leah, are you okay?"

"Define 'okay.'"

"Do I need to arrange for medical assistance?"

"I can walk." She tried to take a step. Failed. "Or hop?"

"I'll call for help."

"No, no, please. The weekend's been bad enough already without having to sit in the ER for hours. And all they'll do is give me an ice pack and tell me to take it easy."

Which was sensible advice, but Leah wouldn't be taking it easy if she was hopping around a field.

"Then we need to get you home."

"But Brian will miss out on his run." Which would be Brian's own fault, but sadly he didn't understand the concept of actions and consequences. "And I'll miss out on the fresh air. My roommate's cooking fish again this morning, and it smells *soooo* bad."

"In which case, that leaves us one option."

"I should sit on the gate and wait for Brian to tire himself out?"

"Okay, two options."

"What was your option?"

Now that Lennox actually considered it for longer than half a second, he realised that speaking without thinking had been a mistake.

"Uh..."

Leah elbowed him in the side. "Kevin..."

"Uh, I was going to suggest I give you a piggyback."

"A...piggyback?"

"A fireman's carry would be uncomfortable, a farmer's carry would be undignified, and a bridal carry would prove difficult for long periods because your centre of gravity would be in front of mine. With a piggyback, I could lean forward slightly and...never mind. Sitting on the gate is an excellent suggestion."

But Leah hesitated. "A piggyback *would* be fun."

"Would it?"

"My little brother used to give me piggybacks. Well, I say

little, but he's actually eight inches taller than me, just younger." Leah sized Lennox up. "How do I get on?"

Did that mean Leah saw him as a brother? A disappointment, but also a good thing because moving their relationship to a less platonic footing would be a Very Bad Idea.

"Just, uh..." He crouched low enough for her to hop up with her good leg, then stifled a groan as she wrapped her arms around his shoulders. "Comfortable?"

"Yeah, this is good."

No, no it wasn't. This had been a terrible plan. Now Leah was so close that he could smell traces of vanilla from her shampoo, and her breasts were squashed against his back. The only saving grace was that since she was behind him, she couldn't see his thickening cock. Fuck knew what he was meant to do when they got back to the car.

But that was a problem for later. For now, Lennox swallowed his regrets and set off across the field with Brian leaping around his feet. That damn dog had a lot to answer for.

17

LEAH

Getting a piggyback from Kevin had been a bad, bad idea. Oh, he'd carried me around the field for twenty minutes, effortlessly it seemed, but that whole time, the seam of my jeans had been rubbing me in the wrong place. Or the right place, to look at it another way, but definitely an *inappropriate* place. And then just as I was about to come—quietly, I hoped—the next dog had arrived to use the field and Kevin had carried me back to the car.

Luckily, he'd dumped me into the driver's seat and run off to use the bathroom, so at least I could check quite how damp my panties had gotten. Nothing was showing from the outside, thank goodness, but I was definitely squirming.

"What am I gonna do, boy?"

Brian stuck his head between the seats and slurped my face in what might have been a gesture of support. Or maybe sympathy?

I liked Kevin. Okay, I really liked him. The disaster with Darius had shown me that money wasn't the be-all and end-all, and although Kevin could act geeky some of the time, he was sweet and kind and he treated me like a princess.

He'd carried me around a field.

And it wasn't as if he was on the breadline. He worked the same job as I did, and he lived in a nice apartment. No, he wouldn't need to hit me up for a loan. I considered the rest of the items on my "dream man" list. Kevin's personal hygiene was on point, better than on point. Whatever products he used in the shower made him smell really, really good. Not that I'd been sniffing him or anything, but his hair had been two inches from my face and... Okay, maybe I'd sniffed it. And he definitely worked out.

Dress sense... Well, it wasn't *terrible*. His clothes were always clean, and the casual look suited him. Plus I'd never seen him barefoot. He hadn't mentioned his mom once, or women's beach volleyball, and his kitchen didn't contain a single jar of mayonnaise. I had no idea of his musical tastes, but he didn't insist on playing hard rock at painfully loud volumes, so I was going to add a check in the "plus" column. Did he snore? I kind of hoped I'd get the opportunity to find out, and there were always earplugs.

The negatives? Kevin was due to move back to New York in a few months, and then there was the fact that I'd lied to him about practically everything, so why was I even considering this? Our relationship would be doomed from the start.

Relationship? I snorted to myself. Probably he didn't even feel the same way. I was his dog walker, not potential girlfriend material. But we did watch movies together. Eat dinner together. Gah, this was all such a mess!

I was still hot and bothered when we got back to his apartment. Hot, bothered, and a tiny bit sad that I'd met the right man at completely the wrong time and ruined any prospects I might have had of dating him. What if this had been my one shot at happiness and I'd blown it? What if—

"Are you okay?"

"Uh, yes?"

"Are you asking me or telling me?"

Dammit. Darius wouldn't have noticed if I'd zoned out like that. No, he'd have carried on talking about stock prices or whatever. Maybe there were *some* benefits to dating a complete putz.

"Oh, I'm just a little concerned about how bad my apartment's gonna stink when I get home. But it's no biggie— I can air it out for a while." I forced a giggle. "Or stay in my car."

"Want to come in and watch a movie? I can pick up something for lunch."

That was an even worse idea than the piggyback. My ovaries wouldn't take it, not today. But my stupid mouth had developed a life of its own.

"I'd love that."

Brian panted in my ear as I pulled into the parking garage. Funny how I'd come to like the big furry goofball. Sure, he was clumsy and over-exuberant, but he had a good heart, the same as his owner.

Kevin helped me out of the car and wrapped an arm around my waist for support. How long could I realistically keep limping? I'd have to look that up. Hell, I'd faked so much else about my life—why not an injury too? This felt so...so comfortable.

The elevator arrived, and the moment the doors closed, Brian yip-yip-yipped and ran a couple of high-speed laps of the tiny space, which would have been funny if Kevin hadn't been holding the leash in his free hand. Now we were tied together, and—oh my gosh—I could feel *everything*. Body heat, muscles, half-hard dick.

Wow.

Kevin bit out a curse, but rather than untangling us, he

just locked his gaze onto mine. Time stood still. Hell, even Brian stood still.

"We shouldn't," Kevin whispered.

"No, we definitely shouldn't."

But then he kissed me, and sparks shot all the way through my body to my toes. He wasn't messing around, either. I thought that perhaps he'd have been a bit more...fumbly, but he teased my lips open with practised ease. This was *not* helping the panties situation. I grabbed his arms for support as my knees went weak, and maybe it was a good thing Brian had bound us together? Kevin held me tight as our tongues duelled, and when the elevator dinged for the third floor, I was thoroughly breathless.

Brian bolted into the hallway and nearly pulled us both over, but I wedged my arm against the wall while Kevin released us. He hadn't said a word, and I couldn't speak. A second later, I was in his arms as he strode toward his apartment, centre of gravity be damned.

"Are we still doing lunch and a movie?" I asked as I rummaged through my purse for the key to his door.

"Do you want to do lunch and a movie?"

I jabbed the key at the lock, got it in on the second attempt. "I'd rather do you."

He didn't answer, and I thought that maybe I'd overstepped when he didn't head for the bedroom. Instead, he settled me onto the new sideboard.

"Stay there."

How could I possibly move? Quite apart from my sore ankle, my legs had turned into overcooked noodles.

Carrots? Why did Kevin have carrots? I didn't mind a bit of kink, but the idea of having a carrot shoved—

Kevin tossed the carrots onto the living room floor. Phew.

"There you go, buddy. Enjoy."

Then he picked me up and carried me into the bedroom,

and the second he kicked the door shut, we began tearing at each other's clothes, both of us breathing hard. Why wouldn't his damn belt buckle come undone? Why did he even wear a belt? Hadn't he heard of tailored pants?

The buttons on my shirt went flying, but who cared? Secretly, I'd always wanted a man to rip my clothes off, and Kevin was getting pretty freaking close to doing that. I got the fly on his jeans undone, then changed tack for long enough to pull his shirt over his head. He really did have very nice muscles, and later I'd study them properly, but at this moment, I only had one goal. And that was to ride Kevin like a rodeo bull until I *finally* got the release I'd been so close to earlier.

"Tell me you have a condom," I gasped.

"I have a whole box." Jackpot. "Do you want to slow this down a bit?"

What? I stilled. "You want to stop?"

Now he looked horrified. "No, not at all. But studies show that women enjoy foreplay, and also that they appreciate being asked about their feelings and their likes and dislikes in bed, so..."

"Right now, I'm feeling horny and I'm feeling frustrated. I want you to stick your dick into me and hammer me into the mattress. Are you good with that?"

Oh boy, that was one dirty smile Kevin kept hidden away. "I'm good with that."

He threw me onto the bed, freaking *threw* me, and I worked my jeans carefully over my feet while he shucked the rest of his clothes. He'd really lucked out in the dick department, which meant *I'd* lucked out in the dick department, and I didn't know whether to stroke it or suck it or ride it into the sunset.

But then Kevin knelt in front of me and stroked himself, and I could do nothing but watch.

Oh my.

When he opened the drawer in his bedside table, it turned out he believed in getting value for money because he'd bought the economy-sized box of condoms. This truly was my lucky day. I didn't do hook-ups, and my dry spell had lasted longer than I cared to remember, but I was about to break it in style.

"Spread your legs for me, sweetheart."

Outside of the bedroom, Kevin Haygood was quiet and easy-going, but this new, pushier version of him was pure fire. I did as instructed and held my breath as he eased into me. Stretched me. Filled me. Kissed me with all the intensity of our earlier smooch in the elevator.

This was dangerous, I knew it was, because how could it last? But in the moment, I pushed aside my worries and my doubts and my fears for the future and wrapped my arms around him as he began to thrust into me. Wrapped my legs around him too. There was this connection between us, an energy I'd never felt before, and I needed skin against skin, as close as I could get. I was him, and he was me. We were one.

My orgasm built quickly, and when it burst, I saw stars. Kevin followed me over the edge as I gasped his name, filling me with heat until I thought I might melt from the inside out.

That had been... I'd never... Oh, hell, I was *ruined*.

Now Kevin kissed me softly, tenderly, the flames temporarily reduced to a smoulder.

"Do we have the zing?" he asked.

Oh my gosh. Tears threatened to fall, and what the hell was wrong with me? I tunnelled my hands through his messy hair, pressed my lips to his.

"We have *all* the zing."

18

LEAH

I'd never felt hunger like it. Not for food and not for a man. But after four rounds in the bedroom, each growing gradually less frantic as we learned each other's bodies and how to make them sing, I was flagging. Kevin dug up a menu for Il Tramonto, and we ordered enough carbs to feed six people. I fully intended to eat a third of the feast myself.

Quiet snoring came from the living room. The run at the freedom field followed by a carrot hunt had tired Brian out, and he hadn't eaten a single item of furniture while we were busy in the bedroom. It had been a *really* good day.

"Sorry about your shirt," Kevin said as he laid the table. "I'll buy you a new one."

"Forget it."

Hell, I was keeping the tattered shirt as a souvenir. Maybe I'd even frame it. I glanced toward the painting on the wall above the dining table, the frame hiding its nasty little secret. Nate better not have been kidding when he said the microphone only picked up sound from one direction. I'd suggested eating on the couch, but Kevin said we'd have more dishes than would fit on the coffee table, and I couldn't argue with that.

No, I'd just have to keep my voice down.

"Should I open a bottle of wine?" he asked. "I can call a cab to take you home."

Home? He wanted to send me home? Well, that sure took the shine off dinner. My apartment probably still smelled icky —I hadn't been kidding about Stefano and the fish—and worse, it didn't have Kevin in it.

He put down the cutlery he was holding. "What did I do? I said something wrong, didn't I? You're teetotal?"

How could I explain that I knew our time together was limited? That I wanted to spend every possible moment with him before the inevitable break-up, even if I destroyed my own heart in the process?

The answer? I couldn't.

And then there was the guilt. Guilt that we'd slept together and I hadn't been entirely truthful about my identity. Well, my job. And the fact that I'd bugged his apartment. But I hadn't lied about my feelings—those were very real, and almost overwhelming.

"No, no, you're right. It's too soon for a sleepover."

"You wanted to stay here tonight?"

"I just thought..."

"Thought what?"

Spelling things out definitely worked best with Kevin, didn't it?

"I just thought that drifting off in your arms would be a nice idea."

"Oh. Right." The pause lasted so long that my mouth went dry. "Uh, you can borrow one of my shirts to sleep in. Plus I should change the sheets—those ones are sweaty—and I only drink coffee in the mornings, so I don't have proper breakfast food, but I can go—"

I put a hand on his arm. "Kevin, relax. You don't have to do any of that. The sheets are only gonna get sweaty again, so I'll put them in the laundry tomorrow. And I can get breakfast at work."

He gave me a funny look, and I wondered if I'd overstepped by offering to do his laundry. Then I realised. Shit, shit, shit!

"Work?" he asked. "I thought you were a student?"

"Aah, yes, I *am* a student. Work is the name of a café near the university. Like a joke? You could say you were going to work when really you were going to pick up a cookie. *Was* the name—now that I recall, they changed it last year." I gave what I hoped was a nonchalant shrug. "New management. It's called Java these days."

Kevin stared at me for a moment, and I sent a silent plea to the heavens. *Please, please stop me from being so freaking dumb.* But finally, he cracked a smile.

"My favourite Italian restaurant in New York changed its name from Luigi's to Crunchy Mango."

"Crunchy Mango? But mangoes aren't crunchy *or* Italian?"

"Exactly. Haris thinks they used a random name generator."

"Who's Haris?"

"Uh, Haris... He's a friend of my boss's. And the new owners at Crunchy Mango put as much effort into making the pizzas as they did the name, so it's not my favourite Italian place anymore."

I shuddered. "Well, I just avoid all Italian places in New York, so it's not mine either."

"You had a bad meal there?"

"The food was actually great, but the experience... Truthfully, I'm probably more freaked now than I was back then."

"What happened?"

"I was with my sister. First time in New York for both of us, and we were on a super-tight budget, and do you know how expensive everything is there? I guess you do. Anyhow, we were staying in a crappy hotel in a crappy location—it didn't look so bad on the website, I swear—and we arrived late in the evening because our flight got delayed, but we were so hungry that we thought we'd grab a bite at the nearest restaurant. Which turned out to be this dusty-looking Italian place, but we figured the shabbiness wasn't a bad thing because that meant it would be cheap, right? So we went inside, and it was empty except for these four guys sitting at a table in the back, but Laken—that's my sister—said the service would be fast if there were hardly any other customers, so we sat down and picked up menus. And they were dusty too, like nobody ever opened them."

"And you thought everyone just ordered the specials?"

"How did you know?"

Kevin's lips twitched. "A lucky guess."

"I was young, okay? I grew up in rural Missouri, and the only restaurant in town had been run by the same family for, like, fifty years. And when I say family, I mean Grandpop, Pappy, and Junior, not the freaking Gambinos."

Kevin's grin turned into a full-on chuckle. "You really ate dinner in a Mafia front business? How long did it take you to realise?"

"A while," I admitted, not wanting to confess the whole truth. That until I met Dan and she filled me in on the activities of the New York crime families, I'd just assumed the chef had been off sick that night. "One of the men came over, and we asked for two margheritas and a jug of water, and he chuckled and looked over at his friends, and they laughed too. Then the oldest guy pointed at the door, and the first guy left and came back twenty minutes later with a couple of pizzas in takeout boxes and a big bottle of mineral water." I put my head in my hands. "We even left them a tip."

"Il Tramonto's bona fide. It was recommended by someone at work."

"I know—the food's amazing." This time I avoided putting my foot in it and telling Kevin I knew one of the owners. Emmy and Black's lawyer was a silent partner. "Maybe you could open that wine now?"

Kevin picked up the bottle, but before he found a corkscrew, he pressed his lips to mine.

"Thank you for staying."

"There's nowhere else I'd rather be."

Help myself to any of his shirts, Kevin had said. At least I knew his secret now—he didn't wear the same jeans and sneakers over and over—he had twenty pairs exactly the same, neatly lined up in his cavernous closet, and he rotated them as required. T-shirts were folded on a shelf above crisp white dress shirts and half a dozen suits.

Really nice suits in different weights, black, dark grey, and French blue. All his? I just couldn't imagine him wearing them. Idly, I flipped through the hangers. Brioni? Kevin bought suits he never wore from Brioni? But those cost at least five thousand bucks a pop—I knew that for sure because Nick favoured Brioni suits, and I had to go through his credit card statements when I reconciled his expenses.

"Take whatever you want," Kevin said from behind me, and I leapt a foot in the air. *I shouldn't be nosing through his freaking stuff.*

I grabbed the top T-shirt from the pile on the shelf, a black one promoting some kind of engineering conference.

"These are nice suits."

"Are they?"

"They're by Brioni."

"Is that a designer?"

"One of the best."

"Oh. Uh..." Kevin took a step back, and I hated that. Hated the space between us. "A while ago, I dated a woman who worked in the fashion industry. She got a lot of promotional items, and she brought me the suits. I don't wear them often."

His ex had picked out his clothes? I didn't much like that, but what was the point in dwelling on it? Right now, I had Kevin and she didn't. And I planned on keeping him for as long as I possibly could.

19

LEAH

"What the…?"

I fell on my ass as a rainbow of colour exploded out of my desk drawer and hit me in the face. Glitter, streamers, and…condoms?

"Okay, who did this?" Keeping my dignity was impossible as I scrambled to my feet. "Who messed with my drawer?"

From the silence, the little smirks, and the way most of my colleagues looked away, I suspected it had been a group effort. Well, I'd have the last laugh. I flipped the entire room the bird and began stuffing the condoms into my purse. Those would keep Kevin and me going for at least a week. The lube would also come in useful, but I wasn't sure about the furry handcuffs or…the magic cock ring? What was magic about it? I picked up the package out of curiosity, then froze.

Wait a second.

Wait a *second*.

Why would they even think we needed this stuff? What had they heard?

I must have stiffened because Dan's voice came from behind me. "Chill, nobody knows the details."

"Then how...?"

"We're keeping a man nearby in case Garner ventures out anywhere. He saw you go into Belvedere Place last night, and his replacement saw you leave this morning. The guys in the control room put two and two together and..." She waved a hand toward the glitter. "Voila."

I followed Dan into her office. "The microphone...?"

"Worked exactly as Nate said it would. Which means that last night, we heard Garner mention how difficult it was to find buyers for gold jewellery these days, and we absolutely didn't hear anything you might have been doing with Kevin."

Thank goodness. I processed the rest, and a buzz ran through me. "Jewellery? The necklace? Who was he speaking to?"

"At the moment, we have no idea. But Garner said he'd do his best to move the stuff in the next few weeks."

"Stuff?"

"You know as much as I do. Garner's still a definite possible on our list of suspects in the Molly Sanderson case, but there's another guy we can't rule out either. A part-time food delivery driver."

"Did Molly get food deliveries?"

"No, but her neighbours did. Molly's daughter understands that progress in a case like this one can be slow, so she wants us to keep going. And as long as her fiancé's willing to pay..."

My heart sank. "Okay."

Dan laid a hand on my arm. "You're doing great. Don't worry."

"How can I not worry? I like him," I blurted. "Kevin, I mean. I really like Kevin, and every day I have to tell him more lies."

I loved working at Blackwood, truly I did, but now I felt as if my job was coming between me and my happiness. And I had no idea what to do about that.

Dan's expression turned sympathetic. "We only need a few more weeks, maybe just a few more days, and then we can get the recording equipment out of there."

"How will that solve the problem? He thinks I'm a student. What am I meant to do? Study for an actual degree?"

"We could fake your transcript."

"So I just keep lying to him forever?"

"Okay, then how about this? Tell him you were undercover as a student, surveilling a totally different apartment, and when Brian ran into you that first time, you didn't want to give the game away."

"And how would I explain sitting in Kevin's apartment with Brian every day?"

"Say you're a real dog lover?"

"I ditched my good-paying job as a PI to dog-sit for minimum wage?"

Dan snapped her fingers. "Got it! You're on sick leave. Brian bruised your ass when he knocked you over, and you didn't want to tell Kevin in case he felt guilty that his dog hurt you. Then there was the incident with the door, and the problem with the treadmill... All you need to do is injure yourself a little more. Trip down the stairs or whatever."

"Oh, sure, I'll just break an arm, shall I?"

"You don't *actually* have to break it. We can have Dr. Beech put on a cast and write you a sick note."

That was crazy.

Wasn't it?

Could it possibly work? Yes, it would mean one more big lie, but then I'd be able to come clean about most of the small ones. Would it be worth it? By the time I took the fake cast off, Kevin would probably be back in New York. But long-distance relationships were feasible, even common nowadays, and the Big Apple was only a short flight away. Laken would welcome me visiting more often.

"You really think Dr. Beech would write me a note? What about X-rays?"

"Yeah, he'll mock something up. I'll call him right now."

Later that morning, I felt more optimistic than I had in weeks. We had a plan, and although there would be short-term discomfort while I wore the cast and unravelled the web of half-truths, I'd gladly put up with that for a chance at long-term happiness. After I'd printed and bound a pile of reports, Dan told me not to worry about taking minutes in her next meeting—she'd make notes herself—so I headed for Belvedere Place to change the microphone battery and take Brian out.

My stomach grumbled as I left the parking lot at Blackwood headquarters, and I figured I'd pick up lunch on the way. Kevin didn't keep much to eat in his kitchen. There were six kinds of doggy treats, a seemingly endless supply of carrots, and a giant bag of gourmet kibble, but nothing much for humans. He appeared to buy food day-to-day, usually by ordering takeout.

Java came up on the left, and I lucked out with an on-street parking space. A minute later, I was in line waiting to pick up a panini and a double chocolate muffin. Actually, make that two muffins. I practically had to drive past Hydrogen Labs on my way to Kevin's place—okay, yes, I'd checked out the location—and he'd surprised me with so many little treats at lunchtime. It was about time that I returned the favour. If he was busy, I could just leave the package at the reception desk and ask them to mention that I'd dropped by.

And at least he'd know I was thinking of him.

At Hydrogen Labs, I found a visitor's slot in a lot in front of the lobby and headed toward the doors. The building was more modern than Blackwood's headquarters, glass and steel rather than brick, with solar panels on the roof and what I assumed was a wind turbine to the side. Three reserved director slots lay right next to the entrance. Solomon King's was empty, Haris Kohli's held a neatly parked electric SUV, and in Hayden Lennox's, there was a bicycle chained to a post. I had to giggle—the idea of Emmy or Black or Nate or Nick cycling to work was hilarious. Where would they put all their guns?

The building's lobby was part jungle, part minimalist. A single receptionist sat at a sleek wooden desk, and a small seating area held a pair of chic leather couches and a dinky coffee machine on a side table. Several other employees walked to and from the bank of elevators—the lunchtime rush.

"May I help?" the girl at the desk asked. She was younger than me with a ready smile and a perfectly sleek brown bob.

"Is Kevin available? Kevin Haygood?"

Rather than answering me or checking her computer, she turned toward the elevators.

"Hey, Kevin!"

From the back, the guy did look a little like Kevin, but he was wearing suit pants and a dress shirt, not jeans, and when he turned, he was definitely a different guy. Sure, his beard was similar, but his eyes were brown rather than Kevin's grey-blue-green and his brows were bushier. Not such good bone structure either. He studied me with an expression of puzzlement that quickly morphed into...well, it almost looked like shock.

"This lady is here to see—"

"Thank you, Jessie. I'll handle it."

Now he smiled and motioned me toward a potted palm.

The fronds blew gently in the breeze from the air conditioning, and the sweet fragrance of flowers wafted past too.

"You're here to see Kevin?"

"That's right. But then I thought the receptionist called you Kevin, and..."

"Oh, no, no, no. Kevin's my executive assistant. I guess she thought I could take a message." He held out a hand. "Hayden Lennox."

Bicycle guy? "I'm Leah. It's good to meet you. I don't know if Kevin's ever mentioned me, but—"

"Trust me, we've heard *all* about you."

They had? Kevin had never struck me as the type to gossip, but even Black participated in the office betting pools at Blackwood, so I guess you never could tell.

"I just brought him a muffin."

"You want to take it up?"

Did I?

Yes, I wanted to see him, but when I dreamed up the muffin plan, I'd thought that he'd come down to the lobby so we could spend a few moments together in relative privacy. Appearing at his desk seemed kind of intrusive, and what if he was busy? But if his boss thought it would be okay...

20

DOG GUY

"Explain it to me again. Explain it like I'm six years old."

Lennox hadn't seen Tally this excited in, well, forever. She waved her hands, and sugar from the donut she was holding sprinkled all over the break-room table like tiny snowflakes.

"There's a possibility we can make the olfactory cell lines *immortal*."

"Like vampires, yes, I got that part. *How?*"

"Not like vampires because vampires don't exist." Tally rolled her eyes. "More like HeLa, except the mechanism's quite different. HeLa originated from a cancerous tumour. ORN2708 was created in a lab via expression of a viral tumour antigen."

"How many six-year-olds do you know who understand the meaning of 'viral tumour antigen'?"

"Okay, okay, fine. The researchers took nose cells from a dead puppy, then gave them a virus so they'll replicate over and over and over and over ad infinitum given optimum growth conditions. Voila: immortality. Just think..." Tally spread her arms wide. "In twenty years, the ghost of Fido can watch as his former nose detects explosives at Dulles International and stops a plane from being blown out of the sky."

Tally had graduated high school two years early, but Lennox was beginning to suspect she'd missed out on elementary school altogether. And she'd definitely skipped the lessons in tact.

"If we ever get as far as marketing this product, can you do me a favour and avoid any mention of dead puppies?"

"*If* we get as far as marketing? Do you doubt my abilities? Do you doubt *your* abilities?"

"We've always known this would be a long-term project."

A long-term project combining cutting-edge engineering, nanotechnology, and biochemistry. He had faith that they'd eventually achieve their goals, and undoubtedly they'd made gains so far, both scientifically and financially. Ninety-three new patents and counting, plus three seven-figure licencing deals off the back of those patents.

"Yes, but we're both gifted workaholics," Tally reminded him. "And I like to finish everything early, so..."

The "gifted" part was conceivably true, but Lennox was starting to rethink his workaholic tendencies. So far today, all he'd been able to think of was Leah, studying at home in his apartment with Brian. That was where he wanted to be, not sitting at Hydrogen Labs waiting for Kevin to come back with his lunch.

"How can a cell live forever?"

"Not the individual cell, the cell *line*. Do keep up." Tally looked past him, through the glass window that separated the break room from the open-plan office behind. "Hey, did we get a new intern?"

"Not that I'm aware of. Why?"

"Then who's that with Kevin? She looks kind of young."

"Says the woman who got her first PhD at the age of twenty-two."

But he turned anyway, and...*fuck*.

"Hey!" Tally leapt backward as he dropped his mug and coffee splashed everywhere. "If I'd wanted a mocha donut, I'd have bought one."

This time he cursed out loud, then quickly ducked behind the counter as Leah started to turn.

"Have you lost your mind?" Tally asked.

"That's *Leah*."

"Huh?"

"Out there with Kevin. What the hell is she doing here?"

"Oh, oopsie-daisy. Hold on a moment... Is she the reason you've been spaced out all morning? Yes, yes, of course. And you still haven't told her who you are, have you?"

"The right moment never came up," Lennox mumbled.

And he'd felt sick about the lies all day. Sick and scared. Scared that if—*when*—he told Leah the truth, he'd lose her. Did she realise the depth of his feelings? Possibly not yet, but he sure as hell understood the extent of his stupidity.

"Your love life is a disaster," Tally told him.

"Thank you for that insightful observation."

"You're very welcome. Do you want me to get rid of her?"

"Yes! I mean, no! What the hell am I meant to do?"

"You could, I don't know...try talking to the girl?"

A valid suggestion. But one that would involve knowing what to say, and at this moment, Lennox scored a big, fat F in that particular subject. A first for him, although it shouldn't have been a surprise given his dating history. In hindsight, the reason his relationship with Liliana had lasted so long was because she hadn't shown much interest in conversation. No, she'd been more interested in sex and cash flow.

But Leah... Leah cared about his personality rather than

his bank balance, which was both wonderful and supremely awkward.

"What's Kevin told her?"

Another eye-roll from Tally. "How should I know?"

"Maybe I could try texting him? Or calling?"

"That's a good— On second thought, don't bother. He's heading in this direction."

"With Leah?"

What was Lennox meant to do? Squeeze into a drawer? Fold himself into a cupboard? Why hadn't the architect included a fire escape from this room? That was a serious design flaw and one—

"No, he's on his own."

Thank goodness.

"Tallulah, my sweet, have you seen Lennox?"

She looked pointedly at her feet, and a moment later, Kevin peered over the counter.

"What are you doing on the floor?"

"I lost something."

"What did you lose?"

"His sanity," Tally helpfully put in, either oblivious to or completely ignoring the dirty look Lennox gave her.

"Why did you bring Leah up here?" he asked Kevin. "Are you trying to ruin my life?"

"No, I'm helping."

"You and me, we have very different definitions of that word."

"She was in the lobby, okay? I think she brought you a cookie or something. And Jessie behind the desk saw me walk past and called my name, so I had to make up a story for Leah about how you're my assistant and Jessie was only asking me to take her upstairs to meet you."

"Wait, wait, wait..." Tally gave up on the donut and

dropped it onto her dainty china plate. "Kevin, are you saying Leah thinks you're Lennox?"

"Well, what else was I meant to tell her?"

"This is fantastic." Tally began laughing, holding her sides. "You've actually managed to make the whole situation worse. And don't look now, but Haris just went into Lennox's office."

Oh, son of a gated recurrent unit, no! Lennox intended to tell Leah everything, truly he did, but not right now. Not like this. He'd break the news gently in a day or two, once they'd become more comfortable in each other's company. And, he hoped, inseparable.

"Help me. Please, just help me."

"You're an idiot," Tally told him. "You know that, yes?"

"Fine, yes, I'm an idiot. But will you help?"

Kevin chuckled to himself. "You know, this could be fun. It's not every day I get to be a brainiac multimillionaire as well as devastatingly handsome. Maybe I could give myself a pay raise?"

At this moment in time, Lennox would sign off on anything. "Get into my office and stop Haris from spilling the beans. Hurry. Hurry!"

Thankfully, Kevin picked up on the urgency and strode out, followed by Tally, complete with her plate and half-eaten donut. This was such a damn mess. As an undergrad at Columbia, Lennox had thought all of his problems would be solved if he only had a million bucks in the bank, but it turned out that while wealth certainly resolved some issues, it also created different ones. Making friends was hard, and dating was riskier than Russian roulette. Did people like you or your money? Your personality or your connections? With Leah, he knew the answer. In spite of Lennox's many, many faults, she liked him, just *him*, and he liked her right back.

The basics were there. The chemistry. If they had a solid foundation built on love, the rest would come in time.

Wait a second... Love?

He thought maybe things were heading that way, which meant he couldn't lose her.

He *couldn't*.

Forget thinking about mistakes of the past and hopes for the future—if he didn't get over there and help with the damage control, there would *be* no future. He hurried after Kevin and Tally.

"I found him," Kevin announced as he walked into Lennox's office, and Haris's brow creased into a frown.

"Found who?"

"*Kevin*."

"But you're—"

"Have you been introduced to Leah yet? She's Kevin's girlfriend."

By then, Tally had managed to position herself behind Leah, and she pointed frantically at Lennox. "Yes, *Kevin's* girlfriend."

Comprehension finally dawned. "Ah. Ah, I see now. *Kevin's* girlfriend." Haris turned to Lennox. "And this is Kevin."

"She already knows that."

"Yes, yes, I realise this."

Leah was also looking puzzled, and understandably so. "I'm not sure we've actually put a label on things yet, but..." She broke into a grin. "I thought I'd surprise you with a chocolate muffin."

Lennox forced a smile of his own. "Consider me surprised."

"I guess I should have called first, but I was driving right past, and..." She looked around the office. "Is this a bad time? Maybe...maybe I'll just leave."

Kevin dropped into Lennox's ergonomic desk chair. A friend from Columbia had come up with the design, and it adjusted in seventeen different ways. Lennox watched in horror as Kevin moved the armrests that had taken him weeks to position perfectly.

"Oh, no, my lovely, this isn't a bad time at all. In fact, why don't we have coffee and we can get to know each other?"

Why was Kevin staring at him? Tally sniggered silently, and realisation dawned. *He* was Kevin. *He* was meant to make the damn coffee. Kevin—the real Kevin—was enjoying this, wasn't he? Great, now Haris was smirking too.

"Sure, I'll make coffee."

"Tea for me," Tally said. "And don't forget to use the right cup."

Yes, *all* of his friends were enjoying this. Now what was he meant to do? He couldn't simply leave Leah with the three of them—they'd probably scare her off to Proxima Centauri.

But how could he extricate her from their clutches? Figuring out the logistics of housing Tally's immortal cell lines would be an easier problem to solve. How many lines would she need? Dogs had four types of olfactory receptors, so—

"Want me to help carry the drinks?" Leah offered, and Lennox could have kissed her. No, really. But he wasn't about to lock lips with an audience.

"That would certainly make things easier. After you."

He ushered her out of the office and over to the break room, where they'd installed a full kitchen because some people—okay, Lennox and Haris—spent far too long at work. Before he adopted Brian, Lennox used to sleep on the couch in his New York office five nights out of seven, and his diet had been atrocious, Mrs. Karowicz's casseroles excepted. Brian had helped him to discover the benefits of fresh air and vegetables.

"Oh, gross. Someone spilled coffee everywhere and then just left the mess."

Dammit, he should have wiped up after himself. "Shocking. I'll send a memo around."

Where was the roll of paper towel? He blotted up the liquid, mouthing silent thanks that the mug hadn't smashed everywhere too. Recycled plastic certainly had its benefits.

"Want me to make the coffee? Hey, weird—this place has the same coffee machine as you do at home."

Yes, because when Kevin had bugged Lennox to pick out coffee machines for the new office and his temporary home, Lennox had been right in the middle of a complex set of calculations, so he'd simply pointed at the first model on the list and said, "Get two of those." Which had probably been Kevin's plan all along because he was something of a coffee connoisseur, and that was the reason Lennox brewed his morning caffeine fix in a ten-thousand-dollar Nuova Simonelli Prontobar. A fact Leah thankfully hadn't picked up on.

"Uh, sure. Crazy coincidence, huh?"

"Which cup is your colleague's? Sorry, I don't know her name."

"Tallulah. Actually, it's Tallulah Belle, but we just call her Tally. And before you ask, yes, her parents were on drugs, but she's quite sensitive about it, so..." He put a finger to his lips. "She never smokes anything stronger than brisket now."

Actually, even the brisket had been a mistake, but the fire department's response time had been impressive.

"I won't say a word, I swear."

"Her cup is the one with the pink flowers and the saucer." No way was Lennox going to suffer the indignity of Kevin's "I don't even know what I'm doing here" mug, so he tossed the paper towels into the trash and lined up four plain white mugs on the counter. "We stopped using disposable cups several years ago."

"Same with— Uh, at home, I also stopped using disposable cups."

"You used disposable cups at home?"

Even Lennox hadn't stooped that low, although he was partial to takeout straight from the carton, much to Sol's disgust.

"Can't afford a dishwasher, hate washing up."

"I know that feeling. Come here."

Lennox beckoned her toward the refrigerator, closer, closer. Out of the corner of his eye, he glimpsed Kevin, Tally, and Haris watching through the glass walls and sorely regretted not having gone for a frosted alternative, but with a little creativity... When Leah came within alpha radiation range, he opened the refrigerator door, neatly blocking everyone's view, and hooked an arm around her waist.

"I've been thinking about you all morning."

She stood on tiptoe and gripped his biceps. "Same. Last night... That was..."

He cut her off with a kiss because, quite frankly, there were no words to describe it anyway. Her breathy little gasps turned his cock hard in an instant, and perhaps this was a mistake, but hell, he'd made worse ones. At least the open refrigerator cooled things by a degree or two. Although they *had* installed gender-neutral bathrooms with generous-sized stalls, so if they could just sneak—

Someone cleared their throat, and Leah stepped back, red-faced.

"Oops," she mumbled.

Lennox recognised a member of the robotics team, one who liked to talk a lot, which meant everyone in the company would know he was off the market by close of play that evening. Because Lennox *was* off the market. He had a hell of a mess to clear up with the whole Kevin thing, but Leah was worth the effort.

"Doesn't matter." He wanted to tell her to drop by any

time, but he couldn't, not yet. Instead, he gave her hand one last squeeze. "Rain check?"

"Can I stay at your place again tonight? Or you could come to mine, but my roommate snores, and even through the walls, it's still so loud."

"My place. Come at my place."

"Don't you mean 'come *to* my place'?"

A Freudian slip. "No."

Leah fanned herself with a hand. "Maybe you could open that refrigerator again?"

Tempting, but the Three Stooges practically had their faces pressed to the glass.

"Unfortunately, the drinks won't make themselves."

How long would it take to rig up a remote control? If Lennox got the robotics team on the task, then—

Leah giggled. "Does anyone take sugar?"

No, but he dumped five spoonfuls into Kevin's mug anyway. And when Leah set the drink on Lennox's desk and Kevin took a sip, the look of disgust on his face made Lennox's smile grow even wider.

But it quickly faded with Leah's next question.

"Hayden, why do you have a photo of Brian on your desk?"

Kevin managed to laugh and glare at the same time. "Oh, Kevin put that there for a joke, but what's not to like about Brian?"

"Everything," Tally muttered. She still hadn't forgiven him for the shoe incident.

"He *is* really cute," Leah agreed. "Maybe I should have a picture of him on *my* desk?"

Phew. "I'll get you one. Hey, why don't we go out for lunch?"

Kevin tapped his watch. "Because I have a meeting in thirty minutes, and I need you to take notes."

Ah, yes, two researchers from Stanford were coming to discuss a new type of polymer with the potential to be used in organic solar cells. The material would offer greater photochemical stability, and until yesterday, Lennox had been looking forward to the discussion. Then Leah happened, and suddenly, revolutionising the solar energy market didn't seem quite so exciting anymore.

"Dinner, then?" he suggested, and Leah beamed at him.

"A date?"

"Absolutely. Where do you want to go?"

"Surprise me." She checked her watch too. "I should make a move. Brian's probably eaten the couch by now, and I need to pick up more carrots. Uh, sorry for disturbing everyone's day."

She blew Lennox a kiss as she backed out the door, and she was gone before the full horror of her statement dawned. *Surprise me*? Those two words struck fear into Lennox's heart.

"Lennox has a date," Haris sang as Kevin poured the rest of his coffee over the roots of a sansevieria plant Tally had bought to purify the air in Lennox's office. It didn't work. Nothing could defeat Kevin's cologne.

"At least she seems relatively normal," Tally said. "Which is a minor miracle in itself."

"This is true. Kevin won't need to spend his mornings hunting for the right brand of oat milk anymore."

Kevin snorted. "Or rolling out a little red carpet in front of the elevator. Liliana was a pain in everyone's ass."

Okay, so Liliana had been demanding in many ways, but in others, she'd been easy. For example, "surprising her" wouldn't have been an option. She'd have expected the best table at the best restaurant in town, nothing less.

"Where am I meant to take her?"

"Liliana?" Kevin asked. "How about Jupiter?"

Ambitious, but right after the break-up, Lennox had

seriously considered investing in a space program to do precisely that.

"No, you fool. *Leah*. Which restaurant?"

"Oh, simple. I'll make reservations for you at Claude's. Or maybe Rhodium?"

But Tally shook her head. "No, no, no. Firstly, just booking the most expensive place is such a cop-out, and secondly, you want to check she isn't a closeted gold-digger. Go mid-range."

"Or even cheaper," Haris put in. "If you pick somewhere quirky but good, that makes you look thoughtful. At least, that's what Saira says."

Ah, Saira. Haris's personal assistant and the girl he'd been not-so-secretly in love with for the past six months. The problem? Saira was engaged to a bodybuilder named Axe, and everyone was scared of him. But Lennox had no time to consider Haris's disastrous personal life today, not when he had more important things to worry about. All three of his friends' suggestions had merit, but which would be the best choice for Leah? And what the hell was a "quirky" restaurant, anyway?

Decisions, decisions...

21

LEAH

Why had I told Kevin to surprise me?

I'd lost my mind; that was the only explanation.

The last time a man had surprised me on a date, he'd taken me boating. And I don't mean on a yacht. No, he took me to a park, and in the park was a lake, and at the side of the lake were those little boats you had to pedal. I should also mention that this happened in November.

Me and water, we didn't get along so well. I'd managed to get into the boat by sitting on the edge of the wooden jetty and lowering myself slowly, but that tactic didn't work in reverse. The guy who rented the boats had held out a hand, and I'd been so desperate to get back onto dry land that I'd leapt for safety like a long-jumper taking off, but I hadn't realised that my date had stood up to steady me. When my enthusiasm sent the boat rocking, he overbalanced and belly-flopped into the water, and after he'd scrambled out, he bore more than a passing resemblance to Brian on the first day we'd met.

Needless to say, there hadn't been a second date. And to add insult to injury, the splinter in my ass got infected and I had to sit on one of those rubber haemorrhoid rings for a week. Even now, people still left pink-glazed donuts on my desk as a joke.

But tonight, I'd be on the receiving end of another surprise, and I had no idea what to expect. Kevin brought me muffins, but he also brought me snails. And when I'd asked what I should wear, he'd said it didn't matter.

Didn't matter?

Of course it freaking mattered.

There was a huge difference between a cocktail dress and jeans.

But when I'd tried to explain that, he'd just told me I looked beautiful in anything, and also that he was going into a meeting but if I texted him my address, he'd pick me up at six. Gah! Kevin Haygood was the easiest man to spend time with, but he definitely needed to improve his communication skills.

With little other choice, I fed Brian, made sure he had a good supply of carrots and plenty to chew on that wasn't furniture, footwear, or clothing, begged him to behave himself *for once*, and hurried back home.

Should I go with pants? A dress? No, a dress was too risky, but what about a skirt? What if Kevin decided to take me go-karting or some other nightmare? In the end, I settled on slim-fitting black pants, low-heeled boots, and a pink top with a few frills. That would be safe, right?

"You're going out?" Stefano asked from the couch.

"No, I thought I'd dress up to watch Netflix."

His forehead creased in puzzlement, and then he pointed a finger at me. "Ah, you are making a joke, yes?"

"Yes, I'm making a joke."

"You have a date?"

"That's right."

"With a man?"

Why did he have to sound so surprised?

"Yes, with a man. Can you please take your underwear off the heater and put it in your bedroom?" I waved toward the radiator, where half a dozen assorted thongs were draped like wilted tulips. "I want to make a good impression if he comes in later."

"It's not dry yet."

"But you have your own radiator. You'll have to put it on there."

"The room was too stuffy, so I turned it off."

"Just for tonight, you'll have to turn it back on again. And can you air out the kitchen? It still smells of fish."

"I'll light a candle."

Give me strength.

"Please, not one of those pink ones that make me sneeze."

"I have the grapefruit and neroli."

"Wonderful." I took a deep breath and picked up my purse. If I met Kevin downstairs, Stefano wouldn't be able to start an awkward conversation. "I'll see you later."

I made it out the door just as Kevin raised a finger to buzz the intercom.

"Hey, perfect timing," I said out loud, and inside, I thought *thank goodness.* Kevin had gone for smart-casual attire too, so wherever we were heading, it couldn't involve any kind of sports.

He'd booked a cab again, even though the ride turned out to be less than a mile. Although I was grateful—the twinges of pain in my ankle hadn't subsided, even though I'd taken painkillers this afternoon.

"Will you tell me where we're going yet?"

"Right here."

He pointed at a plain black door in a plain black wall with a silver sign over it in fancy script, and I craned forward to read it.

"Noir Absolu? What's that?"

It sounded like a brand of vodka, and a date to a distillery would be okay as long as there was food to line my stomach. I couldn't afford to spend tomorrow with a hangover, not when I had a meeting at Blackwood in the morning and Brian to deal with in the afternoon.

"It's a restaurant. A friend recommended it."

Phew. It couldn't be that bad, then. Fingers crossed it didn't serve molluscs.

"What type of food does it serve? *Noir* is French, isn't it? It means black?"

"*Noir absolu* is pitch black." The door slid silently to the side as we approached. "After you."

We found ourselves in a luxuriously appointed room. Sumptuous velvet banquettes lined the walls, deep red in colour, and a chandelier hung from the ceiling, low enough that I could reach up a hand and skim the crystals. Soft classical music played from hidden speakers, and the smell of garlic drifted on the air.

But where was the food? The other diners? There was only one table in the room, and there were no napkins, no cutlery, just two glasses of water and a vase of white roses. A man dressed entirely in black sat on a banquette, and he rose as we approached, but rather than making eye contact, he looked past us.

"Good evening. My name is Anton, and I'll be your host tonight. Please, take a seat."

Kevin touched a hand to the small of my back, and we sat side by side on the banquette. Where was everyone? This was super weird. For a moment, I wondered if we'd meandered into a trap, but Kevin seemed perfectly calm.

"Where's all the food?" I blurted.

"Once we've discussed your menu choices and you've made yourselves comfortable, I'll show you through to the dining room."

So this wasn't the dining room? It was more of a...lobby? Anton still wasn't looking at us, and when he carefully slid two small brass keys across the table toward us, feeling his way, I realised he was blind. Kevin pocketed the keys, then twined his fingers through mine and smiled. My world shifted. The way he looked at me... It felt as if I were his whole universe, and a lump came into my throat. Yes, our meeting had been unconventional, but maybe the stars had aligned that day. Kevin Haygood was the man I hadn't been looking for, the complete opposite of everything I'd thought I wanted, but I didn't feel as if I were giving up on my dream. No, I'd just woken up to a new reality, and who wanted to sleepwalk through life anyway?

"We have three menus available," Anton told us. "Meat-based, fish-based, and plant-based. The plant-based menu is completely vegan. And if you'd like to mix dishes from the menus, we can do that."

"Where are the...you know, the menu cards?"

"Oh, nothing's written down. This is a sensory experience, designed to help you savour the food in a way you never have before. Before you go inside, we'll also ask you to leave anything electronic in our cloakroom, including your watches. Time isn't a constraint here." He nodded at us. "You already have your locker keys."

Kevin said he'd eat anything, just let the chef decide, and I opted for a mixture of the meat and vegan menus. No fish, because if they slipped some seafood in, I'd gag. Oysters might have been an aphrodisiac, but they turned my stomach rather than turning me on. And I didn't need any help in that department either. One glass of wine, and I was Kevin's. Actually, I didn't even need the wine.

When we'd filled our lockers, I took Kevin's hand again as Anton led us through a pair of padded doors that would have been more at home in a castle. Still we weren't in a dining room. This was more of a cupboard.

"What the...?"

And then the lights went out.

Kevin's grip tightened. "We eat in the dark. This'll be fun, huh?"

"The *dark*?" I asked, as if this were a joke and the lights would turn back on at any second. But suddenly, it all made sense. The name of the restaurant, the blind host, the way they'd carefully stripped us of our phones so we couldn't use them as flashlights.

"But...but... How will we see the food?"

"We can't. I bet it'll taste better when our other senses are fully engaged."

"Each dish is crafted to provide a unique culinary experience," Anton told us. "Our chefs play with different temperatures and textures, and we use local, seasonal ingredients to provide an intensity of flavours. Please, follow me."

"How?" My voice rose. "How? I can't even see you!"

"Listen to the sound of my voice. In a moment, we'll cross the dining room, and I'll seat you at your table. Here at Noir Absolu, we prefer communal tables so you can meet new people. In this world of smartphones, people so rarely talk to each other anymore."

So now we had to do this with *strangers*? Oh, hell. Next time, I'd suggest we try go-karting instead.

But it was too late to back out now, and I wasn't a coward. Kevin tugged me forward, and we walked into the dark.

22

LEAH

The same music played in the dining room, and now I could hear the buzz of conversation over the mournful caress of the piano. Before he left, Anton had pressed a small remote into my hand and told me to buzz him if I needed anything. The temptation to push the button and tell him I needed a flashlight, a candle, a match, anything, was almost too much. The darkness wrapped around me like a blanket, reminding me of those nights at home when Mom had gone out to some bar or another and the electricity had been shut off yet again. I used to curl under the covers with Louis and Laken, quiet, so quiet in case a loan shark hammered on the door looking for his cash. Back then, I'd hated the dark, and I didn't much like it now. I wasn't scared. Just...uncomfortable.

But Kevin didn't know that, and I could hardly tell him about my past without also telling him about my present.

So I gingerly felt for the table in front of me and worked my fingers across the wooden surface, hoping for a glass of water to moisten my dry mouth. We'd been seated next to each other, and the slight curve of the table's edge suggested it must be quite large. How many people were around us? Eight? Ten?

Twelve? Cutlery clinked against dishes, which told me they had food already. *Please, don't let there be snails.* Noir Absolu —the name was French, but was the cooking? I ran a thumb over the buzzer, itching to press it and explain to Anton that I didn't eat molluscs, I merely pretended to study them. But would that hurt Kevin's feelings? Dammit, why hadn't I suggested going for pizza?

"Is this a quail egg?" a female voice asked. "I think it's a quail egg, with...a tiny tomato."

Okay, a quail egg didn't sound so bad.

"I have sushi," a man announced.

A giggle. "I thought the food would be, like, French."

At least I wasn't the only one. But I could deal with sushi, as long as it wasn't massive chunks of raw fish, and I'd skipped that menu. And fish was sashimi, right? Akio from Blackwood's executive protection team had told me that when we ate lunch together one time. Sushi was the rice.

"Are you okay?" Kevin asked softly, slipping an arm around my waist.

I laid my head on his shoulder. "I think so?"

"You don't sound very certain."

"I... I thought that you'd take me somewhere like Il Tramonto or maybe Rhodium. Or Claude's if you wanted to really splash out. This is...different."

"Good different or bad different?"

"I'll let you know once I've tried the food."

Kevin wove his fingers through my hair, then leaned in and pressed a soft kiss to my lips. Which quickly turned into something altogether harder, and I began to see the benefits of dining in the dark. Well, not *see* them because it was pitch black, but when I steadied myself with a hand on his thigh, I definitely felt them.

"Is this dessert?" I whispered.

"What if I said it was the appetiser?"

Tempting, so tempting... I stroked his length through his jeans, shocked to find I was actually considering the offer. Only one little zipper stood between me and my favourite part of Kevin's anatomy. But what if a diner had snuck in a contraband flashlight? Or management turned the lights on for a fire drill? Or someone had brought night-vision goggles?

Night-vision goggles?

Freaking heck, I'd been working at Blackwood for too long. Emmy might have carried thermal imaging equipment in her purse, but regular people didn't do that.

"You'd ruin my mouth for all other food."

I felt rather than saw Anton appear beside me, and a soft *clunk* told me he'd put a glass on the table.

"Enjoy your wine, ma'am." The *clunk* was followed by a *thunk* I'd have missed if my ears hadn't been working overtime. "And an amuse-bouche."

Just for a moment, I stopped to reflect on how weird this all was. Right now, I was sitting in the dark with a man I barely knew and a bunch of strangers whose faces I couldn't see, about to eat food that could be French or Japanese or anything in between. And I was a *planner*. From a young age, I'd had my goals mapped out—work a good-paying job for a few years, long enough to put my siblings through college and find myself a rich husband. Then I could relax, take my foot off the gas and enjoy life, see more of the world and hopefully become a mom. But Kevin had derailed my carefully laid-out timeline, and what was more, I wasn't even upset about it. He was kind and thoughtful and, okay, a tiny bit weird in some ways... No, quirky. Quirky was a better word. But he cared for me and he challenged me, nudging me out of my comfort zone and showing me there was more to life than the pursuit of money.

I was beginning to think I could fall in love with him.

Hell, maybe I already had.

I felt for my plate and found a triangle of...cheese? The

sharp tang of Parmesan exploded on my tongue, tempered by something sweeter… Onion relish? Oh, there was a kick to it—chilli pepper—not blow-your-head-off hot, but a definite tang.

"Is there any water?" I asked the void.

A woman answered from next to me, her voice sweet and cutesy, like Elle Woods in *Legally Blonde*. I loved that movie, and so did Laken, mainly because at college, she was the Elle Woods of the Biological Sciences Department. *She* should be the one faking it with molluscs, not me.

"There'll be a glass in front of your place setting, hun. Feel real gently."

"Thank you." I slid my hands forward again, gingerly, until my outstretched fingers hit the cool curve of a tumbler. "Did anyone else get the cheese with the chilli jam?"

"Sure did. Wait until they bring the salmon on the little cracker—I could eat an entire meal of those."

"I chose to skip the fish."

"Aw, I'm sure you'll still get something good."

I took a swallow of water, ice cubes clinking in the glass. The glass itself was textured, covered in a series of tiny bumps that could have been Braille or just a pattern.

"Leah, is that you?" a man asked, and I swallowed funny. Water went the wrong way, and I spluttered and coughed until Kevin thumped me on the back.

Shit, shit, shit! Who else was at this freaking table? The voice was familiar but not instantly recognisable.

"You okay? Because my first-aid refresher isn't due until next week, so my Heimlich skills are a little rusty."

Ryder. It was Ryder, former Navy SEAL, member of Emmy's Special Projects team, and all-around hot guy. An Abercrombie model with a gun.

"I'm"—cough—"fine."

"You two know each other?" Kevin asked.

"We work together," Ryder said before I could speak again. Dammit. Dammit!

I couldn't kick him under the table because I didn't even know where he was, plus his shins were probably made of titanium because the guy was basically the Terminator in chinos if the rumours were accurate. And he was about to blow my cover.

"I sometimes pick up shifts at the Brotherhood of Thieves. That's a bar not too far from here," I added, desperately hoping Kevin hadn't heard of the place, let alone visited it. He didn't strike me as the type who'd go for Friday-night drinks in a biker bar, even if the place catered to white-collar wannabes rather than actual Hell's Angels these days. Better yet, it was part-owned by another guy from Emmy's team, and he'd definitely fake me a payslip if I needed one. "Ryder's been employee of the month three times."

It was the best story I could come up with on the spur of the moment, and I didn't think it was terrible until a new voice spoke.

"What the hell, babe? You told me you were a bodyguard."

Oh, no, no, no. Ryder was here on a date? Why hadn't I thought of that? Probably because he only had to smile at a woman and she dropped her panties—he didn't need to wine her and dine her first.

"I can explain—" he started, but the crack of flesh on flesh echoed around the now-silent dining room.

"I don't date liars." Wood screeched against tile as she pushed back her chair. "Or waiters."

Well, that was a nasty thing to say, especially in a restaurant.

"Ma'am, are you okay?" a man asked, and I assumed it was a host. Not Anton, though—the pitch was lower.

"Get the hell out of my way."

Judging by the crash, the sound of breaking glass, and the

cursing, she was trying to find her own way out of the darkened room.

"Ow, that was my foot."

"Sit down!"

"Where's the freaking door?"

"Just stay where you are."

In the chaos, I felt hot breath against my ear. Ryder didn't have a problem moving around in the dark—a side effect of being superhuman.

"We'll talk about this tomorrow," he hissed, and then he was gone.

23

LEAH

What had I done?

Now I felt sick. By attempting to scramble out of the hole I'd dug myself into, I'd ruined Ryder's evening and possibly his whole relationship. Another crash, and someone turned on a flashlight. Ryder, I suspected—of course he'd break the rules. Hosts materialised from the gloom, apologising and checking we were okay, and a square of light illuminated shocked faces as Ryder's date finally found the door and hauled it open. I caught a glimpse of his silhouette as he followed, and then they were both gone.

What should I do? I couldn't even text him to grovel because my phone was in a freaking locker. And a restaurant wasn't the place to confess my sins to Kevin, not unless I wanted to cause *another* scene.

"Holy moly," Elle Woods said. "So much drama."

Kevin cupped my cheek and kissed me on the forehead. "Are you all right?"

"Yes." *No.* If this hole got much deeper, I'd need to take up spelunking. "I didn't mean to...you know..."

Another woman chimed in, this one with a New York accent. "Serves him right for lying. What an asshole."

Okay, so he *had* told a little white lie—Ryder was so much more than a bodyguard—but he *was* trained in executive protection. Which made *me* the asshole, not only for ruining Ryder's evening but for deceiving Kevin too. I wanted to come clean, but I also wanted to find Molly Sanderson's necklace and see the Rat go to prison where he belonged.

When Laken, Louis, and I were growing up in Missouri, our mom had been fond of quoting Jesus. Oh, she only lived by the parts of the Bible she found convenient, but she sure knew how to invoke God's word to make a kid feel guilty. Our refrigerator had been covered with magnets bearing kitschy pictures and inspirational verses. "The truth will set you free," she'd say whenever she caught one of us in a fib. "Lying is a sin."

Divorce was a sin too, and she hadn't had a problem with that one. Or adultery, or getting drunk, or—ironically—hypocrisy, another sin, at least according to Matthew, chapter twenty-three, verse thirteen.

And who cared about freedom, anyway? I kind of liked the idea of being shackled to Kevin.

"Maybe there was a misunderstanding," I suggested.

"Oh, please," New York said. "There's a big difference between a waiter and a bodyguard."

Elle Woods replied, her voice dreamy. "I think I saw that guy come in, and I'd let him guard my body even if he *is* a waiter."

"Uh, Kinsey, did you forget I'm here?"

Another giggle. "He'd have to fight you for the job, obviously." Then lower, loud enough for me to hear but perhaps not her companion, "He'd probably win."

New York spoke up again. "Never date a liar."

"What if there's a good reason for the lie?" a guy asked.

Local accent, so I christened him Richmond. "Like he didn't want to hurt your feelings?"

"Nope. Nuh-uh. If he can't tell the truth about the minor stuff, he'll lie about the major stuff too."

Gee, this wasn't an uncomfortable conversation at all. I squirmed in my seat, wishing Kevin would voice some sort of opinion so at least I'd know how he felt about the whole fibbing thing.

"So if you asked him how a dress looked, and it made your ass look fat, you'd want him to tell you?"

"Yeah, duh, because then I could change into a different dress that didn't make my ass look fat."

Except she didn't say "dress" and "ass," she said "dresh" and "ash," and I realised she must've drunk a lot more wine than I had. Lucky for her.

"Oh, right." To Richmond, New York's words seemed to be a revelation. "I'll have to remember that."

A new voice, also local, but female. Richmond's girlfriend? "Did you let me go out in a dress that made my ass look fat?"

"Of course not, honey."

"Never date a liar," New York reminded us.

"A compliment isn't a lie."

"Oh, you think? It always starts small, trust me. First, he tells you that you look great when you have the worst VPL ever. Next, he tells you he loves going to art galleries when really, he prefers video games. And then—"

"Tina, these good people don't need to hear all this."

Oh, so she wasn't here alone. Poor guy.

"Shush, shush, someone needs to warn them. And then... then he tells you he's a high-powered restructuring consultant, and it turns out he's jusht a...jusht a personal assistant."

The way she spat the words made my blood boil. *Just* a personal assistant.

"What's wrong with being a PA? I'm dating a PA."

"Are you sure about that?"

Kevin put a hand on my arm. "There's no need..."

"The hell there isn't." I squared my shoulders and faced where I thought New York was sitting. "Yes, I'm sure. I've been to his office and met his boss and his colleagues."

"Well, aren't you the lucky one? My ex *stole* from his boss. Had to pay for his swanky apartment somehow, and—"

"Tina, we're leaving."

"But I haven't finished my wine."

"I don't think you need any more."

"But the rest of us sure do," Elle Woods aka Kinsey muttered.

"Don't you tell me what I do or don't need. Doug, get off me!"

"We're leaving right now. Where's that damned buzzer?"

"Here, use ours," Richmond offered.

New York bitched her way across the dining room, and when the door finally closed behind her, our whole table breathed a collective sigh of relief.

"Who wants to chip in for a sympathy card?" Kinsey's date asked. "Doug has the patience of a saint."

A small laugh tittered around the group, more relief than anything else. *Ding-dong, the witch was dead.*

I leaned into Kevin. "I'm sorry I snapped at her, but I just couldn't sit there while she insulted you."

Insulted *us.*

He tightened his arm around me and kissed my hair. "Next time, I'm ordering pizza."

"We are *so* on the same wavelength."

Even as the words left my mouth, the guilt wedged in my throat. Because despite her many shortcomings, New York had been right. Lies were no basis for a lasting relationship. I had to be truthful with Kevin, and I had to do it sooner rather than later.

Oh, and I also had to grovel to Ryder.

But for tonight, I tucked those horrible thoughts into the back of my mind and concentrated on enjoying the evening. The other four people at our table—together, we'd dubbed ourselves "the survivors"—turned out to be surprisingly good fun, although Elle Woods wasn't a law student, she was a journalist who'd just joined the *Richmond Chronicle*, and one of her responsibilities was a new food-and-drink column, hence the visit to Noir Absolu.

"This evening was more exciting than I thought it would be," she said, giggling. "The *drama*."

"Better than a trip to the movies, huh?"

"Definitely. And probably cheaper too when you consider the price of movie theatre popcorn."

She wasn't a blonde either. No, she was a brunette, as I found out after the meal when we were led into the Noir Bar, which had actual lights as well as an extensive cocktail list.

"Are you staying for a drink?" she asked.

I glanced at Kevin. After the problems with Ryder and New York, all I'd wanted to do was get out of there, but once things had settled, I'd actually enjoyed myself. Kevin was shy in company, not so much of a talker, so I guess we complemented each other because talking was definitely one of my strong points. He'd get along well with Laken—she was the quiet one in my family.

Now he shrugged. "Whatever you want."

What I wanted was a second dessert, this time Kevin-shaped, but a strawberry daiquiri was also tempting.

As if he could read my mind, he leaned in to whisper, "Are you staying at my place tonight?"

"I'll have to pick up some clothes on the way. Will Brian be all right for a while longer?"

"If he's going to eat the couch, he'll have done it by now. We can take him out for a walk when we get back."

"Okay, then one drink."

One drink became two, plus the bartender took a bunch of souvenir photos for us, and I swapped numbers with Kinsey in case I wanted to join her on one of her restaurant-testing jaunts. She was new to Richmond, and she barely knew anyone here yet. In the bathroom, she confided that her date was a guy she'd met on Tinder last week, and although he was the life and soul of the party, when the two of them were alone, he turned into a bit of a drag. No spark. None! Today had been their third date and also their last.

"Where did you find Kevin?" she asked.

"In the park."

"That's so old-fashioned. Did your eyes meet across a crowded bench?"

"No, his dog knocked me down."

"Aw, like in a Hallmark movie?"

"Only if the Hallmark movie includes pond slime."

"Oh my gosh, are you kidding?"

"I wish. So I guess it was part Hallmark, part horror movie."

"Whatever, you found a good one. I mean, have you seen the way he gazes at you when you're looking the other way? No, duh, of course you haven't." Kinsey gave her head a shake. "But it's so *dreamy*."

Kinsey's date just looked at his phone every time she glanced away. Probably he was checking out Tinder again. A chill ran through me—she was right, Kevin *was* a good one, and I was so, so scared of losing him.

"I should go. The dog's at home..." *Home.* Funny how comfortable I'd grown in Kevin's apartment, wasn't it? "And it's getting late."

"Call me, okay?"

"I will."

But how could I? I'd lied to Kinsey tonight. She thought I was a student too, and I cursed Dan and Blackwood in my head as I walked out of the bar with my arm linked through Kevin's. I'd spun a web of deceit, and now I was luring even more people into the sticky strands. But ultimately, there was only one creature who would end up the victim in this trap, and that was the spider herself.

24

LEAH

"Should I wait in the cab?" Kevin asked.

Did I want him to come up to my apartment? There was only a fifty-fifty chance that Stefano had moved his underwear. Thongs on the radiator would be bad enough, but I also couldn't discount the possibility that he'd invited one of his boyfriends over, and seeing a thong on Stefano's pasty ass would be a hundred times worse. The man had no shame.

"That's probably a good idea." I leaned in for a hasty-but-hot kiss. "I'll just be two minutes."

Make that ten minutes. The first two were spent finding my earplugs to block out the sound of Stefano and his boy toy grunting in the next bedroom. Until he moved in, I hadn't realised quite how thin the walls were. Then I had to find a bag and decide how much to pack. If I took an extra change of clothes, I might be able to avoid coming home tomorrow, but any more, and I feared I'd jinx my future with Kevin. What if he freaked out and thought I was moving in by stealth? Or worse, what if he kicked me out after I'd made my big confession?

Hurry up, hurry up, hurry up... I raided my closet and

underwear drawer, then grabbed the goody bag I'd brought from the office. Might as well make the most of my colleagues' generosity. Soon I was hobbling down the stairs, and I promised myself that somehow, someday, I'd live in an apartment block with a working elevator.

And in a better neighbourhood.

I heard the scream right before I opened the front door, and I nearly stayed inside. But somebody was in trouble—a woman—and I was a Blackwood girl, albeit one with limited capabilities. Blackwood girls didn't look the other way.

It only took a second for me to work out what had happened. Farther along the street, the woman was still screaming as a man pounded along the sidewalk toward me, clutching a pink leather purse that definitely didn't match his tattoos.

Dan would have chased him down. Emmy would have tackled him to the ground. Ana would probably have glared at him, then watched disdainfully as he withered at her feet. Me? I threw a bag of sex toys at him. Logically, I knew my pathetic attempt wouldn't stop his escape, but I had to do something, okay? He jinked sideways as the bag bounced off his shoulder in a hail of glitter, and I watched in slo-mo horror as the magic cock ring rolled across the pavement.

Should I retrieve it? Or just die of embarrass—

Crack.

Kevin opened the cab door, and the mugger bounced off it with enough force to end up at my feet, groaning. The asshole's eyes rolled back in his head. Shit, was he dead? Should I check for a pulse? I didn't want to touch him, but then I spotted the pair of fluffy pink handcuffs in the gutter and snapped one bracelet around his wrist.

Kevin was at my side in an instant. "Are you okay?"

"Can you help me to move him?"

We took an arm each, and ten seconds later, we'd dragged

his sorry ass over to my apartment building and secured him to one of the metal railings that flanked the steps. Only then did I realise how fast my heart was beating. And only then did Kevin begin asking the awkward questions.

"Where did the handcuffs come from?"

"Uh..." My cheeks burned. "I just thought that maybe... You know, they might be fun?"

"Right." Now he turned red as well. "Do you think they'll hold? Being a novelty item, I mean."

To give my colleagues their credit, none of them would purchase inferior-quality handcuffs. I'd put money on them being police-issue.

"They'll hold. So, uh, I guess we should call 911?"

On any other occasion, I'd have called the Blackwood control room and let them handle everything, but that was out of the question tonight.

"911, yes. Yes, I'll do that."

Where was the woman? The one whose purse got snatched? I spotted her stumbling toward us, minus one shoe.

"Are you all right? Did he hurt you?"

She had blood on her cheek, but where had it come from?

"I... He pushed me. My purse..."

"We have your purse. Why don't you come sit down? Uh, not on the steps. Maybe in the cab?"

The driver was on the sidewalk, muttering under his breath as he examined the damage.

"See what that asshole did to my door? Now it doesn't shut properly."

He wasn't kidding. The top was bent, probably due to the guy's head hitting it, and there was a dent near the bottom too. If I'd been able to call Dan, she'd have arranged to fix the problem. Blackwood had invested in an auto shop not so long ago. Emmy told me it worked out more economical because of how often Dan crashed, and although she'd laughed when she said it, I hadn't been entirely sure whether she was joking.

"I'm so sorry. If you give me your number, I have a friend who might be able to help."

"Same here." Kevin appeared behind me. "You won't be left out of pocket. And the cops are on their way."

Thank goodness. "This lady needs to rest."

"Should I call back for an ambulance?"

She shook her head. "No, no ambulance."

"But you're bleeding."

"Do you know how much an ambulance costs?"

Too much, and I nearly confessed to my lies right then. Blackwood had a hardship fund for things like this. Emmy and Black had set it up last year in exchange for Bradley toning down the Christmas celebrations—after the Thanksgiving turkey incident, Emmy had threatened to spend the festive season in Iraq if Bradley went ahead with the live-action nativity scene he'd planned, so Black had taken over the negotiations and reallocated a portion of the Christmas budget.

"Hydrogen Labs has a hardship fund," Kevin said, and I could have kissed him. "We can cover the cost."

But still the woman shook her head. "I just want to go home."

The blood was coming from her hands. When the mugger pushed her, she'd fallen and scraped her palms on the sidewalk, and now they were full of grit. While Kevin and the driver kept an eye on her, I ran inside to get my first-aid kit—a Secret Santa gift I suspected had come from Black because (a) it wasn't fun and (b) it contained so much stuff it was good for minor surgery—so I could clean up the wounds. When I made it back outside, the mugger was awake and whining about glitter in his eyes. Good. Served him right.

By the time the cops arrived, we'd bandaged the woman's

hands—Tonya, her name was Tonya—and I'd also retrieved my weapons of choice from the sidewalk. Kevin's eyes had widened when he saw me pick up the cock ring, but that conversation would have to wait until later. First, we had to speak to the cops. Two of them showed up, a younger guy who looked as if he'd gotten lost on the way to a bachelorette party and a veteran with grey hair who punctuated his speech by sucking on his teeth.

The first thing they did was separate us. Standard procedure, I knew that, and actually a relief because when the grey-haired cop verified my identity, he also asked about my employment status, and I had to tell him I worked for Blackwood. That news was met with a roll of the eyes and an, "I shoulda known," although relations between us and the Richmond PD were slowly improving under the new police chief. The previous one had been a member of a paedophile ring that Blackwood had busted—awkward—and even before that episode, the local cops hadn't liked us much. We'd highlighted their shortcomings more times than they were comfortable with. But the new chief, Broussard, he had a different attitude. Getting criminals off the street took priority, and he was happy to accept Blackwood's help as long as we didn't get caught doing anything illegal. And we didn't. Get caught, I mean—Emmy and Dan were far too careful for that.

I agreed to visit the station tomorrow to give a formal statement, and the cop let me go with a warning not to discuss the incident with any other witnesses, meaning Kevin. I glanced to the side, and he was nodding at the younger cop, so I had to assume he was receiving similar instructions. Whatever, I only wanted to go home, and Brian was waiting.

Midnight had come and gone when we walked through the door. Brian opened one sleepy eye and managed a *woof*—he'd raided the laundry hamper and made himself a nest out of

Kevin's clothes along with some stuffing from one of the armchairs.

"It's just an inanimate object," Kevin said when he saw the damage. "It could be worse. Are you okay? After tonight, I mean."

"I could use a hug," I admitted. Now that the adrenaline had worn off, I felt drained. How did Emmy and Dan and the others do this every day? Their insides must be made from granite.

Kevin wrapped me up in his arms, and as I laid my head against his shoulder, I realised that this was the true meaning of a relationship. Friendship and support through the good times and the bad. Before I met Kevin, I'd assumed that any future marriage of mine would be more of a transactional affair. That I'd do my best to become a Stepford wife in exchange for financial security. But I'd been wrong, so wrong, and I knew now that money didn't matter. Kindness mattered. Patience mattered. Integrity mattered. Passion mattered. Kevin had all of those qualities in spades, plus he was smart, and adventurous, and he had a sense of humour, and yes, he was great in bed, which was definitely a bonus.

"So," he murmured. "Are we going to talk about the handcuffs yet?"

"Do we have to?"

"Satisfy my curiosity—were they meant for you or for me?"

"Hell, I don't know. Some friends found out I was seeing you, and they decided to surprise me with a few gifts. Surprise *us*, I guess."

"Which would also explain all the condoms? And that ring thing? Am I supposed to wear that on my—"

"Only if you want to."

"Right. Right, okay. But maybe tonight, we could just do things the regular way? I have to attend an important meeting at work tomorrow, and it'll look bad if I yawn the whole way through it. Hydrogen Labs is on the brink of another substantial licencing deal, so Sol's coming down from New York and a delegation of money men is flying in from Europe."

"Does that mean you'll be back late?"

"Sorry, yes."

"Do you want me to make dinner? I can stay with Brian for as long as you want."

Was the armchair repairable? I'd need to take a better look at it in the morning.

"I'll eat at work, but yes, stay here with Brian. Stay all night. This building has better security than yours. Do muggings happen often on your street?"

"It's not the first. But I took a self-defence course, and I carry pepper spray in my purse." And perhaps in the future, I'd start packing emergency glitter too—it had been surprisingly effective. "I know we're not meant to talk about it, but it was super lucky you opened the car door when you did."

"I didn't want to get into a fist fight in case the man had a weapon, so it seemed sensible to use his momentum against him instead. Mass times velocity. Let's say he weighed a hundred kilos, and he was travelling at eight metres per second. I figured a force of twelve-point-five newton seconds would be sufficient to knock a man out, although I'll admit I don't have much expertise in that area."

"I love it when you get all geeky on me."

"You do?"

"Yes." Because there was that passion. Not sexual passion —although he did channel that energy into the bedroom— but genuine enthusiasm over something he enjoyed. "It shows you care."

Once, I'd met a guy who prided himself on being a "real

man," and he'd turned out to be an empty vessel. He told me he'd never cried, not once, not even at his mother's funeral. No emotion, no empathy, no spark.

No zing.

I'd survived three dates before deciding I couldn't face a fourth, and I'd only made it to the third because he drove a Ferrari. No, he didn't get excited over the car either. He'd only bought it because he'd once read an article titled "Top Ten Cars for the Successful Businessman" and that was at number one.

And even then, it hadn't clicked that I might have my priorities wrong. Stupid, stupid me. Like a fool, I'd carried on chasing the money, too focused on my dumb life goals to re-evaluate. It had taken a dog to make me see sense. I'd done a lot of growing up since Brian knocked me down, and I kind of liked the new Leah.

"I care about the important things." Kevin's arms tightened as he spoke, and he kissed my hair. "I care about you."

The warmth of happiness flowed through me. This was new, so new, but it was right. Now all I had to do was pretend to break my arm, then come clean regarding my job, and we could live happily ever after. No biggie.

"I care about you too." It wasn't quite the L-word, but we were definitely heading in that direction. And when Kevin kissed me, properly this time, there was no mistaking the depth of his feelings. Or mine. Every time our lips met, I lost another piece of my heart. When we broke apart, I was breathless. "So me, Brian, and math, huh? I'm part of an elite club."

"Momentum is more physics, but yes."

"I guess if that's your thing, you picked the right place to work. Hydrogen Labs is full of super-smart people, right? Did you ever consider going back to school? Switching over to the tech side?"

"Go back to school? I can honestly say I've never considered that. But—"

"Maybe you should?" A yawn crept up on me. "Tomorrow. We can talk about your career tomorrow. Tonight, let's take Brian out and then go to bed. You have a big day ahead, so you can lie back, relax, and I'll start making a dent in the mountain of condoms."

Kevin glanced over at Brian, snoring upside down in his makeshift bed like a furry cockroach with his favourite zebra plushie by his side. "I suppose I do owe him for bringing you into my life."

"We *both* owe him for bringing me into your life."

25

DOG GUY

"Champagne?" Kevin asked.

"I have a headache."

"Ah, well. More for me."

"It's ten thirty in the morning." Lennox checked his watch. "Ten forty-five."

"It's cocktail hour somewhere in the world." Kevin swallowed a mouthful, then tossed a package of Tylenol onto Lennox's desk. "Take these. I knew you'd get a hangover."

"Alcohol isn't responsible for this. Not completely, anyway."

"Things didn't go well with the police?"

No, they didn't. Telling an unsmiling cop that Leah had hurled a gift bag filled with glitter, contraceptives, and sex toys at a mugger had been difficult enough for Lennox, and then had come the awkwardness of explaining that his girlfriend thought he was called Kevin. On Monday evening when the officer had asked him for ID, he'd actually considered pretending that he hadn't brought his billfold with him, but lying could have jeopardised a prosecution, and he wasn't prepared to risk a criminal getting off scot-free. So he'd handed over his passport card, ignoring the officer's advice not to carry so much cash. But he needed the cash. How else was he meant to pay for dinner when he'd lied to the woman he was falling in love with about his entire identity?

"The visit could have gone better."

On second thought, maybe more alcohol wouldn't be such a bad idea?

The champagne was left over from yesterday, from the late-night celebration after the ink had dried on a deal that would leave him roughly fifty million dollars richer over the next three years, according to Sol. But it wasn't just about the money. Every licencing deal they signed represented another step toward a greener future. A better world for the children he might one day have.

Speak of the devil... No, not children, but Sol. He strolled in, wearing a suit and tie even though he had no meetings scheduled this morning. But his choice of attire was nothing new. For as long as Lennox had known Solomon King, he'd used clothes as a shield—quite literally on the streets of New York. Walking while Black could be hazardous to a man's health, and Sol had figured the cops would be less likely to target a brother dressed like a stockbroker than one wearing a hoodie. For the most part, it had worked. Sol had escaped arrest until a year ago when he made the mistake of climbing into his Porsche one morning after spending the night with a girlfriend. But by that point, he'd been halfway to making his first billion, and once the lawyers had gotten involved, the police had regretted the incident far more than Sol did.

There were probably a dozen more times during those early days that Sol *should* have been arrested, but he'd been street smart as well as smart-smart. Still was, and always would be.

Now he dropped into a visitor's chair and crossed his legs at the ankles.

"Good night last night?"

"You know it was. You were there."

"I meant afterward."

"Afterward?" When he arrived home, Lennox had crawled into bed beside Leah, too tired and drunk to do anything else. She'd curled into his arms, and they'd just slept. He could have stayed there forever. And when the alarm went off, she'd blown his dick and his mind, but that was no business of Sol's. He might have been one of Len's oldest friends, but there were some things a man didn't discuss. "Afterward was also good."

"No issues?"

"You're talking in code."

A smile played at the corners of Sol's lips. "I thought you liked that?" Then he sighed. "Gustav asked me to speak with you."

"Gustav?"

The head of H2's information systems department? He liked code too, but a different kind, and Lennox wasn't aware of any security issues.

"Yeah. Well, he actually asked Haris to speak with you, but Haris delegated sideways."

"Speak with me about what?"

"Gustav's sister married a urologist. The guy's competent and discreet, if you need help with...you know." Sol glanced at his lap. "Down there."

"What the hell are you talking about?"

"When you consulted Dr. Google yesterday morning, you tripped the firewall."

"Dr. Goo..." Lennox trailed off. "Ah, shit."

Kevin watched the two of them over the rim of his champagne glass. "If you have a UTI, you should drink cranberry juice. Want me to go get some?"

"I don't have a UTI." Lennox gritted his teeth. "There's no problem."

Sol kept his expression oh-so serious, but Len knew that inside, he was laughing. "How long did you leave the cock ring on for?"

Kevin spat champagne across the room, and Lennox began to consider the feasibility of life off-grid. Just him, Leah, Brian, and an array of solar panels with appropriate energy storage. They'd need a water filtration system, of course, and possibly some kind of hydroponic cultivation arrangement to maximise productivity, and...

"Are you using that mega-IQ to think up a way to avoid the question?" Sol asked.

"I didn't put the cock ring on at all." Not yet, anyway. "I was merely curious."

And could anyone blame a man for wanting to check it wouldn't cut off the blood supply?

"Curious?" Sol snorted. "Okay. So, when will I get to meet the lady with the miraculous ability to distract you from work?"

"Soon."

"I don't head back to New York until tomorrow. Dinner?"

"Not tonight. There are things I need to sort out first."

"Like telling her his name," Kevin muttered.

"What?"

Sol's confusion was understandable. Lennox might have left out some of the unfortunate facts when he'd divulged the existence of his new relationship because he knew exactly what Sol would say: that he was a jackass. But thanks to Kevin's habit of oversharing, now he had no choice but to confess.

"I'm going to tell her. I almost did on Monday night, but we needed to take Brian for a walk, and then... Well, it wasn't the right time."

"So this woman is sleeping at your place, in your bed, and she doesn't know your name? What the hell does she call you?"

"Uh..."

Kevin spoke up again. "She thinks he's me."

"Why would she think that?"

"Because that's what Len told her."

Sol looked between Kevin and Lennox. "This is a joke, right?"

When neither of them answered, Sol put his head in his hands.

"Len, you're a fuckin' jackass." See? "What were you thinking?"

"He wasn't," Tally said helpfully from the doorway. "Coffee, anyone? Seeing as Kevin—actual Kevin—seems to be asleep on the job."

Haris peered in from behind her. "Did you ask about...you know?"

Lennox's brain was ready to explode out of his skull. What were the symptoms of an aneurysm? Something else to google, but not at work. He'd learned his lesson there.

"Can everyone just get out of my office?"

Sol stood, in command as always. "Yeah, and that includes you. Because you're gonna go find this girl and tell her the truth."

"What if she takes it badly?"

"You fall on your damn knees and beg for forgiveness. Or when will it end? With her screaming Kevin's name as she comes? When you walk down the aisle and she says 'I, Leah, take thee, Kevin'? When you name your first child Kevin Junior? Since your balls apparently didn't drop off, get out of here and grovel."

"She's at college this morning."

"She'll be back soon," Tally said. Why did people keep talking? They were only making this situation worse. "When I saw her yesterday, she said she'd finish her classes in time to let Brian out at lunch."

Sol folded his arms, triumphant. "That gives you time to pick up flowers on the way home. Need a ride?"

"No."

"Did you start taking driving lessons yet? Or are you gonna trade your bicycle in for a tandem?"

"Don't you ever stop?"

"Tough love, buddy."

Haris nodded. "Exactly."

But when Sol turned to him, the smug smile soon slipped off his face.

"And how is Saira?"

"Uh, I just have to...check on something."

Sol was right. Lennox knew he was right—when Leah whispered Kevin's name in bed, it did nothing for his performance—but it didn't make what he had to do any easier.

"What type of flowers should I get?"

"Give the florist a generous budget and tell them you need to apologise."

"Smooth." Tally rolled her eyes. "You've done that a lot, have you?"

"Sol never stays around long enough to apologise."

His "relationships" were measured in hours rather than days, but that's the way he preferred it. No attachments, no deep-and-meaningful conversations, no problems. His first love was making money. Not because he needed any more of it, but because he enjoyed the logistical challenge, much as Lennox and Haris wanted to build smaller and smaller batteries with ever-increasing capacities.

"Then is he really the best person to be dishing out relationship advice?"

Lennox merely shrugged. "I trust him."

Years ago, when money had been tight and H2 was still in the R&D phase, the venture capitalists had come sniffing around. Sure, they'd offered to lend the funds that Len and Haris so desperately needed to complete the project, but the fledgling company would have paid for it later with eye-watering interest rates and redemption premiums. Nothing unusual in that. It was how VC worked—for every ten companies a venture capitalist invested in, only one or two would make it, and they had to recoup their money somehow. But Sol had come up with a different plan. He'd asked Lennox and Haris to trust him, and then he'd quietly short-sold stock in a pharmaceutical company right before it went under. If he'd miscalculated, there would have been no battery patents and the three of them would have spent the rest of their lives eating ramen, and not by choice in Sol's and Len's cases. But the gamble had paid off. When H2's first product was ready for market, the three of them had still owned ninety percent of the company with full control.

By trusting Sol, all of their dreams had been realised.

Which was why, an hour later, Lennox found himself fending off Brian with one hand and balancing a mammoth bouquet in the other. The florist had filled a vase with everything pink and white and added gold ribbon with a mini box of French truffles in the middle.

"Brian, get down. Not the flowers!"

Had Leah gotten home yet? The apartment was quiet apart from Brian's panting, tidy other than the mangled sneaker in the middle of the living room floor. Len's or Leah's? Lennox took a closer look and breathed a sigh of relief when he recognised one of his Nikes.

"She'll be here soon, buddy. Want to take a walk while we wait?"

Dumb question—Brian always wanted to take a walk. But a half hour later, there was still no sign of Leah, and Lennox had more nervous energy than the dog did. Where was she?

Brian deposited a slimy tennis ball in Len's lap and waited expectantly, head tilted to one side.

"No, I don't know why she's so late either." He tossed the ball, only for Brian to bring it right back again. "All we can do is wait."

26

LEAH

"I can't do this. I just can't lie to Kevin for six more weeks."

Dan, Black, and half a dozen managers from Blackwood's investigations division looked on uncomfortably as I melted down in a conference room. I was meant to be taking minutes at the biweekly status-update meeting, and instead, I was...freaking out. I'd tried to pull myself together, only for my breath to start coming in pants as fear got the better of me. Yes, I'd only known Kevin for a few weeks, but he was the sweetest man I'd ever met, and the thought of losing him...

I'd been okay until Dan went through the notes on the Molly Sanderson case. Two suspects left, team in a holding pattern, Leah's doing a great job juggling the surveillance alongside her other duties, blah, blah, blah. But I wasn't. I wasn't doing a great job. Sure, I managed to get my work done, but every time I looked at the skyline print hanging on Kevin's wall, I wanted to throw up.

This morning, I'd been to the hospital, and now my left arm was encased in a fibreglass cast. Dr. Beech had even created an X-ray with my name on it, and Dan had gotten a bunch of people to write me sympathy cards because, hey, attention to detail was important. She might have been able to hold her nerve through the subterfuge, but this was only day one and I was already cracking.

I was an executive assistant, not a spy.

Undercover work was definitely not my calling.

"Let's take a five-minute break," Dan said.

Five minutes, five hours...as if it would make a difference. I still couldn't go through with all the lies.

"I'm sorry. I'm so sorry. I just... I just..."

"Why don't you sit down?" Black suggested.

When did I even stand up? As the managers filed out, I slumped back into my seat, wishing I could carry right on and sink through the floor. What was wrong with me? Was I too tired? I hadn't gotten much sleep the past few nights, but could that explain the overwhelming feeling of dread?

Or was it yesterday's visit to the police station? The officer I'd spoken with had promised he wouldn't tell Kevin where I worked, but what if he let something slip? Kevin was meant to be giving his statement this morning, and he still hadn't replied to my "what do you want for dinner?" text, the one I'd sent an hour ago. Maybe he was just busy? But what if he'd found out I wasn't a student, and—

"Drink this." Dan handed me a cup of water. "And breathe. In and out, in and out."

"Can someone tell me what the issue is?" Black asked.

"Leah fell in love with the guy whose apartment we're borrowing for surveillance."

"We're not borrowing his apartment! We've hijacked his wall to install a listening device."

"This is the Hydrogen Labs guy?"

I nodded.

"And for clarification, he's not the same asshole who tried to hit me up for money over dinner last week?"

"Please, just shoot me now."

"I'm not sure that's the best solution in this case." Black leaned back in his seat, steepling his hands. "So you've known this man for two weeks?"

"I know it's fast, but not everyone takes a whole decade to work out how they feel." I clapped both hands over my mouth. "Sorry! I'm so sorry, I... I..."

I'd lost my damn mind. First, I'd disrupted a meeting, and now I'd insulted the big boss. Forget the minutes—I should start drafting my resignation letter.

"It was Emmy who took the decade; I knew within five minutes of meeting her. But she'd have made me choke on my own testicles if I'd admitted how I felt at the time," he added under his breath.

Dan pulled up a chair next to me. "We only need a couple more weeks. Probably not six."

Same difference. It felt as if I'd reached the point of no return. "If I come clean now, I might stand a chance with Kevin, but if I leave it a whole month... He's sensitive, and so, so smart, and so is his dog, and when I come back to work, Brian will be on his own again, and—" A tear rolled down my cheek, and could this be any more embarrassing? "How do people do this every day? Fake it, I mean?"

Dan smiled sweetly. "Some of us are just natural-born psychopaths."

Okay, that part was true.

"And it's not only me this is affecting. I ruined Ryder's date on Monday."

"Yeah, I heard about that."

Which meant everyone in the office knew. Great.

"Plus Kevin's colleagues all think I'm a student. One of them dropped by his place yesterday and started asking me questions about sea slugs. It's not freaking funny!"

Dan straightened her face. "Yes, this is a very serious situation. Did you manage to bullshit your way through it?"

Fortunately, I'd spent my coffee breaks studying mollusc facts on Wikipedia, and Tally had only paid a flying visit to drop off a gift from Kevin. Most women got flowers and candy; I got a personal attack alarm shaped like a magic eight ball "just in case." According to Tally, it was super loud, and she'd warned me not to test it on myself if I valued my hearing.

The gift had been one more example of Kevin's caring nature, and yet another reason why it would be so difficult to let him go.

"Yes, but she's a scientist, and I'm sure she knows a lot more about biology than I do. Next time, I might not be able to bluff."

"So, what are we looking at?" Black asked. "A fifty percent chance of finding a stolen necklace versus Leah's future happiness?"

Dan nodded. "That sums it up."

"Take out the recording equipment. Garner isn't talkative anyway, and we can continue the surveillance externally. If he's planning to shift merchandise, he'll need to do that physically, and we can monitor his movements. Leah, will that work for you?"

Without the microphone in place, I could go with the sick-leave story for the time I'd spent in the apartment so far, and we'd be able to get through this. I nodded, welling up with tears of relief that the end might be in sight.

"Could I take a day of leave to find a solution for Brian? He's used to me being there now, and he'll need a dog walker or daycare so he's not on his own. I'll still take care of my emails."

"You don't need to be in the office all the time anyway," Dan said. "I bet you can do half of your work remotely. Just check with Nick that he's okay with the arrangement too."

"Or bring the dog to the office," Black suggested. "As long as he's house trained, he can take some of the pressure off Barkley."

Ah, Barkley. Ever since Black had accidentally adopted a dog last year—well, Emmy said the dog had adopted him— she'd become Blackwood's unofficial therapist. Everyone had treats in their drawers, but someone always took her for a lunchtime run so she didn't get fat. If Brian and Barkley got along, and I could bring him with me occasionally, that would be the perfect fix.

"Thank you."

Now the tears fell properly, and Black handed me a handkerchief.

"Now can we continue the meeting? I'm scheduled to go through the kill house at noon, and Logan hates it when people fuck with his schedule."

I managed to nod. Once I'd written up the minutes, I could cut the stupid cast off, hotfoot it over to Kevin's apartment, and switch out the doctored painting for the original. Then this nightmare would be halfway over.

No more lies.

"And once again, I'm so, so sorry. I just didn't think."

Ryder hadn't been in the office yesterday, so today, I spent a full five minutes grovelling while he hunted for the right tool to remove the cast. I'd tried hacking it off with scissors, and when that didn't work, Sloane had sawed at it with a multitool from Logan's desk drawer until Ryder ordered us to, "Stop, stop, stop before you both end up in the emergency room for real this time."

"I figured by the desperation in your voice that you had a

good reason for saying what you did, plus I recalled Tanner mentioning you were trying out undercover work. Does this mean I'll need to find someone else to laminate my workout plans?"

"I'll laminate anything you want. This was my first undercover job and also my last. Did your girlfriend see the funny side?"

"No, she didn't. Keep still if you don't want me to cut through bone. Just relax."

Relax? How could I freaking relax?

"Maybe I should speak with her? Explain that it was all my fault?"

"She didn't see the funny side because I didn't tell her about the misunderstanding."

"You didn't? Why?"

"Because there's nothing wrong with being a waiter. I used to bus tables when I was in high school, and fuck her if she thinks that's not good enough. Let's call it a lucky escape."

"You're not mad?"

"No, but I'm still keeping the box of cookies."

I giggled with relief. "Chocolate orange chip is your favourite, right?"

Ryder peeled the remains of the cast off my arm, and the relief was indescribable. Half a day, and this horror story would be over.

"First choice is salted caramel. Chocolate orange is second." He winked at me. "Remember that next time."

"I swear there won't be a next time."

"Good luck with the guy. If he doesn't make good use of all that shit Sloane and Logan put in your desk drawer, he's a fool."

What?

"Sloane and Logan did that? Really? I thought it was Dan and Emmy?"

"Guess Sloane wanted payback for that online-dating fuck-up over the summer, but at least they bought quality equipment."

"I'm not sure whether to thank them or yell at them."

Yes, they'd nearly given me a heart attack, but the ribbed condoms had definitely hit the spot, plus the glitter had helped to catch a mugger. And I still felt guilty over the online-dating thing. All I'd wanted was for Sloane to be happy, and she was now, but I'd gone about helping in completely the wrong way.

"Go walk your dog while you consider it." Ryder grinned, and if I hadn't been crazy over Kevin, my heart would have skipped. Okay, maybe it skipped anyway. "Have fun."

Have fun... Ryder's words echoed in my ears as I loaded the bug-free painting into the back of my car. At that moment, I had no idea that fate was waiting to kick me in the teeth with steel-toed boots. If I'd known, perhaps I'd have kept on driving. Past Belvedere Place, out of Richmond, off a cliff.

But I didn't.

Ignorance was bliss, and I was as ignorant as they came.

27

LEAH

"Hey, boy! I brought you a—"

The words died in my throat when I saw Kevin sitting at the dining room table. He wasn't eating. No, he had a screwdriver in his hand as he examined... Oh *fuck*. The mangled remains of the skyline print lay on the floor beside him—the twin of the one in my hand—and when he looked at me, his eyes swam with hurt and confusion.

With pain.

And like a fool, I made things worse.

"I thought you'd be at work all day."

His gaze dropped to the painting in my hand.

"Yes, I can see that." Kevin's voice was flat. Distant. "What is this, Leah?"

He already knew, didn't he? There was none of the curiosity I might have expected to hear in his voice, only disappointment. This was a test. Would I lie to him again?

"It's a listening device."

"Why did you bug my home?"

"I—"

"Are you working for a competitor? Is that what this is about? Trade secrets?"

"No, I..."

I sank onto one of the new dining chairs that we'd bought online, and Brian whined and put his head on my knee. Kevin muttered something that sounded like, "Traitor."

"I didn't bug you; I bugged your neighbour. The microphone sat against the wall and picked up vibrations or whatever, I don't freaking know! I'm not a PI, I'm an executive assistant just like you are. My boss is the PI, and I'm way, way out of my depth here." Like, drowning. "I was going to tell you today, about my job, I mean, and I came to switch the painting back, and...and..." Uh-oh, the tears were gathering again. "This is all such a damn mess."

"My neighbour? What does he have to do with anything?"

"He might have stolen some jewellery. We don't know for sure, and that's what we're trying to find out with the..." I waved at the microphone. "With that."

"Isn't that illegal?"

"Uh, probably?"

"Give me one good reason why I shouldn't call the police."

Honestly, I didn't have one. My mind was blank, but panic was rising inside me like dirty floodwater.

"I... I can't."

"You lied to me."

"At the beginning, I thought it would be okay because you were never here, only Brian, and I didn't leave the mic overnight, and then... I'm so, so sorry."

"You engineered a shopping trip to buy a damn painting to hide your recorder."

"Yes."

"You used me."

"And for the rest of my life, I'll regret doing that."

Tears trickled out, and I wiped them away with a sleeve,

but they kept coming. I'd been so freaking close to fixing this whole mess, and now I'd lost Kevin, and I'd lost Brian... I'd lost everything. And I couldn't even be angry, not at Kevin. Every point he made was valid. I was furious at Dan, at Emmy, at Black for putting me into this position, but right now, the overwhelming emotion was despair.

Kevin rose and began pacing.

"I thought you were different. That you were a regular girl and we could have a regular relationship." He scrubbed a hand through his hair. "*Fuck*. I'm so *fucking* stupid."

"No, no, you're not. This was totally my fault, and—"

"Are you even a student at all? Part-time or something?"

When I shook my head, he muttered another curse.

"I couldn't afford to go to college. My siblings, they're the smart ones, I'm just..." I spread my hands wide. "I'm just the family screw-up."

Kevin didn't contradict me, not that I'd really expected him to.

"You should leave. Oh, for crying out loud, Brian." Kevin grabbed Brian's collar as the dog dragged a pair of pantyhose out of my purse. "Give those back."

He made a grab for them, and Brian danced out of reach, thinking this was a game. At least someone in the room was happy.

"Forget it," I tried, but Kevin won the tug of war and stuffed the now-torn pantyhose back where they belonged, his steely gaze fixed on mine. I'd never seen him all tough like that, and on any other day, it would have been a turn-on, but... Freaking hell, I'd lost my damn mind. Kevin pointed at the door.

"Go."

I made one last, desperate attempt. "Could we just talk this through? Please?"

"What is there to discuss? You lied about the most basic

parts of your life, and you used my apartment as a surveillance post. Nothing you might say can undo that."

No, it couldn't.

And I had no choice but to do as Kevin asked and leave. How could I feel both sick and empty at the same time? A wonder of biology, not that I knew anything about that, as we'd established. I picked up my purse and headed for the door, trying to maintain some shred of dignity and also not trip over Brian. But when he licked my hand, the tears only fell harder.

"I'm sorry," I whispered as I gave his head one last scritch and stepped out into the hallway. The door clicked behind me. Now what? What should I do? My knees wobbled, and I fought the temptation to sink to the floor and bawl my eyes out. I'd have to call Dan and confess to my failure and— My phone buzzed in my hand.

Blackwood Control: Error code received from microphone in Haygood appt. Did removal proceed as planned? Please advise.

Too late, too late, too late.

Instead of replying, I sent a message to Dan.

Me: Everything went wrong. Taking a personal afternoon.

Perhaps I should have gone back to the office and tried to fix things, but I didn't have the energy. Or the capability. Or the courage to face the colleagues I'd let down. No, it was far better to go home and drown my sorrows. Stefano had left half a bottle of peach schnapps on the coffee table despite me asking him twice to put it away, so I could start with that.

At this moment, a hangover would be the least of my problems.

28

DOG GUY

"This is actually a neat piece of kit." Haris sat at Lennox's dining table, poking at the remains of the surveillance device Brian had knocked off the wall. "A ceramic stethoscope microphone, a miniaturised amplifier, a wireless transmitter, and these additional microphones look like a noise cancellation system. Of course, it could be improved by using one of our batteries, but overall, it's well made."

An attempt to fix Haris with a glare only made Lennox's head pound harder. Perhaps he should have lined his stomach before he drank the bottle of Scotch, but the last thing he'd wanted to do was eat. Not on Wednesday, not yesterday, and not this morning either. Tally had brought him a breakfast bagel, but it was cooling in the bag while Brian drooled under the table.

"I told you the woman I cared deeply for turned out to be a liar and a spy, and that's your takeaway? That the bug she installed is well made?"

"Credit where credit's due. Do you know where she got it? I haven't seen anything like this on the market."

"Of course I don't know! You think I wanted to sit and

chat after I found out what she'd done? How could I have been so stupid? Again? After all the lies Liliana told, I thought I'd learned my lesson." Liliana's most egregious lie, of course, being that she'd loved Lennox, and he'd been fool enough to believe her. But there had been plenty of other untruths too, almost as if fibbing was a game to her. "I thought Leah was different."

Hoped she was different.

Was there a sign on his forehead saying "please take advantage of me"? Or did he just make a terrible boyfriend? Liliana had said so, but he'd almost convinced himself that she was being deceitful, as was her habit. And although he'd only known Leah for a couple of weeks, once his feelings had surfaced, he'd tried to spend a reasonable percentage of his time with her. Looking back, she'd probably have preferred it if he wasn't there at all.

Tally took a seat on the couch opposite Lennox. "You know, that day I visited Leah here, I thought it was strange that she didn't know the difference between Arcidae and Anomiidae, but I figured not everybody can be gifted."

"Thanks, that makes me feel so much better."

"Well, you asked the question. And if you want your self-esteem boosted, I'll say she was a good actress. She really did seem to care about you, which was why I assumed she was merely a poor student and not an imposter." Tally gave a low whistle. "A private investigator, huh? I thought they only existed in movies."

Yes, Leah had been a good actress. A *great* actress, so perhaps she'd pulled this sort of stunt before? Although she'd then tried to claim she was an EA and not a PI—which was undoubtedly another lie.

"Well, clearly PIs exist in the real world."

And Leah was certainly proficient when it came to doing

her job. Without Brian's clumsiness, Lennox would never have suspected a thing.

"Do you think her name's even Leah?" Tally asked.

"How should I know? She lied about everything else. I mean, she said she was bugging the guy next door, which all seems very convenient. What if she was spying for a competitor?"

"Did you spend much time discussing technological developments in your apartment?"

Lennox's silence provided Tally with her answer, and then Haris gave the knife another twist.

"This microphone was designed to hear through a wall. And if she'd wanted to listen to your conversations with Brian, wouldn't she have installed a unit centrally? Did you even check?"

"Give me a little credit." Lennox had dismantled every piece of furniture and electrical equipment in the apartment, and he waved a hand at the remaining shambles. "Behold exhibits A through Z."

"Oh, I just thought Brian had chewed up the couch again. And the phone. And the refrigerator. And the bookcase. And the—"

"Okay, okay, we get the picture," Tally told Haris. "I'll ask Kevin to order more furniture. So, what did Leah say the guy next door was up to? Is he dangerous?"

"It's possible he stole some jewellery, so I doubt he's a murderous psychopath."

"What kind of jewellery warrants a surveillance operation? The Hope Diamond?"

"She didn't get into the specifics." But it must have been one hell of a trinket for Leah to go to the lengths she did to embed herself in Lennox's life. Although she was wasted as a private detective. If she took up acting, she'd make a fortune because her performance had been Oscar-worthy. Not only her words but the physical side of things. Or had she faked her orgasms too? Fuck, he felt sick. "Can we stop talking about this now?"

"Depends. Are you going to try and give yourself alcohol poisoning again?"

On Wednesday afternoon, Lennox had sent Haris a text saying he'd work from home for the rest of the day, and yesterday, he'd called in sick. If alcohol hadn't dulled his brain, he'd have come up with a better excuse, because feigning illness meant Tally had shown up in the afternoon with chicken noodle soup, a large bag of over-the-counter remedies, and questions about why Leah wasn't providing appropriate sympathy.

When she arrived, she'd found him still in his pyjamas.

In hindsight, he should have taken a cab to the airport and flown far, far away. If he'd done the sensible thing and checked into a hotel, the staff wouldn't have dragged him into the bathroom by his lapel and insisted he brush his teeth because his breath stank. Oh, and apparently his armpits hadn't smelled any better.

Then today, Tally had come back with reinforcements—Haris and Sol, who'd delayed his return to New York in order, it seemed, to make Lennox feel even worse.

"Playing devil's advocate, is what Leah did so much worse than the time Haris bugged our neighbour in New York?" Sol asked. "Didn't hear you complain then."

"That was different."

"Was it?"

Well, sort of. The situation had certainly been more serious.

"He was pimping out minors." They'd all seen the young girls coming and going. By listening in on a number of conversations, they'd managed to glean some specifics—names of the pimp and his supplier, addresses of the clients, confirmation of precisely what the underage victims were being asked to do—and they'd reported the information to Crime Stoppers. After late-night raids on three properties, including the apartment next door, half a dozen girls had been returned home to their families, according to the local news station. "That's hardly comparable to missing jewellery. And Haris didn't try to conceal the equipment behind a painting."

"What if the jewellery was stolen in a home invasion? Or a mugging? People might have been hurt."

Wasn't the idea of friends that they lifted your spirits after a break-up? Because this wasn't helping.

"Don't you need to get back to New York?"

"I cleared my schedule until tomorrow."

Terrific. "And it's not just the bug—Leah lied about her background too."

"Oh, sure, and that's a heinous thing to do, *Kevin*."

When Lennox didn't reply, Sol dropped onto the couch beside Tally. "You didn't tell her, did you?"

"Only because I found the bug first. I came home intending to confess. I even bought the flowers."

"But you get my point? She's not the only person who bent the truth."

Sometimes Lennox hated that Sol was always right. "Lies aren't the basis for a lasting relationship."

"Isn't that what I said on Wednesday? Sure, Leah's transgressions came in one hit, but you can't climb all the way to the moral high ground. Halfway up the slippery slope is your limit on this one, bro."

"Why are you taking her side on this?"

"I'm not taking either side. I'm saying you both fucked up. Does that mean you should forgive and forget? Not necessarily, but underneath all the lies, there was heat between you, right?"

There might have been an element of truth in that statement. "Maybe."

"You blew off work to go to Pottery Barn."

"Actually, it was several independent furniture stores."

"Plus Leah put up with this mutt." Sol ruffled the wiry hair on Brian's head. "That takes a special kind of woman."

"So, what are you saying? That I should ignore the fact she misrepresented herself?"

"I'm saying you should talk to her."

Lennox couldn't help wincing. Talking had never been his strong point, and where would he even start? He'd been in love with the woman, yet their entire relationship had been built on a foundation of quicksand. True, those feelings were hard to turn off, which was probably why he felt so shitty today, but that didn't mean it was appropriate to forgive and he certainly couldn't forget.

"I'll think about it."

Tally rolled her eyes. "Don't think for too long. If you're going to repair this, you need to do it quickly."

"But what should I say?"

"Ask for her side of the story, from the beginning, no lies this time. And then you need to tell her all about Hayden Lennox."

"Maybe the lies will cancel out?" Haris suggested. "Imagine they're sound waves experiencing destructive interference."

If only it were so easy. Lennox understood physics, but the female mind? No, that was still a complete mystery.

29

LEAH

"Laken? What...? Why...?"

My sister stood in the hallway, holding a small suitcase. Her lips twitched as if she was trying to suppress a smile.

"Surprise! I know this isn't a joyous occasion, but..." She dropped the bag and flung her arms around me. "It's so freaking awesome to see you."

"Am I hallucinating? How did you end up outside my apartment?"

"Some guy downstairs held the door open."

"I meant in Richmond. How did you end up in Richmond?"

"Oh, your boss called me and said you needed company. She even sent me an airplane ticket. What happened? You had a bad break-up?"

"Do you mean Dan? Because she's not my boss anymore."

Why had she sent Laken a plane ticket? Out of guilt? I backed inside the apartment because I definitely didn't want to have this conversation in the hallway where all my neighbours could listen. Not that the apartment was a vast improvement. Thanks to the paper-thin walls, the sound of my oh-so-energetic neighbours going at it for nearly two hours had reduced me to tears last night. That should have been me.

Me and Kevin.

Laken followed me inside, dragging the suitcase behind her. "One of the wheels fell off," she explained as she hefted it the last few feet and dumped it beside the coffee table. "What do you mean, Dan isn't your boss anymore? Did you move to a different department?"

"No, I quit."

Laken's jaw dropped. "Why would you do that? You love working for Blackwood."

"*Loved*, past tense."

"Oh, oh, let me guess... You were dating one of your colleagues, and he screwed around on you? That's why you can't face going to the office?"

"Worse. So much worse."

"He screwed around on you *with a colleague*? Ohmigosh!"

I sank back onto the couch and poured myself another glass of schnapps. Stefano might have been a pain in the ass most of the time, but at least he knew how to handle a break-up. Once I'd sobbed out a slurred version of the story on Wednesday evening, he'd produced a huge box of fancy candy from somewhere, cued up Gloria Gaynor and Cher and Taylor Swift on his Bluetooth speaker, and made me dance until I fell over. On Thursday, he'd shown up during his lunch break with candles (not the pink ones), bubble bath, a fluffy bathrobe, and another bottle of schnapps. My hero.

"No, Kevin didn't screw around with a colleague, but my colleagues were involved in the whole...the whole..." Really, there was only one word for it, and I channelled Emmy. "The whole clusterfuck."

I summarised the mess for Laken—the undercover job, the feelings that had crept up on me for a man who was so utterly wrong on paper, and the nightmare ending to my oh-so-brief fairy tale. Somehow, it sounded even worse when I said it out loud.

"Holy crap. You gave up on your 'I must marry a prince' dream? Wow. And after all that, Blackwood didn't even find the missing necklace?"

I shook my head, which only made me realise how bad my hangover had gotten. "No, but at least Kevin didn't call the cops."

I mean, he might have done, but they hadn't broken my door down yet, which I was taking as a good sign. And Dan hadn't yelled at me. No, when she showed up at my apartment on Wednesday, I'd yelled at her instead, and she'd just stood there and let me. And when Emmy stepped in and tried to mediate, I'd yelled at her too. Then I'd told them I quit and slammed the door in their faces, something I felt a little guilty over now because when it came to the crunch, I was the one who'd agreed to Dan's stupid plan and then screwed it up by falling in love. Dan wouldn't have made that mistake. I mean, she did go head over heels for a murder suspect in the middle of an investigation once, but she hadn't been using his home as part of a surveillance operation.

And now Dan had flown my sister in from New York. Did she expect me to thank her? I thought that perhaps I should. A groan slipped out, but I managed to hold the tears back today. How had everything gone so, so wrong?

"Here, let me pour you another drink." Laken picked up the bottle of schnapps. "And then I'm taking you out for lunch—I worked extra shifts at the diner last week, so I can afford it."

"No more drinks. I think I might puke."

"Go take a shower. Although you smell better than I thought—when I split from Gavin, I didn't get out of bed for a week."

"You didn't tell me that." In a heartbeat, I switched into big-sister mode. "You said things weren't that serious and there were plenty more fish in the sea."

"Yeah, well, I didn't want to worry you."

"Didn't we promise to always be honest with each other?"

"I didn't lie; I just left stuff out. And today isn't about me, it's about you. What do you want for lunch? Pizza? Burgers? Tacos?" Laken pulled a face. "Salad?"

Tacos... Kevin had taken me out for tacos. The stupid tears made another appearance, rolling down my cheeks and plopping onto my pink bathrobe, and Laken squashed onto the couch with me.

"Aw, it's okay. Salad makes me feel miserable too."

Although you'd never know that by looking at her. Laken's philosophy in life was science first, everything else second. Who cared about appearances? Any potential suitor had to value her brain over her body, but despite that tenet, and also eating whatever she wanted, she still managed to stay rail thin. Although I noticed she was wearing lipstick today, which was a first.

"The tacos are the problem, not the salad. I ate tacos with Kevin once, and...and..." I waved a hand in front of my face. "Now I can never eat them again."

"Aren't you being a teensy bit melodramatic?"

"He was the only man I've ever wanted a future with."

Laken sucked in a breath. "Okay. Okay, so we'll go out for a salad."

30

LEAH

An hour later, I picked at arugula in the Garden Grill, wishing I'd gone with the "pizza" or "burger" suggestion instead. What did a few extra calories matter when it came to mending a broken heart? At least I could stuff carbs into the cracks. Shredded carrot? That just didn't have the same effect. The restaurant was nice, though. Unusual, but nice. Whoever designed it had bundled four shipping containers together, two by two, and filled the space with plants. A small waterfall provided a soundtrack, and big skylights in the roof let in light from an overcast day.

My phone buzzed with a text from Johanna. Another kitten picture. She was stuck in Sri Lanka on a layover, probably sunning herself on a beach or shopping for local handicrafts—her apartment was full of knickknacks from her travels—but she was still trying to cheer me up from afar. Hey, perhaps the airline she worked for was hiring? Being a flight attendant would be exciting, right? I'd get paid to see the world, and the uniforms were cute. But—I recalled Johanna's stories—I'd also have to deal with belligerent businessmen, drunken frat boys, and out-of-control kids, *and* do it all with a smile. Not so much fun.

"Want one of my fries?" Laken offered. "They're made from parsnip and sweet potato, so they're not, you know, *real* fries, but they're still better than lettuce."

"I'm just not hungry."

"You can't live on air."

"I ate a whole box of chocolates yesterday, and now I feel sick."

"Was it milk or dark? Because dark chocolate contains phenylethylamine and tryptophan and anandamide—"

"Again, but in English."

"Mood-enhancing chemicals that make you happy."

"Whoever told you that, they lied."

"My chemistry professor told me that, and he literally wrote a paper on it." Laken tilted her head to one side, studying me. "Maybe the chocolate just made you a little less miserable?"

No, I still wasn't feeling it. "Can we change the subject?"

"Sure. What do you want to discuss?"

Anything but me. "How's college going?"

"Uh, good?"

"You don't sound very sure?"

And that made me nervous. Since I hadn't gone to college myself, I'd become invested in Louis's and Laken's educations, not just financially but emotionally as well. Perhaps *too* invested. If things weren't going well for Laken, that would be another blow, and I was already on my knees.

"I've been meaning to talk to you about college."

"You're dropping out?"

"What? No!"

Oh, thank goodness. "Sorry, sorry, I guess I've been conditioning myself to expect the worst. Did you flunk a paper?"

"My grades are perfect."

"Then what's the problem?"

"It isn't like, a *problem*, problem." Laken closed her eyes for a second, and when she opened them, her gaze locked onto mine. "I want to study for a PhD. I know I promised that when I graduated, I'd get a job and start paying you back for my tuition fees, but...but this is my *calling*. There's so much we don't yet understand about cell division and replication, and I want to be one of the people who finds the answers."

"That's...that's...great." Surprising, but awesome. Laken had always been the smartest out of the three of us—goodness only knew how because our mom and her dad had the combined IQ of a grasshopper—and she loved to study. "So, when do I get to call you Dr. Burgess?"

Even though we were half-sisters, we shared the same surname, as did Louis. Until the paternity suit when I was six years old, we hadn't realised we weren't full siblings, although my dad obviously suspected something was awry, probably because Louis began to resemble our then-landlord more with each passing day. Turned out that Mom had been drinking half the rent money and spreading her legs for the difference. Our childhood had been such a freaking mess.

"I won't earn my doctorate for years, but I swear I'll carry on working part-time. And I'm going to apply for grants. I totally don't expect you to carry on giving me money every month because you need to live too. And I'll start paying you back somehow, but possibly in smaller instalments?"

I leaned across the table and took both of Laken's hands in mine. "You don't need to pay me back. I never said you had to —that was all your idea."

"But...but you've given up so much to save me from student loans, and Louis, and I know he plans to pay you back too."

He did, but after the baby came along, I'd told him I

wasn't accepting a cent until his daughter started kindergarten. His fledgling family needed the money far more than I did at the moment. Well, perhaps not *right* at the moment. My savings would last a few months, but I'd have to get another job sooner rather than later.

"Yes, and I told him not to."

"But now you've quit your job, and...and..."

"I'll get another job. It might not pay quite as well, but I'll survive. Hey, maybe I could move to New York?"

Blackwood had been the only thing keeping me in Richmond. When I first started working there, my shabby résumé had offered limited options, but I had experience now, and Dan wouldn't screw me over with a bad reference. Even though I'd left under a cloud, she just wasn't that type of person.

"Really?" Laken asked. "You'd leave Richmond? I mean, I know I only have a single room in a shared apartment, but I could squash a futon in beside my closet if you need a place to stay for a while."

"My lease is due for renewal in two months." And with the exception of Johanna, whom I'd met when we accidentally dated the same guy, at the same time—what a sleaze—all my friends in Richmond came through work, so perhaps a fresh start wouldn't be such a bad idea? Stefano might take on the lease. I'd need to speak to him about it. "Let's see what kind of job I can find."

Laken pushed her chair back and walked around the table to give me a hug. "When I make a groundbreaking discovery and publish a paper and somebody pays me millions to be their science bitch, I'm gonna rent us the best apartment ever."

"I thought research paid shit."

Laken snorted out a laugh. "I didn't say the process would be fast."

"As long as you're doing something you love, that's all that matters."

"Leah, you've changed. What happened to doing a rich man in pursuit of the almighty dollar?"

My turn to snort. "Yeah, I *have* changed. The thing with Kevin might have been short-lived, but he opened my eyes to the type of man I should be aiming for. Although not right now, obviously. I'm gonna try celibacy for a year or two first."

And the next time I tried dating, I'd be careful to guard my heart. And also to tell the absolute truth from the very beginning.

"There're, like, four million men in New York, so at least one of them must be half-decent."

"Have you been looking?"

"Me? Gosh no. I'm talking statistically, that's all. My studies come first."

I mimed putting on lipstick. "I just thought..."

Laken's cheeks reddened as she went back to her seat. "Oh, the make-up?"

"You never used to wear any. What changed?"

"I need to attract funding."

"With lipstick?" My mind cycled through the possibilities and immediately came to the worst possible conclusion. "No, no, no... Not *that* sort of funding. We'll find another way. I'll get another job real soon, you'll see."

For a moment, Laken looked puzzled, but then her fork clattered onto her plate and she burst out laughing.

"Wait, you think..." More giggles. "You think I've become a call girl?"

"Well, you wouldn't be the first student to turn to that line of work."

"Honestly, I wouldn't have a clue where to start, I swear. But when I began looking into the logistics of getting a PhD, I talked to a bunch of people at Columbia, and an associate professor told me that when it comes to funding, I have to remember that I'm not just selling my research project, I'm also selling myself. But definitely not in a sexual way," she added, and I sighed with relief.

Not that sex work was necessarily a terrible career—some women undoubtedly thrived on it—but I knew several former escorts through Blackwood, and even Stefanie and Imogen, who'd entered into that world voluntarily, had come to regret their decisions. Stef's roommate had been murdered by a client, for goodness' sake.

"So you changed your image to look...more professional?"

"Exactly. Dr. Berkowitz has a PhD—two, actually—and she said that networking is as important as analysis because without money, you can't do the research anyway. And when the alternative is collapsing under a pile of debt, the lipstick seemed the lesser of two evils."

"That sounds like good advice."

"For sure it is, and Dr. Berkowitz has an amazing sense of style. Pretty, but not slutty at all, more prim, and the schmoozing obviously worked for her because she's managed to stay in academia her whole life, plus rumour says she snagged herself a rich genius along the way. So I guess she never needs to worry about funding again."

"Is that your plan now? To snag a rich genius?"

"Is it such a terrible idea?"

"It sounds scarily like my plan to snag a rich businessman, and that didn't turn out so great."

"Well, my plan is actually to become the rich genius, so there's no need for you to worry. But maybe you could help with the makeover? And some tips for hobnobbing with wealthy folks? Seeing as you spent so long dating loaded jerks, you have more experience at communicating with them than I do. It seems there's a downside to being an introvert for my entire life."

"I can definitely help with the shopping—you're looking at the queen of thrift-store finds here—but the networking... My best piece of advice would be to get a dog and let it mow down your target."

"My landlord doesn't allow pets."

"Okay, so that's a problem. You could try joining a gym?"

"Last month, I ran for a bus and sprained my ankle."

Since I'd be giving up my Blackwood healthcare plan— ouch—and Laken had been covered under it too, inviting further injury was something we both needed to avoid, at least until I could find a new insurance provider.

"Then let's go shopping this afternoon. Did I tell you about the time I scored an Ishmael suit for thirty-five bucks?"

"I don't know what an Ishmael suit is."

"Ishmael is a primo designer. I gave the clerk an extra fifteen bucks out of guilt."

Although fifty bucks would be a stretch today. I'd need to tighten my belt until I got my life sorted out. And I couldn't deny that as the events of the past few weeks sank in, I'd started feeling a little...lost. Not only because of Kevin but because I'd quit the job I always assumed I'd stay in for life. After the disaster at Belvedere Place, though, it had been the right move, the only move. Hadn't it?

So why did I feel hollow inside?

31

LEAH

A half hour later, I walked into Second Appearance with Laken. This was my favourite thrift store in the whole city. Not necessarily the biggest or even the cheapest, but it often had designer pieces that were almost as good as new. Half of my wardrobe came from there, and few people ever realised.

"So, what type of clothes are we looking for?" I asked.

"Uh, modern Victorian?"

"Huh?"

"High-necked blouses, bows, long skirts, tailored pants. I have a mood board."

"Is this based on your Dr. Bershovitz?"

Laken blushed for the second time today. "She's smart in every way. And it's Berkowitz, not Bershovitz."

"Does somebody have a girl crush?"

Pink cheeks turned to scarlet. "Are you gonna help me or not?"

"Sure. Show me the mood board."

I plucked a fuchsia-pink blouse from the nearest rack. It had ruffles. Victorian was some old British thing, right? Did those folks wear ruffles? Probably I should have paid more attention in history class, but I'd always worried more about the future than the past.

"This? I realise it's the wrong size, but do you like the style?"

"If it was in cream, it would be perfect. Here, look."

Laken handed over her phone, and she wasn't kidding about the mood board. She'd put a *lot* of thought into this. A small part of me was relieved because I didn't understand much of the science stuff she studied, and if she developed an interest in fashion, then at least we'd have something to bond over. And the bigger part of me was even more relieved because if she was putting all of this thought into funding, then maybe I wouldn't have to pay tuition fees for another three or four or five years. Immediately after I'd had that thought, the guilt hit. I'd always support Laken, even if it meant curtailing my own social life for a while longer. She and Louis were the only family I had. I mean, technically our parents were still alive somewhere, but none of us knew where or even cared.

I flipped through the pictures my sister had carefully saved into an album on her phone, noting the lace, the kick-ass leather boots and, yes, the ruffles. Then on the seventh or eighth photo, I did a double take and squinted closer.

"Wait, is this Tally?"

Laken peered over my shoulder. "Dr. Berkowitz? Yes, but we're hardly on first-name terms."

But I kind of was. She'd introduced herself to me as Tally, hadn't she? Nobody had mentioned her being Dr. Berkowitz, but if she was working at Hydrogen Labs, I guess it shouldn't have surprised me that she was qualified up the wazoo.

"She's Tally to me."

"Wait." Laken turned to me, eyes wide. "You know her?"

"I wouldn't say I exactly *know* her, but I've met her several times."

"Through Blackwood?"

"No, she was a friend of Kevin's. Well, I guess she still is a friend of Kevin's. They work together."

"Work together? Where? At the university here?"

"Uh, no? Some place called Hydrogen Labs."

Laken clutched both hands against her chest. Why did it feel as if my street cred had suddenly gone up in her estimation? I'd spent years working for a team of superhumans at Blackwood, I was sort-of friends with a couple of billionaires, and Laken had barely batted an eyelid. But sharing coffee with a scientist who wore ruffles impressed her?

"Ohmigosh. Ohmigosh! Kevin works at Hydrogen Labs? What does he do there?"

"He's EA to one of the directors."

"Which one? Dr. Lennox or Dr. Kohli? Or the money guy...I forget his name. Did you know that it's called Hydrogen Labs because of their first names—Hayden and Haris? H2—the molecular formula for hydrogen. Get it?"

"No?"

"Never mind. So, who does Kevin work for? Tell me it's Dr. Lennox. He's dreamy. I mean, Dr. Kohli's cute too, but secretly, I think Dr. Lennox is hiding a wild side under the lab coat. That's probably why Dr. Berkowitz is dating him."

"Who are you, and what have you done with my sister?"

Laken had never shown the slightest interest in men before, and this was the type she went for? Hot nerds? I should have guessed, I suppose, but wow. My little sister was human after all.

"You still didn't answer my question."

"Uh, he works for Hayden Lennox."

"Oh, wow. Are you sure there's no way you can get back

together with him? Because I'd totally be a bridesmaid at your wedding."

She didn't mean to hurt me, but her words still stabbed me in the chest.

"Please don't ask me that."

"Sorry. I'm sorry, but holy crap. Did he tell you that Hydrogen Labs set up a multimillion-dollar scholarship at Columbia? For engineering and applied science, full ride."

"Can we just stop talking about this?"

Tears prickled at the corners of my eyes. I wanted—no, I *needed*—to forget Kevin and Tally and freaking Hydrogen Labs. I hooked the fuchsia blouse back onto the rack and headed farther into the store, pausing to wave to Maria at the register as I went. She'd been volunteering at the store for years, and once or twice she'd held back items she thought I might like. Maria was definitely on my Christmas card list.

Bows... I needed to look for bows... I thumbed through the rest of Laken's mood board, my vision blurry. Full skirts were good, as were florals, and corsets too. How did people even breathe in those?

Hold on a second...

Why was Kevin in this picture?

The phone slipped out of my hand, bounced off my foot, and slid beneath a rack of dresses. Laken cursed under her breath as she knelt to retrieve it, but "darn it" rather than "dammit" because she hadn't been corrupted by a bunch of military men the way I had.

"It's okay, the screen didn't break."

What difference would it have made if it had? One glance at the image had been enough. Kevin and Tally, sitting side by side on a stage next to some guy with a microphone. Kevin was dressed in one of the Brioni suits I'd seen in his closet, and he didn't appear particularly happy to be there.

All the pain came rushing right back.

"Leah? I said it's okay."

"I know, I know. I just could have done without seeing Kevin again."

Laken glanced at her phone, her brow knitted in confusion. "Kevin? What are you talking about? This is Dr. Lennox."

I snatched the phone, just to be absolutely sure. "It's Kevin. They look similar, but it's Kevin."

What was he doing on a stage? Taking notes? Flipping through a PowerPoint presentation? Because surely Tally was capable of doing that herself?

Laken peered closer. "But I don't understand. This was the scholarship announcement at college, and the dean definitely introduced him as Dr. Lennox. And loads of people at Columbia know him. He was a student there for years. But it's a really small picture, and if they look similar, I can see how you might be confused."

"Laken, I was sleeping with the guy!" Shit, half a dozen people had turned to stare at us. I lowered my voice to a whisper. "I was practically living in his freaking apartment. True, we only met recently, but we grew very close, very quickly. I'm quite certain I know what he looks like."

But with that certainty came confusion. Why had Kevin been masquerading as Hayden Lennox? And at an event as important as a multimillion-dollar scholarship announcement? Was Dr. Lennox just camera shy? Or was there a darker reason behind Kevin impersonating his boss?

The tears kept falling, but when I dug through my purse for the tissues that should have been in there, all I found was a slightly crispy plush zebra. Brian's favourite toy. When had he dropped that in there? It must have been during the fight with Kevin because Brian had been chewing on it right before then. The memory only made me sob harder.

"Here you go, sweetie." Maria held out a box of Kleenex. "Is everything okay? I kept a sweater back for you."

"I... I..."

Laken wrapped an arm around my shoulders. "Now isn't a good time."

"Man trouble?"

"Everything trouble," I choked.

"I'll just hold the sweater until you feel better."

At this rate, that would be never. What was Kevin's deal? Why had he lied to so many people?

And how did I fit into his twisted games?

32

LEAH

It was official: Kevin Haygood was a lying snake.

And so was Hayden Lennox.

And Tallulah Berkowitz, and Haris Kohli.

They'd all lied to me.

For weeks, I'd been plagued with guilt over my illicit activities in Kevin's—Hayden's—apartment, but I was the one who'd been used. Toyed with by a genius worth nine figures and counting if the news stories were to be believed. The irony wasn't lost on me—I'd always dreamed of hooking up with a really, really rich guy, and when I finally managed it, he'd turned out to be a total prick.

"How could I have been so stupid?" I groaned.

"It wasn't only you; it was both of us." Laken drained her glass. "I didn't realise they were such...such *assholes* either. Darn it, the bottle's empty."

Stefano eyed us up warily from the other side of the living room. When we arrived back from our aborted shopping trip, he'd been whistling along to Kylie Minogue as he arranged his underwear on the radiator under the window, but after he'd

202

taken one look at my face, he'd wisely gathered everything up and moved it into his bedroom.

"Do you need more of the schnapps?" he asked.

"Yes," we said in unison.

"I will go to get another bottle."

If he kept this up, I might actually start to like him.

And damn, I needed the alcohol to dull my guilt. No, not guilt for the surveillance operation—I was so over that—but for making Laken miserable. She'd idolised Tally, and now I'd shoved Dr. Berkowitz and her frilly blouse right off the pedestal Laken had stood her on.

The front door clicked shut behind Stefano, and I let out a sigh. *One week.* One week, that's all it had taken for my world to fall apart, and one more day to ruin Laken's life too.

"Why did they lie like that? Why?" I swallowed what was left of my drink too. "Was it a game to them?"

According to celebgossip.com, Hayden and Tally had been dating for months, and before that, Hayden was practically engaged to a freaking supermodel. It was official: scientists sucked. Did Tally get some weird kick out of seeing her boyfriend with another woman? I'd heard that was a thing. Some girls even liked to watch. My stomach lurched as that thought settled like maggot-infested meatloaf because what if they'd recorded me for their viewing pleasure? Hayden Lennox was an engineer—he could have hidden a camera.

And we knew for sure that the man I'd fallen for *was* Hayden Lennox. Several of Laken's professors had taught Hayden too, and she'd sent photos to two of them. They'd confirmed the horrifying truth—that I'd been duped. Hell, even Blackwood had been duped, I assumed because the real Kevin Haygood didn't have much of an online presence. The weirdo probably socialised the old-fashioned way: in person.

"Rich-people games..." There was no humour in Laken's laughter. "How would we know anything about that?"

"Precisely."

"Maybe we're better off being poor?"

"There's a lot to be said for ramen."

"All you need to do is add spring onions."

"And if you stand the cut-off root ends in a pot of water, they regrow like magic."

Laken held up her empty glass. "Here's to poverty. Boy, am I glad I didn't buy any clothes today. I'm gonna have to rethink the whole Victoriana thing."

"What about a capsule wardrobe with a handful of nice accessories?"

If I hadn't quit working at Blackwood, I could have asked Bradley for advice—he'd have helped in a heartbeat—but now I was on my own. A part of me wondered if I should try grovelling for my old job back, but I'd said some really mean things to Dan, and when Nick showed up at my door on Thursday, drunk me had just turned up the music and ignored the intercom until he went away again.

"I don't even know what a capsule wardrobe is," Laken said.

"It's where you buy just a few good quality pieces that you love, and then you mix and match them with each other."

"Does that mean we're going shopping again tomorrow?"

Honestly, I wasn't sure I could face that, and Laken must have realised.

"Or do you want to stay home and carry on with the pity party? We could stick pins in pictures of Hayden Lennox, or... or..." Laken let out a giggle. "Or we could cast spells on him. Do you remember that time in elementary school when we both wanted to be witches? And you found some article on witchcraft in a magazine and cursed Becky Willis, and she fell down the school steps and broke her ankle?"

"I felt bad about that for years."

"So, what do you think? Schnapps and spells?"

"Maybe. But do you know who I feel the sorriest for in all this?"

"Yourself?"

"No, Brian. It's not his fault that his owner's a two-faced asshole, but if Kevin..." I took a deep breath to calm myself. "If Hayden breaks an ankle, he probably won't get walked at all. I'll really miss him. Brian, not Hayden. I didn't even think I liked dogs, but he grew on me. What if I start volunteering with shelter animals or something?"

"To take your mind off Dr. Lennox?"

"Yes, exactly."

"Like, walking dogs?" Laken managed her first proper smile since we'd left the thrift store. "That's more constructive than watching sad movies or shopping for clothes I'll never wear."

"I know somebody who works at a shelter." Georgia was connected to Blackwood, but she wasn't part of the central core. And deep down, a part of me wanted to start mending bridges. Even though I no longer worked for Dan, I didn't want to spend the rest of my life on bad terms with her. Which meant I'd have to apologise, but maybe I could write a note? Hmm, a note... I had a few choice words for Hayden Lennox as well. A long sigh escaped. Why were break-ups always so freaking messy? "I'll call Georgia in the morning."

Dear Hayden,

Yes, I know exactly who you are now. You truly thought I wouldn't find out? How long did you plan to keep stringing me along? Actually, don't answer that because I don't want to hear from you ever again. Or your girlfriend.

But I do want to return Brian's toy—he shouldn't have to suffer just because you're an asshole.

Leah

. . .

"What do you think?" I asked Georgia once she'd read through the message draft on my phone. "Too much? Not enough?"

When I'd called Georgia, she'd been only too happy for Laken and me to come and help out at Hope for Hounds. We'd spent most of yesterday walking the younger dogs and cuddling the older ones, plus we'd gotten to play with puppies, which was my new favourite pastime. Sure, they nibbled on you and it could get messy, but those little fluffballs were the cutest things ever. I'd actually been smiling by the end of the day.

Laken had flown back to New York last night, ready for classes this morning, and after I'd forced down a bowl of cereal, I'd found myself in my car, driving back to the shelter again. Anything was better than sitting alone in my apartment. Plus the break room had donuts, and Georgia had proven to be a surprisingly good listener.

Today, she was stroking a goofy little poodle while we chatted over hot chocolate.

"Are you sure writing him a note is a good idea?" she asked.

"Honestly? No, I'm not sure at all, but I need closure, right?"

At least, that's what the self-help article I'd read over breakfast said. Stefano had brought a stack of magazines back with the schnapps, and I'd started flicking through them in a bid to distract myself from the Hayden Lennox disaster.

"I guess."

"And Brian needs his toy back."

"Doesn't he have other toys?"

Yes, and he destroyed one almost every day. Hayden had

never seemed concerned about the cost of replacing them, and now I knew why—he could afford to buy the whole damn toy factory if he chose to. This morning, I'd been making coffee when the business segment came on TV—Hydrogen Labs had signed another multimillion-dollar deal, this time with Volta Technology, and now Hayden was even richer. This morning, he was probably making an Americano in that fancy machine of his—the *ten-thousand-dollar* machine—while I got distracted and poured instant all over the counter.

Asshole.

Once, I'd been a hair's breadth from falling in love with him; now, I wanted to give him a handjob with a cheese grater. But anger was good, right? All part of the healing process. And part of me, a part I wasn't proud of and didn't much like, wanted Hayden to hurt too.

"This isn't about Brian's toy."

Hayden Lennox had made me feel like crap. Yes, I'd deserved it, but his deception had been every bit as bad as mine. I'd only lied about my job. He'd lied about his job and his *freaking name*.

And I needed him to know that I knew that.

"I thought that might be the case." Georgia laughed and twisted out of the way as the poodle tried to lick her chin. "You should definitely lose the 'Dear' at the beginning. And is 'asshole' the best you can do? Haven't we both spent enough time around Emmy to come up with something more creative?"

"Uh..." I racked my brain. "Jizztrumpet?"

Georgia shook her head. "Sounds like an indie band."

"Peckerhead?"

"A little mild? But if you put the word 'absolute' in front of it, I believe that makes it ten times worse."

"Okay, how about this?"

I jotted down an insult and showed it to Georgia.

"What does that even mean?"

"I have no idea, but it sounds good."

And Hayden Lennox definitely deserved everything he got.

33

LEAH

Driving back into the parking garage at Belvedere Place felt strange. As if I was revisiting the scene of the crime, which I technically was. Although the cops still hadn't knocked on my door. A sudden thought seized me—what if Hayden had mentioned my unscrupulous behaviour to his neighbour? To Terrence Garner? I considered that for a moment, then came to the conclusion that he probably wouldn't have spilled my secret. Hayden might have proven himself to be a jerk, but he wouldn't condone theft. Plus he didn't seem to speak to his neighbours in any case. What would he do, pop next door to borrow a cup of sugar and inform Garner that his former dog-sitter-slash-hook-up had bugged the wall between their apartments? No, I couldn't see it.

I'd wondered if Hayden might have deactivated the key card he'd given me, the one that let me into the garage and enabled the elevator, but no, it still worked. Guess security wasn't high on his list of priorities. Either that or he didn't think I'd be stupid enough to come back. Hell, I'd questioned the wisdom of it plenty of times since I finalised the note with Georgia yesterday.

But here I was.

The third floor was deserted, and I propped the toy zebra against the door with the note tucked behind it. No, on second thought, I slid the note underneath—I didn't want a nosy neighbour to read it. Brian whined and scratched at the wood.

"Sorry, boy. Wish I could take you for a walk, but I can't."

I was tempted to open the door and scritch his head the way he loved—Hayden hadn't confiscated my key either—but that was a step too far. I wasn't about to walk into the apartment uninvited, and if I were in Hayden's shoes, I'd have installed a hidden camera to make sure any future dog walker didn't engage in extracurricular activities.

No, it was time to go. I took a step backward and...trod on somebody's foot.

"Sorry, I'm so sorry."

Tell me it wasn't Hayden.

It wasn't.

"No problem."

Terrence Garner put a hand on my shoulder to steady me, and once I was stable on my feet, he carried on walking toward the elevator. Despite the amount of time I'd spent watching and listening to him, that was our first personal encounter. He was just a normal guy, a man you wouldn't give a second glance if you passed him in the street. Late-thirties, brown hair thinning on top, average build, nondescript jeans, and a navy-blue sweater. A little too much nose hair, and glasses with a thin gold frame. Plus he was kind enough to hold the elevator as I walked away from Hayden's apartment for the final time.

"Which floor?" he asked.

"The parking garage."

He nodded but didn't move to press the button, and I

noticed it was already lit. Garner was also going to the parking garage, which was odd because according to Blackwood's research, he didn't own a vehicle. Maybe a friend was picking him up? Whatever, it wasn't my problem anymore. Were my former colleagues still watching him? Was Tanner across the road in the café, picking at his third muffin of the day? Or had Dan found another unwilling victim to freeze their ass off in the park?

Standing in the elevator with a possible criminal wasn't the most comfortable experience, but after giving me a brief once-over, Garner leaned against the opposite wall and stared at his feet. Which made sense—he was a thief, not a psycho, and we were simply going about our business in a semi-public place. When the elevator doors opened, he exited before me and turned left, and I glanced after him out of curiosity. Who was picking him up?

Nobody, it turned out.

Instead of getting into a car, he walked through a door a few yards from the elevator. It closed behind him, and the metallic *clang* echoed around the deserted garage.

The smart thing to do would have been to climb into my car and send Dan a message, letting her know Garner was sneaking around in the basement. What was through that door? Some kind of mechanical room? Blackwood could investigate if they wanted to, and I'd go back to cuddling puppies.

But I really didn't want to text Dan. No, I wanted to put this whole painful episode behind me, and what if Garner had just gone to fix the AC or something? Maybe the building super was inefficient and residents had to take things into their own hands? Johanna had once lived in a building where the super ignored every problem until the front door jammed and he got locked out overnight. Oh, he'd begged to be let in via the fire escape, but the residents had left him in the rain to teach him a lesson. It would only take a second for me to check what Garner was up to. If he saw me, I could say I was looking for the stairwell, which was on the other side of the elevator and had a door that looked almost exactly the same.

And besides, nobody had ever accused me of being smart.

When I opened the mystery door, I'd expected to see machinery, but what I actually got was more doors. A stark corridor full of them, in fact. Uniform blue doors, each with a number painted at eye height. 101, 102, 103, 104... Odd numbers on the left, evens on the right. Were these storage rooms? One for each apartment? Blackwood hadn't checked out any storage rooms. We hadn't even known they existed, just another perk for tenants of an upscale apartment block who might want to tuck a bicycle or a spare couch or their ex's belongings away out of sight. Or even a gold necklace?

I closed the door softly and tiptoed forward to confirm my theory. If I saw 301, 302, 303, then I'd know my assumption was correct.

At least I'd worn sneakers today. The floor was smooth concrete, and the rubber soles sure did make creeping around easier. 301, 302, 303... I was right. These were storage closets, and maybe, just maybe, Dan would be able to find Molly Sanderson's necklace hidden away inside one of them.

Now I'd have to message her, and—

Door 303 swung open.

Terrence Garner stepped out, and as I turned, curiosity got the better of me and I peered past him into his unit. I'm not sure what I thought I'd see—a pile of gold, perhaps?—but I certainly hadn't expected...*that*.

If I'd worked anywhere but Blackwood, I'd have remained blissfully oblivious as to the purpose of the items laid out on the workbench in front of me. But I'd spent too much time hanging out at headquarters, and more than once, I'd taken coffee down to Nate in his basement lair. Although he was a former Navy SEAL who could turn his hand to any job that came up, he was always happiest tinkering around with gadgets. Laser pens, cell-phone tasers, the hi-tech bug I'd installed in Hayden's apartment. And improvised explosive devices.

Maybe I was mistaken about Garner's little project.

But maybe I wasn't.

"Oh, uh, sorry. I was looking for the stairs."

"Didn't you just come down in the elevator?"

"Right, I did. But I left something in my apartment— actually, it's my boyfriend's apartment—and I need to go get it. And I figured I'd run up the stairs because, you know, exercise."

I took a step back, and Garner took a step forward and another step sideways, blocking my escape.

Uh-oh.

"Who's your boyfriend?"

"He just moved here. On the third floor? I should really get going, so if you'll excuse me."

Garner didn't move.

"Ever get the feeling you're being followed?"

"Uh, no?"

But I began to get a strong feeling I didn't want to be in this corridor with this man anymore. He'd turned from benign into something altogether darker. Those bad vibes Dan had talked about seeped from his pores and enveloped me in a noxious cloud.

So I did what any normal woman would do in that situation.

I ran.

I ducked around him and fled, but Garner was faster. He caught me at the door and tore my hand away from the handle, and I saw stars as he slammed me back against the wall.

"Who are you? A fed?"

"Let go of me!"

"Answer the damn question."

"I'm a s-s-student."

"Bullshit." He jerked my arm, and pain shot through my shoulder. "Thought I was being followed the other day, and it seems I was right. I'll ask you one more time..." His other hand came to my throat, and he applied just enough pressure to make me gasp. "Who do you work for?"

I'd been through Blackwood's in-house self-defence course three times, and one time I'd even shoved the instructor onto the floor, but now that I was in real peril, my mind had gone blank. *Think, Leah, think.* Okay, one hand was still free. I could punch him, or gouge his eyes, or...wait, my keys were in my pocket. I had a weapon!

"I'm a freaking student!" My right hand closed around the bunch—keys to my and Hayden's apartments and my car—and I began to slot them through my fingers. "I study b-b-biology. At the University of R-R-Richmond."

Then I touched something else. The key ring Tally had brought me, the attack alarm from Hayden. The magic eight ball. I'd nearly tossed it into the trash, but then I'd figured that free stuff was free stuff, and since he was loaded, it was probably good quality.

"Do I look stupid?" Garner asked.

Well, yes, but I suspected that wasn't the answer he wanted to hear. "Uh, no?"

Okay, I had a plan now. I sucked in as much air as I could, then eyed up the door. *One chance.* I'd only have one chance to get away, and I couldn't afford to waste it.

One chance, and I pressed the button.

34

DOG GUY

Dear Leah,
Words aren't my strong point, so I don't really know what to say, other than: Can we talk?

On Wednesday, I acted in anger without giving you a chance to tell your side of the story, and I'm sorry for that.

I miss you.
Kevin
P.S. Brian misses you too.

Now that he'd had time to think things through properly, and also to take advice from his friends, Lennox realised that perhaps he'd acted slightly too hastily in throwing Leah out of his apartment.

Sol admired Leah's ingenuity, Haris respected her technical abilities, and Tally thought being a PI was cool. Plus Tally had dug right into the crux of the matter in a cringeworthy conversation that involved the word "moist."

And uncomfortable as that chat had been, Lennox had to concede that Tally was right—Leah could have faked many things, but her moistness wasn't one of them.

And nor was their chemistry.

Lennox hadn't forced her to sleep with him, or to go out for dinner, or to take Brian for a run in the field. None of those things had been necessary for her to continue bugging the apartment next door. No, she'd chosen to spend extra time with him voluntarily, and her orgasms had damn well been real too.

"You think I should write more? Try to explain my initial stance?" he asked Tally.

"Better to do the grovelling in person."

Almost a week had passed since Lennox last saw Leah. By Friday, he'd already regretted throwing her out of his apartment, and on Saturday, he'd bumped into his neighbour in the hallway, the one Leah believed to be a thief. At first, the guy had seemed okay, but after he'd casually confessed his relief that his new neighbour was white, Lennox had come to the conclusion that he was an asshole. Perhaps not a thief, but definitely a jerk who deserved everything he got.

No, a little surveillance wasn't the worst thing in the world, although Lennox felt sorry for whoever had to listen to the man's conversations.

"More flowers? Should I get more flowers?"

Tally patted Lennox on the back on her way to the kitchen. "You could try, but I suspect it'll take more than flowers this time, especially when you confess that you lied more than Leah did."

"Maybe I should leave that part until next week? If she agrees to give things another try, that is."

He followed Tally into the kitchen. With the amount of sleep he hadn't gotten last night, caffeine was definitely called for. Where was he meant to leave the note for Leah, anyway?

Putting it in her mailbox seemed so impersonal, and what about the flowers? What if he just got the florist to deliver both items? Leah was more likely to open the door to a stranger than to the man who'd treated her so dismissively.

"Espresso or Americano?" Tally asked.

"Double espresso."

"What's Brian whining about in there?"

"He probably wants to go for a walk. I'll take him after I've ordered the flowers."

"I bet the florist laughs their arse off when you ask for a bunch bigger than last week's pre-emptive apology bouquet."

Yes, Tally was undoubtedly correct. "Good point. I should order from somewhere else."

"No, you should order from the best place, laughter be damned. Throw in a box of chocolates too, and a luxury vacation in Bora-Bora."

"A vacation? You think Leah would go on a vacation with me?"

Tally made a face as she slid Lennox's coffee across the counter. "I'd put the odds at fifty-fifty. If I were her, I'd accept the tickets and take a girlfriend with me instead."

"Aren't you meant to be making me feel better?"

"I prefer to ground you in reality."

Lennox took a sip of coffee and scalded the roof of his mouth. Not a good omen. Although such superstitions had been debunked by science over and over again, so a first-degree burn really shouldn't mean anything, but—

"What's that envelope?" Tally asked.

"What envelope?"

"The one in Brian's mouth."

Hell, had he eaten the Volta contract? The last time Brian had chewed up important documents, the conversation with the lawyer had been painful and also cost Lennox fifteen hundred dollars.

But no, this envelope was smaller and thinner than the one the courier had delivered earlier that morning. Lennox prised open Brian's mouth and removed the now-soggy letter, then wiped the worst of the drool away on his pants.

And froze.

The letter was from Leah. He recognised the writing, and there was no stamp, which meant she'd hand-delivered it. He rushed to the door and yanked it open, but the hallway beyond was empty. Dammit. Dammit!

"What's wrong?" Tally asked.

"Leah was here. She left me a note."

"What does it say?"

"I haven't opened it yet."

Ten seconds passed, and Tally stood there with an expectant expression. "Well? Aren't you going to?"

Bad omens... "What if I don't want to hear what she has to say?"

"The words won't change just because you don't read them. Better the devil you know." Tally headed into the living room, and when Lennox didn't follow, she turned and shrugged. "Or let's play Schrödinger's envelope—no skin off my nose."

Fine. *Fine.* He tore the envelope open and smoothed out the paper inside. There were a few teeth-marks, but the message was still quite clear. Unfortunately. His heart sank to his toes, which Tally would tell him was a physical impossibility, but he felt what he felt.

Fuck.

"Bad news?" Tally asked.

"She knows."

"Knows what?"

"Knows who I am. That I'm Hayden and not Kevin. What's an 'absolute wankspangle'?"

"I have no idea."

"Because, apparently, I'm one of those."

Tally grabbed the note and winced as she read the rest of it. "Ouch. What's this part about a girlfriend? Who's she referring to?"

"How should I know? I don't spend time with any other women apart from..."

Ah, right. Leah had made a reasonable assumption, but still a very, very wrong one.

Tally rolled her eyes. "Fucknuggets."

"You're a woman—help me. How do I fix this? What do I say?"

"Maybe you should forget the luxury vacation and buy her a beach house instead?"

"You really think that would work?"

"Sadly, no. She seems to hate you more now that she knows you're rich."

Lennox had always assumed that if he just had enough money to pay the rent on time every month, he'd be content, but now he knew the old saying was true: money couldn't buy happiness.

"What if we assemble a task force? Gather together a bunch of experts on the female psyche and brainstorm a solution?"

"You can't solve this like an equation. She's not Fermat's Last Theorem."

"I should have majored in psychology."

"A chap I know did that, and at the end of four years, he told me he was more confused by women than he had been when he started." Brian nudged Tally's hand, and she bent to scratch his head. "You know what you should do?"

"I don't have the first damn clue. We've already established that."

"Let Brian take the lead. Leah likes him, right? Sit him outside her door with an apology note."

"He'll run off to the nearest food source."

"Then you need to get a really long leash. Do I have to think of—"

Funny how fast things could change, wasn't it?

In a split second, nothing mattered but getting to Leah. Not Brian's disobedience, not Lennox's foot-in-mouth disease, not Tally's half-baked ideas.

Because Leah had just activated her personal alarm.

Lennox's phone blared with a siren that was nowhere near as loud as the real thing, but the noise still shook him to his core.

"Where is she?" Tally asked, her tone urgent. She understood what the alarm meant—Lennox and Haris had designed it for her, after all—and she also knew its capabilities. Once upon a time in college, a fellow student whose GPA had been nothing to write home about had accused Lennox and Haris of over-engineering *everything*. The guy had meant it as an insult, but Lennox had taken it as a compliment. In his opinion, there was no such thing as over-engineering, not at the prototype stage, anyway.

Which was why Leah's alarm came with full geolocation capabilities. When activated, it would piggyback onto whatever signal it was able to detect—cellular or Wi-Fi—and send its coordinates to any paired devices, namely his phone and Haris's. Lennox checked the screen.

"She's still in the building."

"Which floor?"

Ah. This was a flaw that would need improvement. The map was flat, and it needed to be 3D. They'd have to add an altimeter, and— Why the fuck was he wasting time thinking? Leah was in trouble.

Lennox took off out the door with Brian hot on his heels and Tally hurrying after them. Which floor? *Which floor?* She'd delivered her note and run, which meant there was a high degree of probability that she'd headed to the lobby or the parking garage. And they'd have to go through one to get to the other.

"We'll try the lobby," he called over his shoulder.

The elevator would take too long to arrive, so he hauled open the door to the stairwell, hoping he didn't break his neck as he hurtled down the stairs. Brian gambolled around his feet, barking, which only added another layer of peril. Good thing Hydrogen Labs offered comprehensive health insurance.

Lennox's heart thudded against his ribcage as he took the stairs two at a time with Tally panting behind him. On the first floor, they burst out into the lobby, but it was empty. Well, almost. A guy wearing jeans and a ski jacket was halfway through the front door.

"What's going on?" he asked. "What's that noise?"

"Somebody's in trouble in the parking garage."

Lennox didn't have the time or the inclination to elaborate. With Leah in danger, he ducked back into the stairwell, checking the app on his phone as he went. She was still there. How long ago had the alarm first sounded? Thirty seconds? A minute? A lot could happen in a minute...

Ten more seconds, and they were in the parking garage. Lennox blinked in the glare from the overhead lights. The sales brochure Sol had left on his desk used them as a selling point —no dark corners here, perfectly safe. A lie. Leah sat slumped against her car with a man kneeling over her, the siren still screaming, and Lennox acted on instinct, running for the attacker to haul him away.

But Brian got there first. According to Haris, the noise from the alarm was in the range of a hundred and fifty decibels, but somehow, the man's pained yell when Brian sank his teeth into exposed calf was louder. He tried to crawl away, but Brian wasn't letting go.

"Leah!"

Her eyes were closed, and red marks around her neck left Lennox fearing the worst. His breath caught in the back of his throat as he dropped to his knees. Was she alive? She *had* to be alive.

Nothing else mattered.

35

DOG GUY

Movement in Lennox's peripheral vision caught his eye, and he turned in time to see Leah's attacker fly through the air and land face-first on the concrete. What the...? The guy in the ski jacket, the one from the lobby, he must have followed them downstairs, and now he was twisting the attacker's arm behind his back. The newcomer said something, but the words were impossible to make out over the wail of the siren, and besides, Lennox had more important things to worry about.

Such as finding a pulse. It was there, weak but racing, and he sagged with relief when Leah's eyes flickered open.

"Are you okay?"

He might not have been an expert in lip-reading, but he didn't need to be to understand the word "asshole." *Would someone shut off that damn noise?* Tally was on her hands and knees, scrabbling underneath the car beside Leah's, and finally, finally, they got blessed silence. That didn't mean Lennox could hear anything—temporary hearing loss was common with noise of that magnitude—but at least his skull no longer felt as if it were about to explode.

"Leah, I'm sorry. I'm so sorry."

She let him gather her up in his arms, at least, and when he got her to her feet, she clutched a handful of his shirt to steady herself. Unsurprisingly, she still looked terrified.

"What happened?"

She shook her head, motioning to her ears. She couldn't hear. Weird, it almost looked as if she mouthed the word, "Bomb."

"It's okay. You'll be okay."

There it was again. *Bomb.*

"I'll call an ambulance." Lennox stroked her hair. "You're safe now."

Leah pushed him away and turned her attention to the guy in the ski jacket. Tally had gotten ahold of Brian now, and the stranger was binding the struggling attacker's hands with an oversized zip tie. When the man on the floor turned his head to the side, Lennox got a better look at him and recognised his next-door neighbour. Fuck. The thief? Had Leah been right about his illicit activities, and somehow he'd found out and tried to silence her? Bile rose in Lennox's throat. He hadn't considered the danger, never thought for a moment that the man might have a violent streak.

When Leah shook the stranger's shoulder, he looked up and squeezed her hand, and Lennox felt a spike of jealousy. They knew each other? There was much gesticulating, and then the guy's eyes widened.

"Are you sure?" he asked, probably yelling, but it sounded more like a whisper.

Clearly, the volume of the prototype alarm required a little adjustment. It needed to be loud enough to stun, but tempered slightly so that people could still understand each other in the aftermath.

Leah shook her head and shrugged.

More people were appearing now, curious onlookers

who'd heard the noise and come to investigate. A small crowd had gathered near the elevator.

"Everything's under control," Lennox lied, trying for a reassuring smile.

Nothing was under control.

A brunette in tight pants and a leather biker jacket elbowed her way through the crowd and strode toward them, making a beeline for Leah. She might have been on the short side, but her attitude was ten feet tall.

More arm waving and pointing, and the brunette searched the prisoner's pockets, a move the man didn't appreciate in the slightest. But his ankles were zip-tied as well now, so he couldn't do much to change the situation except writhe on the floor and shout what Lennox assumed were obscenities.

The brunette must have found what she was looking for because she broke into a smile, and then she headed for the storage rooms to the right of the elevator with Leah. Why? That hallway was a dead end. Lennox only used his unit to store his bicycle on occasion—he didn't have enough possessions to need the extra space. When he moved to follow them, the brunette held up a hand.

He stopped, feeling like a spare part.

"What's going on?" Tally asked, and he heard her speak this time. Faintly, but his hearing was gradually returning.

"Leah's hurt, and she still hates me." Those were the most significant issues. "And that guy..." Lennox nodded toward his soon-to-be ex-neighbour. "I want to fire Haris's new laser at his balls."

"Who's the brunette?"

"No idea."

"The guy with the zip ties?"

Lennox shrugged. Had someone called the cops? Or should he try? The problem was, he wouldn't be able to hear what the person on the other end of the phone was saying. Was it possible to text 911?

"I bet this chap can tell us what's happening." Tally pointed at the guy in the ski jacket. "He seems like a knowledgeable fellow."

Did he? Lennox was knowledgeable—he could recite the periodic table in his sleep, including the lanthanides and the actinides—but that didn't help much at this particular moment.

"Hey." Tally took a step forward, and Brian snarled at the attacker. "Uh-oh."

Lennox whipped off his belt to use as a makeshift leash. The last thing he needed was another lawsuit, and his neighbour's pants were already covered in blood. A good lawyer could probably get Brian's first bite excused, but not a second.

As Tally approached, the stranger wiped a hand on his jacket and held it out.

"Tanner."

"Danny?"

"No, Tanner. Tan-ner." They were all still shouting, weren't they? "You're Tally?"

"How do you know that?"

"Leah's mentioned you."

"You know Leah?"

"She's a colleague." Tanner focused on Lennox. "Sorry about the, uh, painting thing. None of that was Leah's fault. Dan put her up to it."

"Who?"

He nodded past Lennox, where the brunette had emerged from the storage area with Leah in tow. If anything, Leah looked paler than she had before. Was she going into shock? Dammit, he should have called that ambulance. He also needed to have strong words with this Dan woman, but that could wait until later.

"Leah, you need to sit down." This time when he wrapped an arm around her, she didn't try to push him away, and he had to view that as progress. "You want to wait in your car? Or we could go up to my apartment?"

She shook her head. "We have to get out of here."

"Yup." Dan nodded in agreement. "Right after we call the bomb squad."

The what? "For a moment there, I thought you said we needed to call the bomb squad."

"Hey, the cops are here." She checked her watch. "Must've been at the donut place along the street. Ford," she called, "did you bring me a bear claw?"

The cops were in plain clothes with badges clipped to their belts, one male in his mid-thirties and a female who looked as if she'd barely finished high school. The two of them obviously knew Dan, and likely Tanner and Leah too. They were a part of Leah's real life, weren't they? The side of her Lennox knew nothing about.

Ford ignored the donut question. "What happened?"

"A guy attacked Leah down here. Tanner was nearby and came to help, along with these dudes and a dog. Kevin, right? You're Kevin and Tally?"

Leah burst into tears.

"My name's actually Lennox, but maybe we could discuss that after Leah's received medical attention?"

Should he try to comfort her? He was way, way out of his depth here.

Dan raised an eyebrow. "Lennox? Not Kevin?"

"It's a long story, and one I'm extremely sorry about."

"Well, I can't wait to hear it. Ford, you need to call the bomb squad."

Bomb. There was that word again... Surely she couldn't be serious?

"What the hell?" Ford took a step back, as if that would help if there were explosives in the vicinity. "Is this a joke?"

"The jackass in the flex-cuffs has been building bombs in his storage locker. Leah saw what he was doing, and he tried to strangle her."

"Bombs? Plural? And we're still standing here?"

Had they fallen into a parallel universe? The multiverse theory was controversial, but it did have a degree of scientific merit. Or was someone merely playing a sick joke?

"Pipe bombs, not *tick-tick-tick* cartoon bombs. You gonna call the bomb squad, or do you want me to get a guy in to do your job for you?"

Ford's turn to pale a shade. "I'll make the call. Tass, get those folks out of here. *Don't* mention a bomb."

"Uh, okay." His sidekick scurried off toward the watching crowd, hands balled into fists at her sides.

Probably Lennox should have been worried by the fact that his neighbour had been outed as a psycho who'd been playing with explosives in the basement of the building they both lived in. Tally was certainly looking nervous. But right now, what terrified him was the thought that Leah might not take him back, no matter how much he grovelled. Yes, she was by his side, but for how long?

The timer was ticking, and he had no idea how to fix things.

36
LEAH

"How are your ears?"

Dan set a mug of hot chocolate on the table in front of me, the good kind topped with whipped cream and marshmallows. I rarely indulged because do you know how many calories that stuff had? But since I'd nearly died this morning, I figured putting on weight was the least of my problems.

"Dr. Kira doesn't think the hearing loss will be permanent."

After Belvedere Place got evacuated, Tanner had given Hayden, Tally, and me a ride to Blackwood headquarters. In silence. I hadn't wanted to go, and I certainly hadn't wanted to go with those two, but I'd been too shell-shocked to argue. And now that I was here, I took a smidgen of comfort in the familiar. This had been my happy place for so long.

Kira Stanton, Blackwood's doctor, had checked me over and decided I didn't need to go to the emergency room. My ankle—the one that had almost been healed—hurt like hell again, but she said it just needed rest. She'd prescribed anti-inflammatories. The bruising on my neck was superficial, and although my hearing was still muffled, apparently that was normal after acoustic trauma. The little hairs inside your ears got flattened by excessive sound, and it took them a while to spring back to their regular upright position.

"If it isn't back to normal in a few days, you should go see an ENT doctor," Dan said.

"Like I can afford that now."

"Blackwood has excellent healthcare."

"I resigned, or did you forget that part?"

"Yeah, well, I was hoping you'd change your mind after you'd had time to cool off, so I didn't put any of the paperwork through yet." She crinkled her nose, sheepish. "Nick and I were gonna come and grovel this evening. I really am sorry about the shit that went down with Kevin. Or is he called Lennox? What's going on there?"

"I don't freaking know!"

It all came spilling out... Laken's girl crush on Tally, the horrible realisation that the average Joe I'd fallen for was in fact a stinking rich genius who was quite possibly dating an equally smart woman—not me, obviously—and I'd been blind to the truth. And now I was partially deaf as well, plus I'd nearly died. I flashed back to the way I'd choked earlier, struggling to breathe as Terrence Garner wrapped his hands around my throat and squeezed, harder, harder... A sob escaped, and Dan pulled me into a hug. I was still a tiny bit mad at her, but she *had* rushed in to help with the bomb situation, and how many other bosses would have done that?

And how many other bosses would have started laughing at the end of the whole sorry tale? Her shoulders shook as she chuckled silently, and I shoved her away.

"It's not funny."

"Sweetie, you have to appreciate the irony. First, that you spent years trying to hook up with a rich dude and then met one by accident, and second, that everybody involved in the whole fuck-up was lying." Dan's phone rang, and she glanced at the screen. "Hold on a second."

I paced the meeting room as she listened to whoever was on the other end of the line. We were on the second floor, overlooking the basketball court. Blackwood's headquarters was on the outskirts of the city, a sprawling three-storey brick building on a two-thousand-acre lot. Years ago, the land used to belong to an eccentric movie star who kept exotic animals, but he'd gone bankrupt and the menagerie got rehomed. Out in the grounds, you could still see the remains of the monkey house, and a flock of ducks called the penguin pool home now. In the summer, I'd often eat my lunch at one of the picnic tables there.

"They found seven complete pipe bombs," Dan announced. "Plus enough materials to build a dozen more."

My legs went weak, and I sank into the nearest chair. At first, I'd only caught the briefest glimpse of the bombs, and I'd thought maybe I was mistaken. After all, I was hardly an expert on explosives. I'd only seen Nate's mock-ups briefly when I took him a coffee, a trio of devices built for an undercover sting operation over a year ago. But Garner's overreaction told me he was hiding something big, and Dan had confirmed my suspicions. I'd been right.

And wasn't that a sickening thought?

"W-w-what was he planning to blow up? Do they know?"

"Garner isn't talking, but the supremacist group his brother-in-law is affiliated with has a militant wing. The cops suspect that last year, they killed a state senator's wife in New Mexico with...you've guessed it..."

"A pipe bomb," I finished. "I feel dizzy."

Coloured spots danced in front of my eyes, and Dan put an arm around me. At least I hadn't drunk the hot chocolate yet—I'd probably have thrown it up.

"If you feel faint, put your head between your knees."

"You think Garner was involved?"

"Seems he found something more lucrative than repairing computers." Dan sighed. "Disappointing that we didn't track down Molly Sanderson's necklace, but you did prevent a bunch of people getting murdered, so there's that."

A hysterical giggle burst out of me. "I'd almost forgotten the damn necklace."

"Emmy would make a bad-taste joke about the Rat versus the Splat, but I'm not gonna do that."

"Please don't." I began laughing again, but then the tears came because my emotions were scattered all over the place. "I... I don't know what's wrong with me."

"Nothing's wrong with you. This is a normal reaction to a difficult week. We'll get through it, okay? We'll get through it."

"We?"

"I don't abandon my friends." Dan gave me another hug. "Whether you choose to work here or not, we'll still support you. Hey, it's all right. Where's Bradley? I don't have any tissues."

Did I want to come back to Blackwood? My head wasn't sure, but my heart knew. When Dan had said I could have my old job back, all I'd felt was an overwhelming sense of relief.

"Laken will be disappointed if I stay. We talked about me moving to New York."

"I need to run a training exercise in the New York office next month. Why don't you come along? We can party in the evenings and write the whole thing off as a business trip."

"I never want to work in the field again."

"I think we've all learned our lesson there. Will you come back?"

Tears plopped onto Dan's boobs as I nodded. "I might need to take the rest of the day as personal time."

"Take the rest of the week. Let's start fresh next Monday, okay?"

"Okay. And thank you for sending Laken a plane ticket. It was real good to see her."

"Anytime. You want to stay here for a while? Or should I get someone to drive you home? Ford's gonna want to talk to you later, and I need to head back to Belvedere Place. Plus your science dick's still in the meeting room downstairs. Should I get rid of him on my way out? For what it's worth, I don't reckon he's fucking the Brit. That's not the vibe I get from them."

Hayden was still here? I'd managed to push him out of my mind for a few minutes, but now he elbowed his way back, front and centre. My employment dilemma might have been resolved, but I still had one massive problem to deal with.

"I sent him a note," I whispered. "Do you think he read it? I wanted him to know that I'd seen through his lies, but now I have no idea what to say to him."

Although I wasn't quite as mad as I'd been this morning, probably because the little gadget he'd given me had saved my life. Where would I be if that alarm hadn't been attached to my key ring? Bleeding out in Garner's storage locker? Would he have gotten his nasty brother-in-law to help dig my grave?

"I can make him leave, but that won't be the last you see of him. He's fucking upset, and every time somebody walks past, he asks them how you're doing. Fifty bucks says he shows up at your apartment tonight."

If I'd learned one thing in my years at Blackwood, it was never to make a bet with Dan.

"Maybe I'll just sleep here."

"Or I could get a couple of guys to wait outside your building and turn him away?"

"Why would Hayden even want to speak to me? He made his feelings quite clear the first time."

Although he *had* helped me in the parking garage earlier. Why had he been there? And Brian, and Tally? Brian was the true hero—I'd been on the verge of passing out when he sunk his teeth into Garner's leg.

"If Hayden Lennox has an ounce of self-awareness, he's realised he behaved like an asshole."

"If you were in my situation, what would you do?"

"Honestly? I'd go talk to him. It's obvious there was chemistry between you, and that doesn't disappear overnight, which means you'd either get hot make-up sex or the satisfaction of kicking him in the balls."

Knowing my luck, I'd break a toe.

"Can you take Tally somewhere else? I don't think I could face both of them."

Dan grinned as she picked up a pen and waved it like an imaginary wand. "Consider it done."

37

LEAH

"Hey."

Hayden looked up from a cup of coffee he hadn't touched, his face impassive. Dan had kept her promise and gotten rid of Tally, but now I was alone with a man I knew intimately and also didn't know at all.

"Are you okay?" he asked.

"Define 'okay.'" I took a shaky step forward. "My hearing should recover, if that's what you mean."

Something touched my hand, something rough and wet, and I leapt back a foot before I realised Brian had crept out from under the table. My heart swelled as I crouched to kiss him on the head.

"Who's the best boy? Do you want a steak? Do you? Or a carrot?" There might be a carrot in the break room. Every so often, Emmy's nutritionist went on a tear and replaced the fun snacks with vegetables. "You deserve a whole truckload of carrots."

"Someone brought him a hamburger, but he spat out the pickles. And I wasn't only asking about your stereocilia."

"My what?"

"The auditory hair cells in your cochlea. Your inner ear," Hayden clarified.

"Of course, my stereocilia. Well, I guess now I understand why you know all this stuff, Dr. Lennox."

He stood stiffly, hands stuffed in his pockets. "Leah, I'm truly sorry that I didn't tell you who I was from the beginning."

"Why didn't you? Why did you lie? Kevin's your assistant, right? Why did you pretend to be him?"

"Because the last time Brian knocked a lady down, I gave her my real name, and when she found out I had money, she threatened to take me to court unless I paid her off."

I gasped. "What? Why? Was she injured?"

"No, but she got a doctor of dubious character to write a report saying she'd torn ligaments in her ankle and suffered emotional trauma."

"So you ended up giving her money?"

"No, I let her take me to court. I don't give in to blackmail. I hired an investigator to prove she was walking just fine, and found an excellent lawyer to represent me, but she still told the judge Brian was dangerous and should be euthanised."

"What? But he's the sweetest dog. I mean, I didn't even like dogs when I met him, but he totally changed my mind." Oops. I looked up, biting my lip. "Uh, I probably shouldn't have told you that."

Hayden managed a half-smile. Actually, it was more like a quarter. "I appreciate your honesty. Anyhow, I didn't think giving you a false name would be a problem, but I also didn't foresee falling in love with you."

My heart stuttered. "You...you fell in love with me?"

"Unintentionally, but yes. The day Brian knocked the painting off the wall, I was there to tell you everything, but then..." Hayden closed his eyes for a moment. "I guess that's why I was so angry. Because I'd been harbouring so much guilt for lying, and then I found out you'd misrepresented yourself too."

"Believe me, I know that feeling."

Hayden turned to stare out the window. This meeting room had a view of the parking lot, and I recognised Emmy's Corvette heading toward the exit.

"This must be the most fucked-up start to a relationship in the history of the world," he muttered.

"Start? Don't you mean end?"

Hayden turned back, and this time, his expression was one of grim determination.

"If you think I'm letting you go without a fight, you're wrong."

"Two wrongs don't make a right, Hayden."

"Two negatives actually can make a positive. Uh, in mathematics, anyway."

"We're not talking math here."

"Yes, I realise that, which is undoubtedly why I'm making such a mess of things again." He took a deep breath. "I wasn't happy about your activities in my apartment, but I understand why you thought it was necessary. And if you hadn't been watching that man, he'd still be assembling explosives in the basement, and…" Hayden shook his head. "I don't even want to consider that."

"What about Tally?" I blurted.

"How does Tally come into this?"

"My sister thinks you two are a couple, and so does the internet."

"Tally and me? No. No, no, no. We went on one date years ago, and there was no spark, not even a flicker. But we do get along very well as colleagues. Leah, I'm not a cheat. Until I met you, I wasn't even looking to date again, not after my last disaster with…" He raised his eyes to the ceiling. "Never mind.

Nobody's ever made me feel the way you do. I realise that sounds trite, but it's true."

Damn that stupid zing. It was still there, wasn't it? We'd both screwed up royally from the start, but all those foolish lies couldn't extinguish the underlying flames. *Hayden Lennox was in love with me.* A bona fide rich guy with his own teeth and a cute dog was in love with me. And no matter how much my head tried to argue, I couldn't change the fact that I loved him back.

"Can we just clarify the basics here? What's true and what isn't? How many lies did you tell me?"

"Three."

Was he always so literal?

"Three? How's about you elaborate?"

"You already know my real name, but everyone calls me Lennox, not Hayden."

"Why? Isn't that weirdly formal?"

"During my first year at Columbia, my roommate was also called Hayden, and people kept getting us confused. Which was unfortunate because he was a womanising jerk, and to cut a long story short, his antics meant one girl threw a slushy in my face and another's boyfriend gave me a black eye. Going by my surname seemed like the easiest option at the time."

"Lennox..." I tried the name out, and it suited him. Strong, but not alpha. "Okay. And I know about your job."

"Hydrogen Labs, yes. I founded the company with two friends a number of years ago. Together, we're still the majority shareholders as well as directors. And I also understated my bank balance, but I didn't fake my lifestyle."

"You don't have a Ferrari hidden away?"

"I have an electric bicycle."

Okay, now we were getting somewhere.

"You really don't drive?"

"I never learned. I probably should've taken lessons, but in

New York, it wasn't difficult to get around." Lennox gave a long sigh. "What about you? Care to confess your sins?"

"The only things I lied about were my job and the original reason I wanted to be in your apartment. I'm an executive assistant to two of the senior staff here, and I spend most of my time organising schedules and making travel arrangements. My bosses and I have already agreed that I'm never working surveillance again."

"Good." A long moment passed. A *really* long moment. What was he thinking? His face didn't give much away. "Because I'd hate for you to spend your time in someone else's apartment when I want you in mine. Although I won't be living in Belvedere Place for much longer."

Lennox still wanted me? The tears welled up again, but this time they came with a weird mix of happy relief plus a hint of panic. And also sadness. He was leaving?

"You're moving back to New York?"

"Not unless you're coming with me. No, I'm going to buy a place that doesn't have a basement."

"In Richmond?"

"Of course."

Oh, of course. Because his bank balance ended in a bunch of zeros. I was still struggling to get used to that part —this was the man who'd taken me to a food truck for lunch, after all. But what had Dan said? That we'd either have hot make-up sex or I'd kick Lennox in the balls? Right now, my body was crying out for the first option. He'd be up for that, right? I mean, he said he loved me, which was *wild*, but also better than a lifetime supply of peach schnapps.

I stepped forward and took his hand, and he smiled properly for the first time since I walked in.

"Come with me."

"Where are we going?"

I didn't answer, just pulled him out the door. Brian tried to follow, and I nudged him back inside.

"Stay there. Good boy."

An intern was walking past, and I waved her down.

"Shelby?" I thought her name was Shelby. "Could you do me a favour? Find a bag of carrots and give them to the dog in meeting room three."

"The *dog*?"

"Yup, the dog."

"Uh, sure."

She gawped after us as I pulled Lennox into the nearest bathroom. Thankfully, Emmy insisted on having proper bathroom stalls with full-length doors, and they were reasonably spacious too. I shoved Lennox into the first one and locked the door, and our eyes met for half a second before we began tearing at each other's clothes.

Lennox paused for long enough to kiss me breathless, then raised his head.

"So, when you said 'come with me'…"

"I meant *come* with me."

"I don't have a condom."

"I'm on the pill, and I'm clean, I swear. And this is serious, right? I don't want anyone else, not ever, and—"

I didn't get a chance to finish the sentence before Lennox dropped to his knees. Deft hands unbuttoned my jeans and wriggled them down my hips. Those same hands held me up while he went to work with his tongue, and when he hit the right spot, I had to bite my own lip to keep from crying out.

"Fuck me," I choked as I tunnelled my fingers through his hair.

He looked up, his gaze molten. "Is that an instruction or merely an expression of surprise?"

"Can it be both?"

"The dictionary allows that."

If it weren't for the whole argument part, make-up sex might have been my new favourite thing. Quick, dirty, forbidden make-up sex. I unzipped Lennox's pants and freed his cock, and he didn't waste any time. As he pushed inside me, stretched me, the bathroom door opened, and knowing somebody was just outside only added an extra edge.

"I won't last long," Lennox whispered.

Another lie, but only a tiny one. The interloper in the next stall finished their business and washed their hands, and Lennox still wasn't done with me. His blue-green eyes focused on mine, and in those unguarded moments, I saw the real him. Strength, kindness, intensity, lust, and yes, love. There were no barriers between us anymore, not physically or emotionally. We had each other, and that was more than enough. That was *everything*.

My legs trembled as I came for the second time, and three thrusts later, Lennox followed me into oblivion. I clung to him, breathing hard as I tried to process the latest crazy turn my life had taken. My future—our future—held so many unknowns, but right now, there was one certainty.

"I love you," I murmured against his neck. "We'd better not screw this up again."

"I love you, I'll always love you, and I'll take classes in how not to screw things up." He kissed my hair. "I always work hard."

I wrapped my hand around the base of his cock. "Yes, I know that."

"I was talking about my academic record."

"I know that too."

Strong hands cupped my ass, and he lifted me to meet his lips. I'd never get sick of his kisses.

"Can I take you out for dinner this evening? Who was that guy in Noir Absolu, by the way? I take it neither of you worked in a bar?"

"Ryder. He works upstairs on the Special Projects team. Maybe we could go somewhere with lights this time?"

"I'll take you anywhere you want to go."

"Rhodium? Blackwood staff get a discount there, and I love the desserts. Or Il Tramonto? The pizzas are the best in the city, but Giovanni's always generous with the drinks, and I've drunk enough alcohol for this week."

"When I said anywhere, I meant anywhere."

"Will Brian be okay on his own? He's had an upsetting day too."

"I can ask Kevin to sit with him. The real Kevin, I mean. Who, for the record, thought that switching identities was a terrible idea."

Good to know, but that didn't matter anymore.

"Forget the past, okay? Let's start over."

"I love you." Another soft kiss. "And I'd love to stay here with you all day, but we should probably go and apologise for whatever havoc Brian's managed to wreak in our absence."

"Plus your cum is running down my leg."

"I'm sorry about that."

"No, you're not."

Lennox grinned, a proper, carefree, knock-me-off-my-feet grin, and I knew then that we'd be okay. This man was everything I'd always wanted and more.

"No, I'm not. Not with one single quark."

"A what?"

"Uh, quarks are elementary subatomic particles."

"Smaller than atoms?"

"Smaller than atoms," he confirmed. "They combine to form composite particles called hadrons, and—" Lennox paused, eyes wide. "Sorry. Not the time or the place."

I had to smile. There that passion again, and he wanted to share it. Learning science with a man's dick in me was a new experience, but I couldn't say I hated it. And the teacher was top notch.

"You can talk geeky to me any time, Dr. Lennox." I pressed a soft kiss to his cheek. "But could we avoid molluscs?"

His turn to smile. "Biology isn't my area of expertise. I know a reasonable amount about olfactory organs, but molluscs only have the most basic sense of smell. Through their tentacles, or rhinospores in the case of marine gastropods, and— Sorry. When I'm nervous, I tend to stick to topics I understand."

He was nervous? That was so...so...sweet. Now I was seeing the real Lennox, and...and... As I pulled up my panties, my heart just freaking swelled. Now that the lies were out, I knew that he wouldn't play any more games with me. It wasn't in his nature.

"Let's go rescue Brian, and then we can head somewhere more private."

"My apartment is likely to be off limits."

I thought of Stefano's thongs and the lingering smell of fish in my own home. "Maybe we could try a hotel room? Blackwood employees get a discount at the Black Diamond because the big boss owns it, although there are definitely cheaper options if—" My cheeks heated. "You probably don't worry about counting the pennies."

"How do you feel about Bora-Bora?"

"Bora-Bora?"

"The more accurate name is actually Pora-Pora since there's no 'B' in the Tahitian language, but apparently it's nice there. Kevin can look after Brian for a few days."

Lennox was offering to take me to Bora-Bora? That was *insane*. Although I did have the rest of the week off, and I had always wanted to— No way, it was too much.

"You don't think that's a little extra?"

"A little extra what?"

Ah, right. Lennox spoke nerd, not slang. "Extravagant. Excessive."

"For you? No."

My phone buzzed as he zipped up his pants, and I checked the screen in case there was an emergency. If Brian had escaped from the conference room, we'd have to chase him down fast. But no, it was Dan.

Dan: Should we close out the betting pool?

They'd been running a pool on us? Oh, who was I kidding—of course there was a pool. And Shelby had a big mouth. I loved my colleagues, really I did, but privacy wasn't high on their list of priorities. Five bucks said Dan and Black were running in-depth background checks on Hayden Lennox as I stood here with damp panties and a dazed expression. But you know what? There was no Blackwood office in French Polynesia.

I stood on tiptoe and cupped Lennox's cheeks in my hands. "Bora-Bora sounds wonderful."

EPILOGUE - DOG GUY

"Brian, you came in from the yard thirty seconds ago." The dog stared up at Leah beseechingly, and a moment later, she opened the back door again. "Fine, but this is the last time."

Lennox just watched them. The past six weeks had been full of changes, but from the moment they'd emerged from the bathroom stall at Blackwood Security, those changes had been for the better. Leah, it turned out, had told one more small fib—she'd been dying her hair. She'd been beautiful as a brunette, but as a blonde, she was stunning. His breath still caught in his throat every time he looked at her.

And when she'd emerged from the sea in a bikini, he'd feared a coronary was on the horizon. The trip to Bora-Bora had been worth every cent. The first-class flight, the over-water villa, the gourmet meals... Lennox had changed his mind about reprimanding Dan for the stunt with the recording device when she offered Leah an extra week off. In the past, he'd always favoured work over vacations, but he was definitely beginning to see the benefits of downtime.

"Maybe we should install a doggy door?" he suggested.

"Can you imagine the trouble Brian would get into? He'd tunnel out of the yard while we weren't looking."

"I could put a lock on it. Build an app to open it by remote control. Then add some cameras to monitor him outside, and a speaker to tell him off, and—"

"Don't you think we should focus on getting furniture first?"

A fair question. So far, they had a king-sized bed, the now-reassembled coffee machine from Lennox's old apartment in Belvedere Place, and the seascape coffee table they'd seen on the fateful day they'd acquired the skyline painting. He'd bought the table with the intention of giving it to Leah once he'd come clean about his identity, but now she'd agreed to move in with him when her lease ended, so it had become *their* table.

"I figured I'd just hire someone to decorate. That's what I did before."

"In New York?"

"Yes."

Leah made a face. "But you hate most of the furniture there."

That was true. With the last traces of Liliana erased, the place was bland and uninspiring, a blank canvas full of neutral tones. Two weeks ago, Leah had spent a few days in New York —a work thing—and he'd headed there as well to catch up with the staff at H2's headquarters. He'd shown her his apartment and taken her to his favourite Mexican restaurant for dinner, and they'd talked about seeing a show. Didn't get as far as booking tickets because Leah noticed the hot tub on the terrace and wanted to try it out, but they could visit Broadway on their next trip. They had all the time in the world.

The initial plan had involved him and Haris splitting their time between the two cities until the Richmond facility was established, and they'd both planned to return to the Big

Apple after that, but three days ago, Lennox had finalised the purchase of his new property, and now... Now, he wasn't going anywhere. The New York location was well-established, and it ran just fine on its own. He could commute when necessary.

This was his new home.

With six bedrooms and seven bathrooms, the house in Rybridge was far too big for one person, but it didn't feel so empty with Leah there too. And maybe...maybe someday, they'd have a family. He'd barely thought about fatherhood before, but these things would need consideration. For now, they just had Brian, and Brian liked the new yard, plus there was a park nearby.

"I'd specify that the furniture needs to be functional this time."

No white couches, no mirrored tables, and no floor-length drapes. Brian left paw prints and nose marks and drool everywhere.

"Or we could shop for the furniture ourselves?"

"Together?"

"No, I thought you could go and send me pictures while I take a relaxing bubble bath."

"In that case, wouldn't it be easier to look on the internet?"

Leah rolled her eyes. "I was kidding." Ah, yes. Right. "Of course we'd go together, but maybe I won't take you to the second-hand store this time. You must've thought I was the biggest fool who ever lived that day."

"No, I thought it was sweet that you were trying to save me money. Don't forget I grew up dirt poor. When we started Hydrogen Labs, our only goal was not to live on ramen for the rest of our lives. Although Haris developed quite a taste for ramen, so he still eats it all the time, but I prefer tacos."

"Pinch me—I can't believe you're rich and also normal."

In keeping with their "no more lies" pact, Leah had revealed that for years, her goal in life had been to land a rich husband so she wouldn't have to worry about money anymore. Her fear of his reaction had been all-too-obvious when she made her confession, but Lennox wasn't concerned. At heart, Leah was no gold-digger. He'd had first-hand experience with one of those. No, she just wanted the same thing he'd always dreamed of—financial security—and he'd happily provide that.

"Some people would contest the 'normal' assertion, but— Is Brian digging out there?"

"Dammit!" Leah yanked the door open. "Brian, get back in here." The dog slunk into the kitchen with his beloved toy zebra in his mouth, leaving a line of muddy paw prints across the tile. "We should get a doormat. Or an outdoor shower so we can wash off the dirt."

"Why don't you drink your coffee while I find a towel?"

"I can do it."

"I know you can, but you don't have to." Quite quickly, Lennox had realised that Leah's fairy tale might have involved a rich husband, but in her head, she'd cast herself in a role of subservience. And he didn't want that from her, not at all. Back when she thought he was Kevin, she'd treated him as an equal, and he much preferred for things to remain that way. He nudged her cappuccino across the breakfast bar and rose from his stool. "This is getting cold."

She stood on tiptoes to kiss him. "Did I mention that I love you?"

"Only three times so far today. I love you too, sweetheart."

Lennox took hold of Brian's collar and led him to the nearest bathroom. This one was a wet room with a monochromatic theme—tiny black and white tiles with silver accents. Luckily, the towels were turquoise rather than white.

"Brian, you need to behave, buddy. We can't afford to mess this up."

The dog tilted his head to one side.

"You realise how good things are now? You go to work with Leah and get petted all day. If you chew stuff and roll in dirt, you'll have to stay at home again."

In the beginning, Lennox had tried taking Brian to Hydrogen Labs, but during the very first week, he'd turned his back for three seconds and Brian had eaten a prototype battery. The resulting trip to the veterinarian hadn't been fun for either of them. But the folks at Blackwood loved having Brian there, and he got so many walks around the grounds that he spent the remainder of the time asleep under Leah's desk. And for the days when Lennox and Leah both had heavy workloads, Leah's friend Georgia had recommended a reliable dog walker.

Everything was falling into place.

Brian whined as Lennox rinsed his feet, but tough luck. This was his own fault.

"If we get an expensive couch, are you going to chew it again?"

What did that look mean? At a guess, Brian was making no promises.

"What if we get you your own couch, huh? We have the space now."

Brian slurped Lennox's face, and Lennox overbalanced into a puddle of water. Mentally, he added a clothes dryer to the shopping list. Or perhaps they owned one already? He hadn't spent too much time exploring the house, and there was a good reason for that—once the bed arrived, he'd spent every spare minute exploring Leah instead. Priorities.

Leah probably knew whether there was a clothes dryer— she'd become pally with the realtor, and this house had been her favourite out of the six they'd viewed. She'd made friends with Tally too, which was a good thing but also a bad thing because Tally loved to talk, and now Leah knew that Lennox had once gotten locked out of his old apartment wearing only his underwear. Although it hadn't been entirely his fault. He'd stepped into the hallway to retrieve Brian after Liliana turfed him out for eating her shoes, and she'd slammed the door behind him. But he'd still been forced to ask the concierge for help, and the concierge had called Haris, and Haris had a big mouth.

"Okay, we'll get you a couch. Maybe from that second-hand store. Just promise you won't eat Leah's shoes."

Back in the kitchen, Leah was speaking on the phone, but she looked up when Lennox walked in.

"I'll be there soon. You want me to pick up muffins on the way? ... Okay, double chocolate." She hung up. "What happened to your pants?"

"Brian happened. Do we have a clothes dryer?"

"We have a whole laundry room. Didn't you see it on the tour?"

"I was distracted."

"By what?"

"By you."

"Oh." She broke into a smile. "*Oh*."

Lennox nodded toward the phone. "Everything okay?"

"Everything's *great*. We found Molly Sanderson's necklace."

"The necklace that started everything?"

Leah nodded. "We always had two possible suspects, and the other guy sold it to Tanner in a bar last night. For fifty bucks! It's worth two hundred times that."

"So all's well that ends well."

The necklace would be reunited with its owner, and Terrence Garner was in prison along with his brother-in-law and a whole bunch of their acquaintances. After Garner's brush with death, he'd started talking, and by "brush with death," Lennox didn't mean the home-made bombs he'd been cooking up. No, the dog bite on his leg had turned septic, and he'd spent a week in the ICU before they amputated the limb. His perforated eardrum had been the frosting on the cake. And speaking of cake, Lennox had ordered Brian an extra-large pupcake from the Doggy Deli to celebrate.

Leah's sister was also celebrating. Tally had agreed to act as her mentor, and although Leah had thanked Lennox in some rather creative ways for facilitating the arrangement, in reality, he'd done little beyond setting up the initial meeting. Laken had already begun making a name for herself in the world of science, and Tally didn't need much of a nudge to take the young woman under her wing. At the moment, they were plotting world domination over Skype, but maybe someday, Laken would end up back in Richmond? Hydrogen Labs always needed good people. Project Kibble was showing promising progress, and a government agency had agreed to provide a generous amount of funding, which meant they'd have to assign a full-fledged development team soon.

Lennox hooked an arm around Leah's waist, and she sighed contentedly as she laid her head against his shoulder.

"Yup. Things sure did turn out well for us."

BONUS CHAPTER

Not ready to say goodbye to Leah and Lennox? Neither was I, so I wrote a little extra scene—it's free to members of my reader group :)

Download the bonus epilogue here:
www.elise-noble.com/hydrog3n

WHAT'S NEXT?

My next book will be the first in the Blackstone House series, *Hard Lines*...

Violet Miller never wanted to be a star, but fate conspired against her when she won the lead role in *Hidden Intent*, the latest experiment from acclaimed director David Jackson.

Part movie and part reality show, the production takes over Violet's life. She's soon battling against a jealous co-star, a horrific script, and an A-lister who thinks the world revolves around him. Then the anonymous gifts start arriving...

As the torment continues, the studio grudgingly hires bargain-basement bodyguard Dawson Masters, a man with his own secrets. Which will catch up with them first—Violet's stalker or Dawson's murky past?

For more details:
www.elise-noble.com/hard-lines

If you enjoyed *Hydrogen*, please consider leaving a review.

For an author, every review is incredibly important. Not only do they make us feel warm and fuzzy inside, readers consider them when making their decision whether or not to buy a book. Even a line saying you enjoyed the book or what your favourite part was helps a lot.

WANT TO STALK ME?

For updates on my new releases, giveaways, and other random stuff, you can sign up for my newsletter on my website: www.elise-noble.com

If you're on Facebook, you might also like to join Team Blackwood for exclusive giveaways, sneak previews, and book-related chat. Be the first to find out about new stories, and you might even see your name or one of your suggestions make it into print!

And if you'd like to read my books for FREE, you can also find details of how to join my advance review team.

Would you like to join Team Blackwood?

www.elise-noble.com/team-blackwood

facebook.com/EliseNobleAuthor

twitter.com/EliseANoble

instagram.com/elise_noble

END-OF-BOOK STUFF

Firstly, just in case you ever need to know this random piece of information, it is indeed possible to text 911 in many locations in the USA—over 3,000 call centres support this feature at the time of writing. If you try and your location doesn't support it, you'll receive a message informing you that you'll need to contact the emergency services by some other means.

Okay, now that's out of the way, thanks so much for reading Hydrogen! It was the third book I've serialised in my newsletter, so thanks also to all those folks who voted on what they wanted to happen next :)

It's been a busy few months for me, not just with writing but with "home" stuff too. If you read the End-of-Book Stuff in Secret Weapon, you'll know I was fostering a German Shepherd named Razor and hoping he'd find his forever home. The good news is that he did indeed find his forever home. The bad news? It's with me. I'm such a failure at fostering. Over the months he was with me, he turned into the loveliest dog, and I'd have been super sad to see him go, so now it's official: this is a three-dog household again. Gah.

I've also been gardening. With food prices sky-rocketing, I've been growing a lot of my own veggies this year, but the lack of rain means I've also had to spend most evenings watering. And with the impending hosepipe ban, that's going to take even longer now. Grrr. Sod Strictly—I need to learn how to rain dance. On the plus side, I do have more courgettes (zucchini in American) than I know what to do with, and the beans and carrots are ready now as well.

Writing-wise, I'm a book behind because Hard Tide (#2 in the Blackstone House series, which is coming soon) ended up twice as long as planned, making it my longest book ever. So I'm going to have a busy autumn to catch up! The first book in the Blackstone House series (Hard Lines) will be out soon, and it's another romantic suspense. Yes, there is a Blackwood connection, but you'll have to wait to see what it is :)

Elise

ALSO BY ELISE NOBLE

Blackwood Security

For the Love of Animals (Nate & Carmen - Prequel)

Black is My Heart (Diamond & Snow - Prequel)

Pitch Black

Into the Black

Forever Black

Gold Rush

Gray is My Heart

Neon (novella)

Out of the Blue

Ultraviolet

Glitter (novella)

Red Alert

White Hot

Sphere (novella)

The Scarlet Affair

Spirit (novella)

Quicksilver

The Girl with the Emerald Ring

Red After Dark

When the Shadows Fall

Pretties in Pink

Chimera

Secret Weapon (Crossover with Baldwin's Shore)

The Devil and the Deep Blue Sea (2023)

Blackwood Elements

Oxygen

Lithium

Carbon

Rhodium

Platinum

Lead

Copper

Bronze

Nickel

Hydrogen

Blackwood UK

Joker in the Pack

Cherry on Top

Roses are Dead

Shallow Graves

Indigo Rain

Pass the Parcel (TBA)

Blackwood Casefiles

Stolen Hearts

Burning Love (TBA)

Baldwin's Shore

Dirty Little Secrets

Secrets, Lies, and Family Ties

Buried Secrets

Secret Weapon (Crossover with Blackwood Security)

A Secret to Die For (2023)

Blackstone House

Hard Lines (2022)

Hard Tide (2023)

Hard Limits (2023)

The Electi

Cursed

Spooked

Possessed

Demented

Judged

The Planes

A Vampire in Vegas

A Devil in the Dark (TBA)

The Trouble Series

Trouble in Paradise

Nothing but Trouble

24 Hours of Trouble

Standalone

Life

Coco du Ciel

A Very Happy Christmas (novella)

Twisted (short stories)

Books with clean versions available (no swearing and no on-the-page sex)

Pitch Black

Into the Black

Forever Black

Gold Rush

Gray is My Heart

Audiobooks

Black is My Heart (Diamond & Snow - Prequel)

Pitch Black

Into the Black

Forever Black

Gold Rush

Gray is My Heart

Neon (novella)

Made in the USA
Las Vegas, NV
02 October 2024